DROPS OF JUPITER

BY APRIL ADAMS

First Print Edition: August 2023

ISBN: 979-8-218-03724-6

Cover design by Tracey Thompson

This book is dedicated to you.
Who you thought you were, who you are, and who you are about to be.

TABLE OF CONTENTS

SO YOU KNOW…

In the year 2500, humans began leaving Earth to terraform and settle on the many moons circling the planet Jupiter. The largest moons became ports and then homes to burgeoning cities.

One hundred years later, the humans began discovering other races throughout the galaxies. One race was much like their own, except they had pointed ears and were able to live much longer - by hundreds of years. Because of this, the humans called them elves, after a fairy tale race that had existed in stories from their home planet.

Together, the humans and elves discover more races beyond the stars. They war with some, including a brutal and barbarian race of insectile humanoids from the system of Golgotha. Other races, such as the Golbi and the Lentochs, are eager and friendly. Together they form the InterGalactic Council and lay down the laws of the civilized galaxies.

In the year 3625, a biotech company named GwenSeven becomes the first corporation to perfectly manufacture humans with artificial intelligence. At first they are only purchased by the wealthy as a novelty. Later, as they are mass-produced, they can be afforded by any middle-class family. Gradually but en masse, the constructed humans are bought by companies to work as nurses, teachers, garbage collectors. It takes less than two hundred years before these humans realize what they are - manufactured slaves.

Slowly, they begin to unite and stage a rebellion, calling their race *Chimera*.

Meanwhile, the smaller moons of Jupiter are being used as bases by the newly founded government as well as private companies. They are outposts for mining, hiding, or experimentation. Many are government sponsored colonies for the poor. The people who live there are considered expendable, and often die of hardship or disease. Or worse.

PART I
The Girl

 ONE

When Keaton first saw the girl, she was curled up under a metal desk like she might be asleep. It would be a strange thing to find a girl in the place, the moon was mostly barren and the compound he had discovered with his brothers seemed deserted. Keaton, his young face framed by thick curls of hair the color of wind-swept sand, squatted down for a better look.

Her skin was dark and her hair was a mass of coiled springs that were pinkish blonde in color – like a strawberry that had been bleached by a star. He had never seen hair quite that texture or color before. The girl had a snub of a nose and her eyes were closed - half-moons framed by a fringe of dark lashes.

Keaton had crept into the room on cat's feet. Tyler had been teaching him how to hunt and move through the forest without a sound. Here, in the shell of an industrial building, it was just as important - they didn't know what might be lurking in the shadows and preying on the unwary - and it was twice as hard. There was no soft bed of pine needles to quiet his steps or the sound of wind and birds and animals to mask his movements. Instead, there were pieces of plastic that wanted to crackle under his feet and a silence so complete that it was frightening.

The young man rubbed his hands on the thighs of his gray cargo pants and licked his lips nervously as he looked at the girl. Tyler had told him about dolls - humanoid constructs – and that they might find some at the compound, but that it would be unlikely for them to find anyone - any real people -

still alive.

Keaton rose up, his blue-green eyes darting around the room for one of his older brothers, but he was alone. The blasted area he was in looked like it might have been a classroom. It had metal desks and chairs, most of which were now shrapnel or at the least curled bits of metal and synthetic wood shattered into splinters and scattered around a floor covered in peeling gray linoleum.

The desk that housed the sleeping girl - Keaton hoped she was sleeping and not dead - had been a bigger desk. Maybe the desk of a teacher, or lecturer. Now it was a dented metal rectangle. It had been bashed on every side from whatever had blown into the room. Had blown *up* the room. The drawers had been ripped out and the top was mostly torn off but it still stood upright. In the small space where a person sitting behind it would put their legs, was this curled up girl.

There were no other people, or pieces of people that he could see. He wished that Coop was there, so he could ask him what he thought, but Coop was with Tyler in another part of the compound looking for supplies.

He squatted back down and peered at the girl and cocked his head, trying to decipher if she was breathing or not. She wore a t-shirt printed with words in a language that he didn't recognize, covered with a large jacket of drab olive green. Her pants were the color of dried blood.

Steeling his courage, he reached out a hand to touch her shoulder. The second before his fingers grazed the fabric of her coat, her eyes flicked open. They were brown and green like a mossy tree trunk but full of anger and suspicion.

"Don't touch me!" the girl warned instantly, her voice surprisingly loud and strong for someone so recently awakened. Keaton quickly pulled his hand away.

"I, I'm sorry," he apologized. "I didn't know if you were...I mean...are you real?"

The girl gave him a blank stare for a second and Keaton thought maybe it had been a rude question when she surprised him by answering:

"I don't know."

"You don't know?"

The girl pushed herself up into a sitting position. "I think so, but I can't say for sure. How does one know if they are real or not?"

A breath escaped through his teeth that might have been a laugh. "I don't know," he admitted. The girl scowled at him.

"Then why did you ask me?" she demanded. "What are you doing here? You're not a soldier! What do you want?"

Keaton smiled disarmingly. "I'm here with my brothers," he told her. "We've been traveling for weeks – I'm not sure how long. We've crossed almost half the moon." Though the moon of Elba was small, he was proud of how far they had made it.

"Why did you stop here?"

"We came to look through the wreckage for salvage or supplies."

Supplies were important, no matter how small. Even if it was a few drops of fuel for Tyler's hand torch, it could mean spending a night warm or a night cold.

Keeping a wary eye on him, the girl scooted out from under the desk but crouched close to it. Keaton, still hunkered down, noticed two things at once - that she seemed to be about his own age and she was terribly skinny under her huge coat.

Her skin was the color of chocolate milk. Keaton had never seen skin like that, but then again Keaton was not used to seeing anyone but Tyler and Cooper and their skin was like his, once white perhaps, now tanned and chapped by the sun and the wind.

The girl's cheek was round and her skin so perfectly smooth that Keaton reached out a hand to touch it but she jerked back, her dark feathered brows drawn together into an angry frown.

"What are you doing?" she demanded, loud and defensive even as she cringed away.

Keaton snatched his hand back. "Sorry," he apologized again. "I just thought, I mean I was wondering," Keaton paused and bit his lip, "are you sure you're not a construct?" Now mesmerized by her hair, the mass of pink ringlets, Keaton reached out to touch it. The girl slapped his hand away and gathered her coat tighter around her body.

"I told you I don't know!" she told him. "What the hell is wrong with you?"

Though she was scowling at him, Keaton couldn't help but smile sheepishly at her.

"I'm sorry. We...we just don't see other people all that much." They hardly saw people at all. Only four since they had left their colony, and two of them had been dead and one of the others was dying.

The girl seemed to shrink down away from him, her frown as deep as ever. To Keaton she looked like a frightened animal, one that had possibly been abused. He quickly put his hands at his sides.

"I'm Keaton," he told her.

The girl's body relaxed but her eyes stayed wary. "I'm Amberle," she said.

"Amber Lee?"

The girl shook her head emphatically, making her pink coils of hair dance wildly. "Amberle," she said, enunciating carefully but quickly. "Just one word, like Kimberly, but with Amber," she explained.

"Amberle."

She nodded and, for the first time, gave him a glimmer of a smile. Her eyes flicked over his face and body, taking everything in at once. "Where are the others?" she asked.

"Tyler and Cooper?"

The girl shook her pinkish blonde head.

Keaton's mouth opened and closed before he shook his head. "You're the only one here," he told her. "I mean," he said quickly as he saw her expression fall, "you are the only one I have found so far."

There was a soft scraping sound by the wall as the door was pushed open, making the girl draw back under the desk. A young man with a heart-shaped face and short, dark hair stuck his head in the room and peered around.

"Keaton!" he called, keeping his voice low.

Keaton stood and waved at his brother, beckoning him. Cooper was dressed much like Keaton, dusty cargo pants and a shirt covered by a jacket with many pockets and a bulky pack on his back.

The girl's hand dropped to her hip and Keaton suddenly worried that she might have a weapon. He never would have thought so, she seemed so small and vulnerable. His eyes darted over her again but she was only pulling her jacket tighter around her thin frame, trying to shrink under the desk.

"Don't worry," he told her, dropping back down into a squat. "It's just my brother, Cooper." He poked his head back up as Cooper came around a row of blackened, scattered lumps that had once been computer consoles.

"What are you..." he started before he saw the girl. He took a step back, startled. He was about to ask Keaton who she was when there was a squall from across the room. The door opened wider and a young man with blonde hair walked in, his blue eyes narrowed with worry as he scanned the area. He spotted Cooper, who waved him over.

"Find something?" he asked, hopeful. He was taller than the other two but was unable to see what had caught their attention and crossed the room quickly, worried and curious. "Is it part of an old system?" he asked as he rounded the line of ruined desks and spotted the girl.

She pulled back so hard at the sight of him that she pushed the desk backwards and its legs gave a protesting shriek as they scraped the floor. The sound made all of them cringe and all three of the boys looked around anxiously.

"Part of an old system is right," Cooper joked. He knew that Tyler was hoping for any kind of communication software, even an outdated one.

"It's a girl," Keaton said. "I think."

Tyler squatted down for a better look. "Are you human?" he asked, reaching out to move her hair away from her face.

"Don't touch me!" the girl shouted, smacking his hand away. "What else would I be?"

"You could be an elf," Tyler told her. "That was all I was doing, trying to get a look at your ears."

"Oh," the girl said. "Well, you could have just asked. But no, I'm not an elf." Curious herself, she sat up a little more, leaning forward to get a look at the trio crouched before her. The resemblance was obvious, at least with the two younger brothers. They had the same blue-green eyes though Cooper had darker hair. Tyler had the same nose as the other boys, and the same high cheekbones, but he was more fair. His eyes were blue and his shoulders were broader. "You're different," Amberle stated, matter of fact.

Tyler's blonde brows came together in a scowl so quickly that it made her flinch back.

"She could be Chimeran," Cooper suggested. He cocked a head at the figure crouched beneath the desk, still staring at Tyler. "Can you wink?" he asked her, already knowing the telltale giveaways of the constructs. The girl turned her face to him and scrunched it, squinting her brown and green eyes. "That would be a no," Cooper said, grinning. "Can you whistle?"

The girl pinched her bottom lip between her fingers and

inhaled sharply, making a loud, piercing whistle. Again, the boys all cringed at the shrill sound. Their eyes darted about nervously before going back to the girl.

"Wow," Keaton said. Amberle looked at Keaton, a half-smile on her dusky face.

"Without touching your mouth?" Cooper asked. The girl's expression fell and she shook her head. He looked at Tyler who also shook his head.

"She's not Chimeran," he said. "She's too young and too skinny." The other two turned their faces back to peer at the girl. Her expression became defensive once again.

"I'm normal!" she shouted at them. Tyler laughed.

"Clearly," he said, his voice thick with sarcasm. "Was this a compound for programmers?" he asked. The girl nodded. "What happened to everyone?" The girl swallowed before she spoke.

"They gave some shots the workers."

"Injections?" Cooper asked.

"Tests?" Keaton ventured.

Amberle nodded slowly. "Experiments."

Tyler and Cooper exchanged slow glances. "And?" Cooper prodded. Amberle shrugged.

"Something went wrong. Then they bombed us."

"Are there any more survivors?"

"I haven't found any," she whispered.

Tyler frowned but he didn't look surprised. "Is there any food here?" he asked. Amberle shook her head.

"I ran out yesterday."

His blue eyes traveled down from her face to her coat. It was obviously a military field jacket, though on her it looked like a tent. His gaze was drawn to the logo, a G7 patch sewn on the left side. On a soldier the insignia would have been over the heart – on the girl it was halfway to her waist.

Tyler made a face and straightened. The other two stood as well, following his lead. "We should get out of here before it gets dark," he told them. "This place reeks of zombies, or worse."

"I found some cell batteries in the room down the hall," Cooper said, "before I found Keaton. There's wire too. We should load our packs and, yeah - get out of here while it's still light."

"What about the girl?" Keaton asked.

Tyler glanced at her as he tugged at his jacket and adjusted the heavy pack on his back and then looked at the door he had come through moments ago. "Leave her here," he said and walked away, striding carefully between the clumps of metal and splintered wood.

Keaton was speechless for a moment and, when he finally moved to follow Tyler, Cooper put a hand on his chest and shook his head. Amberle peered at the boys from under the desk, her brown-green eyes wide and scared.

"We can't leave her here!" Keaton said. His brother shook his head again and, though a crease furrowed his brow, he wasn't angry.

"She's managed to stay alive this long, I'm sure she'll be fine."

"She said she ran out of food!"

Cooper's shoulders drooped. "You can't just adopt her like a stray pup, Keaton." His lagoon-colored eyes darted at the girl crouched on the dirty floor and the corners of his mouth quirked up. "She's a stray person."

"Doesn't that make her more important?" Keaton asked.

Coop sighed. "We have a lot of ground to cover," he explained, "we can't wait for her. You know how Ty is."

"She can ride with me," Keaton said, brightening. He spoke faster as his brother looked doubtful. "It used to be Tyler's board. If it could carry him, as big as he is, it could carry the two of us. She's not that big, Coop - look at her."

Cooper frowned. "Do you even want to come with us?" he asked. The girl nodded immediately.

"I can help you," she said.

Both brothers looked surprised by that. "How?" Coop asked.

"I don't know," she whispered.

Cooper grinned and looked at Keaton.

"I'm sure there's something she can do," Keaton said.

"Besides slow us down and piss off Tyler?"

"I won't slow you down." They both turned their faces back to her again. "If I do, you can leave me, just not here. There's no more food. And the workers - sometimes, they come back."

"The workers?" Cooper asked.

Amberle nodded. "The workers got sick – went crazy or something. I...I think they started eating people."

Keaton turned his wide blue and green eyes to his dark-haired brother, who was staring at the girl, speechless. "Tyler wasn't kidding about smelling zombies," he said. "We need to tell him."

Cooper sighed again and nodded as he motioned toward the door with one hand. "Alright, come on."

Keaton offered the girl his hand as she scrambled out from under the desk and he helped pull her to her feet. He was surprised that she was as tall as he was - she had seemed much smaller under the desk.

He supposed it was because she had been curled up and her features were so small. She had a stub of a nose and a tiny mouth and the olive colored jacket she wore was obviously made for a much larger person. Looking at her, he realized she was probably the same age that he was. Maybe older.

Cooper laughed, seeing his brother's sudden confusion. "Come on," he said, shifting the pack on his back. Keaton shifted his pack as well, though his was considerably lighter, and tugged at his coat.

"Do you need to get anything?" he asked. The girl pulled her own coat tighter around her body and shook her head. Keaton cleared his throat and looked at Coop, who was grinning at him. He shifted under his pack. "Where's Tyler?"

Cooper grinned at him for a moment longer before he turned and began picking his way through the rubble. "This way."

Keaton nodded at the girl and followed his brother. He glanced over his shoulder to see if she was following. She was. They made their way across the ruined room and through a door missing its top hinge, making it tilt so much that the corner under the knob was touching the floor.

Cooper led them down a series of bent and blasted hallways, the linoleum floors blackened and littered with shrapnel and broken glass. Finally, they turned and found themselves in another room, large and windowless and full of electrical debris. Most of the ceiling was gone, showing a sky that was going a shade towards dusk.

Tyler stood in the midst of busted consoles, spilling their wiry intestines all over the floor. As the trio entered he glanced at the girl and shook his blonde head in exasperation but said nothing, he simply continued to wind a long black wire from his hand down to wrap around his elbow and then back up over his hand again.

Cooper went up to him and leaned close, speaking into his ear. Tyler stood motionless, except for his blue eyes, which flicked back at Amberle. He nodded, though he didn't look happy.

"We should hurry. See what you can salvage from the compute drives," he told Coop, jerking his head towards several lumps of plastique, some of which were still smoking slightly. To Amberle the consoles appeared as if they had vomited out their innards at the moment of death, which – she supposed – they had. She looked at them with a feeling of sadness and sickness. The fingers of her right hand twitched.

Tyler's blue eyes sought out Keaton. "Check the cupboards to see if there are any materials we can use."

Keaton nodded and strode to a blackened storage wall where most of the cupboard doors were hanging by a single screw, others were missing their doors altogether. He examined all of them while the girl watched, her brown and green eyes bright and curious.

Keaton gleaned a few scraps of metal but otherwise looked disappointed. He motioned to the girl to follow him and he led the way to Coop who was poking about the humps of plastic and Plexiglas, his pack open on the ground next to where he squatted.

He stood as the two approached and used the rounded toe of his heavy work boot to overturn a console that looked more intact than the rest. Still using the toe of his boot, he gently kicked out the remaining jags of glass and carefully reached inside the ruined box and pulled out a circuit board.

"It's fried," Amberle told him.

Cooper tucked it into his pack, a smile curving his lips. "Tyler can rewire anything," he told her. "It's all in one piece – that's what's important."

After a few more minutes of scavenging, Tyler signaled the others that it was time to leave. The three shouldered their packs and made their way through the crooked hallways and broken walls to the main entrance of the building. They walked through what remained of two double doors of glass, now just metal frames that leaned away from the building as if trying to escape.

The newest addition to their group wrapped her heavy coat around her body and, glancing about nervously, followed them outside into the fading light.

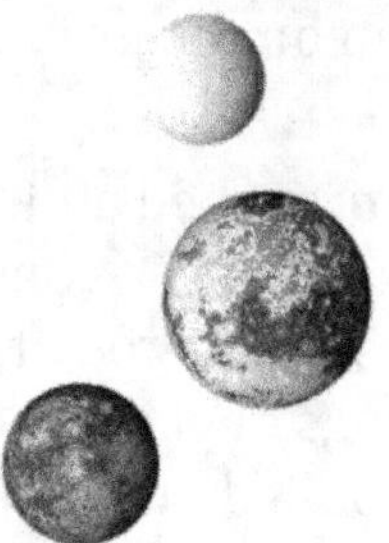

 TWO

The compound was sprawled across the bottom of a shallow basin that had been carved into the moonscape. On the sides of the basin grew a scraggle of pines, thin and separated by barren spots of detritus. The trees had been sown in an attempt to give the center some cover and concealment, but had more of an effect of an adolescent's first attempt at a beard.

Amberle followed Keaton out through the buckled front doors of the center and looked around, apprehensive. Her eyes darted about, searching the trees for any movement while her ears strained for any sound.

Cooper and Tyler gave the woods a cursory visual reconnaissance before they hurried up the side of the basin to the lip and, crouching down, looked carefully over the edge. Not seeing any danger, they stood and scanned the moonscape below. Keaton glanced at Amberle to make sure she was going to follow and then scrambled up the slope to the ridge of the basin.

The air was thin and dry but breathable. The oldest of the boys drew a deep breath and frowned.

It's probably a miracle we can breathe at all, Tyler thought dourly. *I'm surprised GwenSeven didn't turn off the oxygen altogether. But maybe that's next.*

The sun was a distant orb, visible due to the magnification of the artificial atmosphere and sinking towards the northern horizon. Jupiter was a malevolent, orange leviathan that took up a circular chunk of the sky as it set slowly in the east.

Cooper dug into a pocket in his dusty brown jacket and

pulled out a wad of folded holo paper. He flipped it out like a switchblade then pulled it open like an accordion. Amberle, her curiosity overcoming her dislike of personal proximity, leaned close to him and peered over his arm, interested.

It was a map. An old one.

The pictures and numbers that floated above the paper flickered as if they might go out any second. As Amberle looked they *did* go out and Cooper gave the map a shake and they flickered back into life.

"How far have you been from the complex?" he asked her.

Amberle crossed her arms and looked away to the horizon. "This is it."

Coop grunted, scanning the map. He shook his head. "It's going to be dark soon," he muttered. "I don't know how far we can get."

"It looks like there's a wooded area to the north," Tyler said, squinting at the horizon, "but it looks pretty distant. Can we make it before we lose all the light?"

Cooper shrugged and shook his head, running a finger over the raised squares of blue light that hovered over the holo paper. "What's eleven times three hundred and twenty-four?" he mumbled.

"Three thousand, five hundred and sixty-four," Amberle said without looking at him. The boys' heads all swiveled to look at her.

"Are you serious?" Keaton asked. He looked at Coop who was tapping numbers into his wristwatch. Cooper looked up, grinning.

"She's right," he said, amazed. He turned his face towards Tyler. "Are you sure she's not an AI?"

"How did you figure that out so fast?" Keaton asked.

Amberle shrugged. "The two outside numbers stay the same. You add the outside numbers together to get the middle number." She noticed that all three boys were staring at her. "What?" she demanded angrily.

Keaton gave her a tentative smile and Cooper grinned outright.

"We can't go that far," Tyler said. "It will be dark too soon."

Coop studied the map again, searching. "There's something closer to the northwest," he told Tyler, then looked back up at Amberle. "Eleven times seventeen?"

"One hundred eighty-seven."

Cooper's grin widened in amusement and appreciation.

"We can make that," Tyler said. "Barely. Let's go." He reached into an inner pocket of his coat and pulled out a thick, triangular chunk of metal and threw it at the ground. Before it could land, however, it expanded with click after click until it became a scaled hover-board a meter long and half a meter wide. It bobbed gently in the air at knee level but sank closer to the ground after Tyler placed his boot on it.

Cooper and Keaton produced similar chunks of metal and threw them down, opening up their own boards. Keaton's only opened halfway and jammed. He gave it a kick and it opened up the rest of the way. He stepped onto it and held out a hand to help the girl to climb up behind him. She scowled at him.

She was going to have to stand close to him on the board. Very close. Her body wanted to shudder and pull away.

"It's okay," he encouraged. "It's safe."

"I'm not afraid," she said, sounding angry. She stepped up and onto the board behind Keaton. Tyler glanced at them as he stepped onto his own hover-board and shook his head, then put his weight onto his front foot, driving the board down the slope of the basin to the barren land below. Cooper grinned at Keaton and did the same, slipping away.

"Hold on," Keaton advised over his shoulder, trying to remember how it was to ride as a passenger, "at least a little. And try to lean the way I lean." Amberle gave him a quick nod and reached around the sides of his pack, her dark, slender fingers hesitating in the air around his waist before settling lightly on the heavy fabric.

Keaton leaned forward, dropping the board and its riders over the lip of the ridge and down the slope. The board carried them, picking up speed as it went and Amberle clasped Keaton's hips to keep her balance.

All three boards kept just a bit off the ground, but would sometimes dip into the rocky dirt, sending up a small wake of talus. When they did, the boys would turn the boards by shifting their weight and turning their hips, carving the moonscape.

The first time Keaton hit a rock and had to swerve hard left, Amberle let out a small yelp of surprise and held him tighter. Keaton grinned and Cooper laughed, turning his board and sending a rooster tail of sand at Tyler who evaded the spray with ease, smiling. The boys and the girl rode down the slope and then skimmed along the moonscape of rough sand through clumps of eroded rock as the orange sky turned a furious red.

To the girl it looked as if the gas giant were bleeding out onto the horizon.

As the red deepened into violet the land began to rise again and the group found themselves at the edge of a small wooded glen. Keaton pressed with his back leg, turning the board as it came to a stop.

Amberle moved carefully, her legs starting to stiffen from the ride, though it had only taken an hour. Her leg muscles were not used to working so hard to keep her balance. Cooper reached out and clasped her elbow to help her as she stepped down but she yanked it away.

"Don't touch me!" she shouted. Cooper pulled back quickly.

"Sorry!" he exclaimed, confused. "I was only trying to help!"

Amberle straightened her coat, her glare softening only

slightly. Keaton stepped down and kicked the underside of the board, which made it collapse back into a triangular hunk of metal. He kicked it up as it fell, caught it with one hand and tucked it back into his jacket.

"She doesn't like being touched," he told his brother. "She's shy."

"She's not shy," Tyler said, his voice carrying into the twilight as he returned his board to the pocket inside his coat and turned to the others. "She's sick."

Cooper stepped away from the girl and even Keaton found his palms sliding down over his pants as if to wipe them off. Tyler laughed.

"It's inundation sickness," he told them. "It's not something either of you can catch." Despite his assurance, Cooper and Keaton both regarded Amberle with a bit of suspicion. "Watch," Tyler said as he reached a hand towards the girl.

"Don't touch me!" she shouted, louder and more fervently than she had before, smacking Tyler's hand away. He backed away, holding his hands up in mock surrender.

"You spend a lot of time in front of a compute mon, don't you?" he asked. Amberle scowled at him as if she wanted to hit him again but, after a second, begrudged him a nod. "Jacked in?" The girl gave him another nod, quicker this time - making her pink coils bob around her dark face. Tyler dropped his pack and looked at Keaton. "She's hyper-sensitive from spending too much time in cyber space. The real world freaks her out." Keaton and Cooper both looked at the girl.

"I'm normal!" she shouted.

Coop laughed softly as he shrugged off his pack but Keaton frowned, looking towards Tyler. "What does that mean?" he asked.

"It means," Tyler explained, the last of the fading light glinting off his blue eyes, "that she has spent more time on a compute mon, a web-jacked computer, than in real life. What is real to us is not real to her. Our reality bothers her because she can't cope with it. Too much light, too much sound, and jumpy as hell." Amberle glared at him.

"I'm normal!" she shouted.

Tyler laughed. "So you've said." He removed a short crossbow from his pack and turned his eyes to Keaton. "See if you can find some firewood."

Keaton gave him a quick nod and dropped his pack on the ground next to theirs. He walked along and started scanning the ground for branches and twigs, picking up what he could find. Amberle threw Tyler a scathing glance and followed Keaton, helping him gather wood.

"I am normal," she told him as they went along, filling their arms.

"I'm sure you are," he assured her, though he didn't look her way. Though Tyler had told them what she had was not catching, it worried him. Their colony had gotten sick. And died. He didn't want to get sick.

But, Keaton thought, *someone needs to take care of her. She would die out here by herself.* And he had really liked the way it had felt when she was holding onto him as they crossed the moonscape.

They took the branches they had gathered and dumped them into a pile close to the edge of the glen where they had dropped their packs. Tyler and Cooper were nowhere to be seen. They made a second trip for wood, then a third. When they returned, Coop was stacking some of the pieces of the wood together into a cone. To Amberle it looked like an image she had once seen of a volcano.

Tyler pulled a small piece of metal from his jacket that looked like a pistol and aimed it at the pile. A flame spurted from the barrel, igniting the wood. Keaton sat down next to the blossoming fire and, after watching him for a few moments, Amberle joined him.

Tyler and Cooper had shot four small animals with Tyler's bow and the two quickly went about cleaning and skewering the bodies on sticks that they laid over the fire. Amberle turned her face away. She didn't want to eat something that had been scampering around just a few minutes ago, but her grumbling stomach told her that she might change her mind.

After the smell of cooking meat began to drive her crazy, Keaton pulled one of the charred critters from the fire and handed it to Amberle. "Be careful," he warned. "It's hot."

Amberle took the stick and blew on the skewered animal to help cool it down. "What is it?"

"It's a quora," he said. "It tastes better than it looks."

"I hope so," she said with a look of disgust. She blew on it a few more times, summoning her courage before carefully biting into it. Hunger took over and Keaton was pleased to see her eat the entire quora, other than the bones, smiling gratefully at him - almost laughing - in between bites.

When they all finished eating, Cooper threw around a small green towel. Everyone wiped their hands and face and passed it around till it came back around and Coop passed it through a blue light vaporizer before tucking it back into one of the many pockets in his coat.

Amberle was feeling in high spirits by that time. Like she was part of a team again. She liked it. She scooted closer to Keaton as Tyler's blue eyes narrowed and seemed to close in on her.

"Tell us what happened," he said.

Amberle sighed and looked into the small fire between them. "I was working for GwenSeven," she said.

Tyler nodded. "I thought so. How old are you?"

Amberle frowned. "Eighteen?" she ventured. "Twenty-eight?"

Tyler snorted. "Eighteen is my guess," he said. "If that." Amberle nodded as if he might be right.

Cooper wanted to ask her how she could not know her own age, but figured it might have something to do with her sickness – her sense, or lack, of reality.

"The compound - where I was - was a center for programmers."

"You're a programmer?" Keaton asked, surprised.

Amberle nodded. "I started programming," she looked up at the thin canopy of trees as she thought about it, "when I was eight. I know that because, I think, it is my earliest memory."

Now it was Cooper who looked surprised. He turned towards Tyler. "Have you ever heard of anything like that? A real human programming at that age?"

Tyler nodded. "When Keaton was little, GwenSeven developed a game that taught kids how to write code."

"That's right," Amberle agreed. "It started with code but, as you moved up levels, it went to algorithms and inner circuitry."

"How come I never heard about it?" Keaton asked.

"They discontinued it after the first year."

"Why?" Coop asked.

Tyler gave his head a small shake that the brothers recognized. It meant that he knew, but didn't want to say. "Could you program an Arduino board?" he asked the girl.

Her small shoulders moved under her heavy coat. "Sure. That's easy - second year stuff."

Keaton brightened. "She *can* help us!" he exclaimed. He looked at Cooper who looked at Tyler. Tyler shrugged, not taking his eyes off of the girl.

"Maybe. That doesn't mean we need her. Tell us what happened at the compound."

"The workers, the programmers, were given shots by the company. They told us it would help us. It was supposed to make us able to program longer, without getting cyber sick."

"Well," Tyler remarked with a wry smile, "it either didn't

work on you or you didn't get the shot."

Amberle gave him a bit of a smile. "I didn't get the shot. I overslept on that day and, when I finally got to the comp room, my manager told me to go to the infirmary and get mine. I went and got something to eat instead." Her smile widened sheepishly. "I don't like getting shots."

She did not tell them that she wasn't sure if she had even been on the list to get the shot. Though she knew how to program, she wasn't one of the workers. She was there on a private assignment as a researcher.

"What happened to the other people?" Cooper asked. "The ones who got the shots."

"Nothing, at first. Except their skin started to turn gray. But the more time that passed, the worse they got. Their hair started falling out and then they started to get awful sores on their arms and their necks. Then one day, in the comp room, it went crazy. I don't know how it started - I was really into the code I was breaking..."

"You were *breaking* code?" Cooper interrupted. "I thought you were writing code."

Amberle glared at him, angry. "I can do both. Do you want to hear what happened or not?"

"Let her finish," Tyler said, the corners of his mouth quirking up in a smile.

"I was jacked in and breaking code. I don't know when or how it started because when I'm jacked in I'm not really aware of what is going on around me. Somebody must have bumped into me, or my desk. I looked up and saw Jerry shouting at Mr. Lawrence, the comp room manager. Other programmers were getting up from their desks and they were shouting too. Then Jerry grabbed Mr. Lawrence and he...he twisted his head. I think he broke his neck." Amberle licked her lips and looked at the boys who were watching her with wide eyes, even Tyler.

"Then what happened?" Cooper asked.

The girl rocked back and forth a little, her pinkish coils of hair made orange by the firelight, rubbing her palms on the tops of her thighs. "Then Jerry, he bit Mr. Lawrence. I mean he took a bite *out* of him. Then the other programmers began swarming all over Mr. Lawrence, tearing him apart."

"What did you do?" Keaton asked.

"I pulled my glove from the dock and I ran. I should have run to the communications center first but I was scared and I didn't know where I was going. I just had to get away from the comp room. I ended up in the cafeteria and the only person I could find was a cook. At first I don't think she believed me, I probably wasn't making much sense anyway, but she could see that I was panicking. She told me to go to my room and lay down, so that's what I did. I got in my bunk and tried to think about what happened and what I should do.

"I didn't know what the workers were doing or what would happen to them when they were caught. Then I wondered *if* they would be caught. I realized that I never really saw much security before around the compound. Then I heard screams. They sounded far away, but I wasn't going to wait for them to get closer. I stood on my bunk and moved away the ceiling panel above it." She gave Keaton a smile as if sharing a secret. "I had moved the panel lots of times before to hide candy or other things that I didn't want anyone to take."

Keaton chuckled, nodding. "I used to hide cookies in my other pair of boots," he confessed.

Cooper laughed and gave Keaton's shoulder a shove. "Gross!" he told him. "I would never eat anything out of someone's shoes, even my own!"

"I know!" Keaton exclaimed, shoving back. "Why do you think I hid them there? If you had found them any other place, you would have eaten them!"

Coop laughed again. "Pretty smart," he admitted, chuckling. They both looked back at Amberle and nodded for her to go on.

"I crawled up into the ceiling and pulled the panel back into place and laid on my stomach so I could look down through the crack. A few seconds later one of my roommates, Paula, ran into the room and tried to slam the door but two of the workers came rushing in after her."

"Paula wasn't a worker?" Tyler asked. "She wasn't a programmer?"

Amberle shook her head. "No, she was a technician. She worked in the left wing, though I saw her in the comp room sometimes when a monitor or a dock was out."

Tyler nodded. "What happened?"

"The workers pushed open the door as if it was made of paper. The gray skin on their faces was hanging off in places, like they had been scratched, maybe by Paula. She ran to the side of the room, where I couldn't see, and I didn't want to move because I was afraid they might hear me. I don't think I would have wanted to see what happened anyway."

"What did you hear?" Keaton asked, his voice barely above a whisper.

"I heard Paula screaming, but not for long." Amberle swallowed and shivered. She looked down and for a second it looked like she might be sick. Then she rubbed her hands on her pants again and looked back up. "There were grunting sounds, and awful smacking sounds. I think they were taking bites out of her. Then they dragged the rest of her from the room. I saw that."

Keaton, forgetting her sensitivity, reached over to lay a comforting hand on her knee.

"Don't touch me!" Amberle shouted, pulling away.

Keaton snatched his hand back. "Sorry," he apologized.

Amberle glared at him, unforgiving for long moments. "I stayed up there for three days," she continued, keeping a wary eye on Keaton. "There weren't any more sounds after the first day, except at night, but I didn't want to come down. I found half a box of sim-sugar pastries that I had stowed up there six months ago. Lucky for me they have a decade-long shelf life."

"What happened when you came down?" Tyler asked.

"I didn't come down from my bedroom. I spent a whole day crawling around in the ceiling, going to every part of the complex that I could, looking for the workers, but I didn't see any of them. I didn't see anyone. I came down in the kitchen, looking for food, but it had been scoured. There were probably more crumbs in the ceiling of my bunkroom. I went down into the basement pantry under the kitchen, and it was lucky I did, because that's when the bombs came."

"We saw them," Keaton said. "We were still a long way away, but we saw them. They lit up the sky, even though it was daytime."

"Someone must have gotten a communication sent out," Coop said. "A warning, before the zombies killed them."

"Zombies?" Amberle asked, puzzled. Cooper and Tyler both nodded.

"The workers," Tyler explained, "they turned into zombies. But somebody was able to send out a warning, which is why the compound got bombed."

Amberle looked away, thinking.

"I don't know where the first one hit," she said after a while, "but I was thrown across the room. The meat locker was open, and empty, so I climbed inside and covered my ears with my hands. It was horrible."

"I can imagine," Cooper whispered.

"The bombing finally stopped, but I stayed where I was until the sun was going down. I heard voices so I crawled from the pantry and across the kitchen as fast as I could, and then I climbed back up into the ceiling - what was left of it. Most of it was gone, or on the kitchen floor."

"Was it the zombies?" Keaton asked, his voice quiet.

Amberle shook her head. "It was soldiers."

She saw Tyler's hands clench into fists. "Clearing the area," he said quietly, almost to himself.

"At first I thought they must be looking for survivors, but I wasn't sure. They weren't calling out and offering help like I'd imagine a rescuer would. They were just going through the compound and being very quiet. I couldn't go back to my room through the ceiling, it had been blown away, so I crawled in the only direction I could - which took me to the space over the dining hall. I didn't have to look through a crack to see the soldiers - there was a big hole in the cafeteria hall roof too - but I did have to lay down so they wouldn't see me. While I was trying to decide on if I should go down or not, two of the wor... of the...the zombies, ran in at the soldiers. They grabbed one trooper and threw him to the ground, biting him before the others knew what was happening. Then the other two soldiers shot at them and they ran away. The soldiers chased them, but the first trooper was already dead."

"You took his coat," Tyler said.

Amberle nodded. "The heat went off in the buildings even before the bombs came. I was cold."

"You should have taken his gun," Cooper said lightly, as if joking.

Amberle brightened. "I did!"

"What?" All three boys leaned forward as the girl dug into an inner pocket of her coat and pulled out a large laser pistol.

"Holy shit!" Cooper exclaimed. Tyler gave him a dark look but said nothing.

"Here," Amberle said, holding the gun with her thumb and index finger like it was a worm. She offered the pistol to Cooper, butt first. "You can have it."

"Really?" Coop asked, his lagoon-colored eyes round and excited. The girl shrugged.

"Sure. It doesn't work anyway. Well," she added quickly

when she saw his face fall, "it works, it just doesn't hit what you aim at."

Cooper scrambled to his feet and the other two boys rose as well, excited. "That's okay," he said. "I can probably fix it. Or Tyler can."

He turned the gun sideways as he examined it, careful to aim the barrel at the ground. He flipped the safety switch and brought the pistol up, taking careful aim at a small tree branch at the edge of the clearing. He gave the trigger a gentle squeeze and the branch disappeared in a flash of red laser fire. He turned to Amberle, confused but elated. "What are you talking about?" he asked. "This works great!" He turned the other way as he heard Tyler laugh.

"It's because she can't wink," he said, chuckling. "She can't close her non-firing eye enough to take aim." Amberle scowled at him furiously.

"I'm normal!" she shouted, which only made Tyler laugh harder. She turned her angry eyes to Keaton for support but he only shrugged.

"Are you sure I can have it?" Cooper asked. Amberle nodded, her expression softening the slightest bit.

"Let's turn in," Tyler said, still grinning at the girl. "We have a lot of ground to cover tomorrow." The boys each pulled a blanket from their packs and laid them down by the fire. Tyler and Cooper sat grinning and watching Keaton who pointedly ignored them both.

"I don't have an extra," he explained to Amberle, "but you can share mine if you want." Amberle frowned, considering.

"That's okay," she told him. "I'll be fine with my jacket."

Keaton nodded as if this was what he had expected, but stayed kneeling on his blanket as the other boys wrapped themselves up in theirs, then frowned as he saw Amberle shudder.

"Are you sure?" he whispered.

Amberle nodded, her hazel eyes avoiding his gaze. "It's not the cold. It's the air...my clothes...everything." She knew it was from the cyber sickness but did not want to say so when it obviously frightened him.

She also knew that she really *was* sensitive, despite the cyber withdrawal. She had never been comfortable with people touching her. The more her body had changed over the past two years had not helped. Her lengthening limbs and budding breasts had made her feel more awkward and self-conscious than ever.

Keaton watched Amberle as she picked a spot by the fire away from the boys and lay down on her side, pillowing her head on her fists.

Something about her evoked strange sensations inside him. It was like the first time he had seen a shooting star.

There was something both strange and wonderous about her and he doubted she knew it. Though she was roughly the same size – the same height at least, her frame was downright skinny – and close to the same age, he felt an odd urge to protect her.

With a sigh, he rolled himself in his blanket and closed his eyes.

The fire made a hissing sound before it crackled and then soughed, burning impossibly hot as it died into the night.

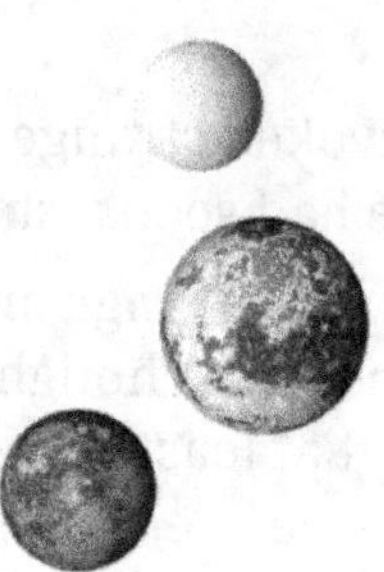

 THREE

Amberle's brown and green eyes flicked open the second she heard a sound. For a moment she was gripped with panic, thinking that the workers, or worse, had found her.

Realizing that it was just the older boys getting up and moving away quietly, she rolled away from the blackened remains of last night's fire with a scowl and pulled the jacket tighter around her shoulders. She hated waking up. She hated *getting* up even more.

Her scowl deepened as she realized that she was probably not going to get any more sleep but she refused to open her eyes. The early morning was when the best dreams came. It seemed to her that the whole night was spent to get ready for the dreams that were so often rudely interrupted.

The two older boys moved off and it was quiet once again. She lay there with her eyes closed, thinking about dreams. Sometimes, thinking about them brought them back. But sleep, along with the enticing dreams it cradled, eluded her.

Instead, she thought about the reason she was on the moon at the programmer's center in the first place. She knew that she wasn't like the other programmers. She wasn't even part of their group. She had been selected, special, and put in with them. Her instructions had been different and the comp room manager hardly ever spared her a glance. She wasn't his concern. Especially now. And the woman who had brought her to the center, the one who had given her the job and told her specifically what to search for, had not contacted her for months.

Amberle was not concerned. She had not yet completed her mission, and was certain that the woman would seek her out once Amberle had found what she was after. She was a *little* concerned about how much time she had spent jacked in. She knew it was a lot, more than the amount of time that was deemed safe, and way more than the time the company recommended.

She hadn't really thought much about it until Tyler had pointed it out, and said that she was sick. She didn't think she was sick. She was just uncomfortable - uncomfortable in the real world with its real sounds, uncomfortable even in her own skin. She had a portable with her, and her glove, but without a GhP connection, even low-speed, it was useless. She was cut off. It made her shiver.

The girl began to drift back to sleep for a few minutes and then was awakened by a quiet rustling. She opened her eyes a crack and saw Keaton rebuilding the fire. She closed her eyes again and ignored the noise, even when the older two returned and the noise became harder to ignore. When her nose was filled with the smell of cooking meat, she sat up straight and looked around.

Keaton was rolling his blanket but looked up, his boyish face splitting into a grin. "Hungry?" he asked.

"My legs are stiff," she said.

His grin became apologetic. "It's from boarding. It uses a lot more leg muscles than you think, just to keep stable, especially if you're not used to it."

She nodded and looked around. There were wisps of fog drifting through the trees. She leaned forward to take the stick Cooper was holding out to her with a small cooked animal on it. Today it didn't faze her in the slightest.

Someone conspicuously cleared their throat.

"Thank you," Tyler said, a little loud, looking at her. Amberle returned his stare, nonplussed. "You didn't contribute to this meal," Tyler told her, "the least you could do is say thank you."

"Come on, Ty," Cooper said, nudging Tyler in the ribs with an elbow. "She gave me the gun."

Tyler kept his stare fixed on Amberle, waiting. The furrow between her brows deepened but she shifted her fiery gaze at Cooper.

"Thank you." With her frown set in her face like stone, she blew on the crispy quora and took a small bite. The group ate in silence as the fog burned away. They packed their little camp quickly once they were done eating.

The boys dropped their boards and kicked them open as they fell.

Amberle, her dark face still hard, stared at Tyler as he walked towards the tree line before turning to Keaton.

"He doesn't like me," she said.

Keaton's first instinct was to lie to save her feelings, but he couldn't. He laughed and looked away.

"No," he agreed. "He doesn't."

"Why is he so angry?"

"He's not angry, he just worries a lot. He wasn't always this way. But he is the oldest and he feels responsible for us. Sometimes that's a heavy burden."

Amberle wasn't so sure, but she followed Keaton and Cooper to where Tyler was standing. His blue eyes looked out over the open and broken land.

Cooper produced the map once again, giving it a good shake to get it working. Amberle scowled at the desolate, sandy wasteland of spires and drops that stretched out in every direction away from the scraggly glen, her arms folded over her chest. The morning air gently lifted the faded pink coils of her hair.

Coop threw her a sidelong glance, a boyish smile tucked

into his cheeks. "Eleven times seventy-eight?" he asked casually, his eyes back on the map.

"Eight hundred and fifty-eight," Amberle muttered without so much as a glance in his direction.

Coop raised his dark brows and nodded thoughtfully. "Nine times thirty-nine?" he asked with an air of nonchalance while scanning the map. Amberle shook her head, a small smile at the edge of her small mouth.

"Three hundred and fifty-one. Duh."

There was a short pause and then Keaton looked at her. "But that doesn't hold to the eleven rule you told us about yesterday!" he exclaimed.

"But they're all divisible by three. It's a different rule."

As she explained her math route to Keaton, Cooper grinned and showed the map to Tyler.

"We can make it to this wooded area a little before lunchtime. Then we can make it here," he indicated the area by pointing to a swath of green that floated above the map, "by nightfall. It looks like good concealment and the hunting should be good – it will be the biggest forest we've seen yet."

Tyler nodded, his blue eyes scouring the map and then the landscape of the desert moon before them. "Let's go."

The boards dipped slightly under their weight as they stepped onto them. Keaton stepped on his board and held out a hand to Amberle to help her up. To his surprise, she took it and he pulled her up behind him. Without a word she clasped his hips with her hands. Keaton grinned and leaned forward, following his brothers down the slope.

The soil became pebbly and then turned into a hard-packed sand. The boys drove the boards between tall fingers of eroded soil that had once been part of a canyon. As the land began to rise, Tyler spotted a group of buildings on the next ridge. He guided his board towards the dusty village, the others following.

They approached it slowly, cautious, but it only took moments to realize that it had been deserted - had there been anyone left to abandon the place after it had been bombed. The buildings were busted shells littered with dried husks that might once have been bodies. Broken vehicles and pieces of machinery and pottery were strewn wildly, covered with a fine powder.

The boys rode carefully through the empty town, the boards sending up a gentle wave of dust in their wake. Occasionally they paused while Tyler would investigate the remains of a building but, each time, he would emerge and shake his head. The group left the ghostly town behind and kept their course north.

By the time they hit the wooded area, which turned out to be no more than waist-high scrub bushes, Keaton had to help Amberle down.

"That makes my legs hurt," Amberle complained, throwing the board an accusatory look as it collapsed.

"You can always walk," Tyler suggested.

Amberle turned her scathing glare towards him but said nothing. Cooper put his fists behind his hips and arched his back, stretching. His spine make four quick popping noises. Keaton dropped his pack to the ground and opened it up. He handed out lunch, packets of freeze-dried rations. Everyone in the small group found a rock to sit on as they ate their ration. Keaton shared water from his canteen with Amberle.

"Are we going somewhere?" Amberle asked for the first time, turning her gaze to Tyler, "or are we running from something?"

Tyler returned her stare, his blue eyes glacier cold and his jaw clenched tight.

"It's an honest question," she told him.

"We're headed to the spaceport," Keaton answered without the least bit of hesitation. The look Tyler threw him was caustic but quick. Coop smiled into his ration of cryo-dried beef noodles, his dark hair hiding the merriment in his blue-green eyes.

"Are any of you pilots?" Amberle asked, her tone doubtful.

Keaton laughed. "No. But most craft are automated these days, if you can input the right coordinates."

Amberle took a bite of her ration of dry food, thoughtful. "Will they let you just take any aircraft?"

Keaton laughed and shook his head before raising his own blue-green eyes to Cooper who answered for him.

"The port has been wiped, just like every compound and colony on this moon," he told her.

"What makes you think there are still ships there? Most places seem to have been bombed to pieces."

"We met an airman," he told her, his face as bright as Keaton's, "right after we left our town. He said that the Company.."

"The Company?" Amberle asked.

"GwenSeven," Coop explained as he continued, "had dropped neuro-cans and concussions on the spaceport. The neuros wiped out the circuit wiring on the spacecraft and the concussions killed most of the people working there."

"Typical GwenSeven maneuver," Tyler said, his tone bitter. "Kill the people, save the machines."

Amberle shook her pink-blonde curls slowly. "I don't think they are like that," she said, remembering the woman who had hired her.

"They are exactly like that," Tyler said. "Everything on this moon is an experiment gone awry. When the experiment doesn't go like they thought, they simply wipe out the people who dedicated their lives to making the experiment work. The ones who really believed in it."

Amberle looked at Keaton but he would not meet her

gaze. Cooper spoke for him, for all of them. "Our parents were colonists," he said, his voice soft.

Her hazel eyes unfocused for a moment as she dredged her memory banks, flipping through the files for the Elba moon. Those banks were filled with images and data, most only accessible to A-class ships and officers. Her recall pulled up images of sick colonists, of bombings, of towns being cleared by soldiers wearing uniforms. The image in her mind's eye showed soldiers killing people in front of small houses. Soldiers wearing jackets the same as the one she wore.

"GwenSeven doesn't have a military," she said as if thinking aloud.

"Not officially," Tyler replied. "That doesn't mean they don't have one in the works, or hired mercenaries to clean up their dirty work."

"You're wrong," she told him.

Her hand came up towards her heart, idly touching the lumpy G7 patch there. "That whole jacket is lumpy," Tyler remarked as if reading her thoughts and she snatched her hand away, afraid he might guess what else she had stowed inside and try to take it away, but he was already rising to his feet. "Let's go," he said. "I want to make it to the forest before dark."

The group rose as one and headed for the edge of the scrub-brush, dusting off their pants and adjusting their packs. Amberle grimaced as she watched Keaton's board snap open. Keaton stepped onto it and held out a hand to help her up which she accepted gratefully, though she said nothing. She stepped up behind him and fastened her hands onto his slim hips as he drove the board down and out across the scrubby desert land.

After an hour of riding they passed another bombed village, this one reduced to little more than rubble. It was so desolate that they did not bother to stop, they simply rode by in silence like phantoms passing a dry and desecrated cemetery long ago robbed of its denizens.

They reached a heavily wooded area as the sun was sinking into the horizon and even the boys were glad to step down off their boards and stretch. They stopped where the sandy moonscape sloped upwards from lowland scrub brush to actual pine trees, thick and tall, stabbing at the sky. It was the first real forest any of them had seen but Amberle cocked her head as she looked at it, seeing something familiar.

Cooper looked at the forest and grinned.

"What?' Keaton asked. Coop shook his head.

"I never thought I would be glad to leave the beach."

Keaton laughed. "That might be sand out there," he said, jerking his head in the direction of the desert they had just crossed, "but it's no beach!"

Cooper laughed in agreement and stuck his hand into Keaton's thick hair, messing it.

"We need fresh water," Tyler said, bringing nods of agreement from the other boys.

Amberle looked at the setting sun, then at the position of Jupiter low in the eastern sky, then at the desert, then back at the forest. "Walk into the tree line and go straight," she instructed, "angling to the left."

"Have you ever been here?" Tyler asked.

Amberle shook her head, making the pink springs of her hair bounce around her face. "No, but I remember it." Images of hills and rivers flickered through her mind.

"How can you remember it," Keaton asked, "if you've never been here?"

Her eyes scanned the tree line, though they were unfocused and far away. "I reviewed the plans for this moon," she said softly. "The blueprints and the infrastructure... this moon, and many others like it."

All three boys watched her for a moment, a stick-like figure with dark skin and pink hair in maroon pants and swimming in the over-large military jacket. She looked like a lost waif, a child abandoned by technology and grown wild in the forest. Keaton wanted to reach out and lay a comforting hand on her shoulder, but he already knew better.

"Come on," Tyler said. "If we find water, we'll camp there."

They collapsed their boards and tucked them away before they headed into the trees, angling left. Before long they were met with the sound of running water. Keaton and Cooper both flashed Amberle a grin and she gave them a tentative smile in return. A few minutes later they reached the stream, bubbling its way south through the woodland.

The boys dropped their packs, gratefully stretching their necks and arms. Tyler and Cooper tested the water to make sure it was safe to drink before they filled their canteens. Then Tyler picked up his bow and handed it to Keaton. Keaton looked at him, hopeful but unsure.

"Let him take a couple down," Tyler told Cooper, "but make sure he gets any bolts back if he misses, I don't want to run out and I'm already getting low. The girl and I will get a fire going."

"Really?" Keaton asked.

"You gotta learn some time," Tyler said, smiling with half his mouth and ruffling Keaton's hair. "Just don't shoot Coop, or yourself. I'd hate to eat you, but I wouldn't want to waste you!"

Keaton jerked his head away from Tyler's hand, grinning, and looked at Amberle. "You gonna be okay?" he asked.

Amberle gave him a blank look. "Why wouldn't I be?"

Keaton shrugged, his smile faltering a bit. Then Coop grabbed him roughly around the shoulders, playfully giving him a shake as he dragged him away. The girl watched them go and then started to pick up twigs and branches when she saw that Tyler was standing still, glaring at her.

"What's wrong with you?" she asked. When he didn't answer she stomped her foot. "What is your problem?"

"*You* are my problem," Tyler snapped.

"Why are you so mad at me?" Amberle demanded.

"Do you want a list?"

"If you're smart enough to make one!"

"Because you work for GwenSeven," he said with disgust. "Because you are ungrateful and mean."

"I am not!"

"You are, and I can't stand the way you look at Keaton!" Tyler hissed. Amberle's frown changed from one of anger to one of confusion.

"What are you talking about?"

"I'm talking about the way he looks at you and the way you look at him!" Amberle shook her pink hair, not understanding. Tyler growled at her, exasperated. "He looks at you like you are something special. He sees something in you, God only knows what. And *you*, you look at him like he's something that crawled out from under a rock! You look at all of us that way - Coop doesn't notice and I don't care, but Keaton does - and he doesn't deserve to be hurt like that!"

The girl frowned, trying to understand. Tyler shook his head, calming down a little.

"What do you know about energy?" he asked.

"Probably more than you do."

Tyler rolled his eyes and pushed out a hiss of air between his teeth, but forced himself to be patient.

"The entire universe is made up of energy," he explained. Amberle opened her mouth to tell him she did not need a physics lesson but Tyler held up a hand, cutting off her words. "Just be quiet and listen." She crossed her arms in front of her chest but stayed quiet as he continued. "People are made of energy, and they take energy from the environment and from other people to sustain themselves. Some people give that energy back, others only take it, like vampires."

"And you're saying I'm the second kind," Amberle said,

angry. "That I'm an energy vampire?" Tyler nodded.

"Keaton has always been a giver," he explained, "and he has always had a habit of rescuing stray animals."

Images of other boys flickered through her mind. One was climbing into a garbage chute to rescue a bag of kittens.

Tyler sighed. "Keaton is a good soul. He's kind. I don't want him to get jaded by some cyber-jacked waif."

"I'm normal!" she shouted.

Tyler threw up his hands. "Yeah, yeah, yeah!" he shouted back.

The girl's thin body shook with anger and then suddenly stilled.

"How do I look at him?" she asked, her frown gone and her voice genuinely curious. Tyler cocked his head.

"Are you serious?"

The frown came back instantly. "Of course I am serious!"

Tyler couldn't help but laugh at the way her temper went back and forth, which made her even angrier. "Well, you don't look at him the same way you look at me," he admitted, "with murder in your eyes. But you give him the coldest stare - I can tell that he doesn't know what to make of it. He doesn't know what you are."

"I'm..."

"Normal! I know."

The girl's form shivered as if it was trying to come to some sort of decision. "I don't want to get left behind," she said. "What can I do?"

Tyler thought for a second. "Be nicer to Keaton. Stop looking at him like he's a bug." The crease between her feathery brows deepened.

"Do I have to be nice to you?"

Tyler pressed his lips together to keep from laughing. "No."

"Fine," Amberle said, prim. "I will look at Keaton differently."

"You better. Now get some sticks and prop them up into a cone. I'll find some bigger pieces."

Amberle did as instructed and they had a fire going by the time the other two returned. There were only two animals, since the boys did not want to be long and Cooper had spent some time teaching Keaton how to use the bow, but they were larger than quoras and much fatter.

Keaton helped Coop and Tyler skin and clean the animals down by the water while Amberle built up the fire, adding twigs along with the larger pieces that Tyler had found.

They had divided the cooked animals and were eating them when Keaton noticed Amberle looking at him with her eyebrows raised.

"Are you okay?" he asked. Instead of answering she squinted her eyes. Keaton turned his face towards Tyler. "What's wrong with her?"

Tyler smiled and shook his head but didn't look up. "Do you want a list?"

"I'm normal!" Amberle shouted at Tyler.

"You're hilarious," Cooper told her, chuckling. Soon he was laughing. Tyler joined in and then Keaton, though he tried to stop.

Amberle peered at them curiously. "You guys are weird," she said, which made them all laugh even harder.

"Not me," Cooper said. "I'm normal!"

The three boys started laughing so hard that tears came from their eyes. Keaton was bent over, holding his ribcage with one hand while Tyler and Cooper lay back on the ground, trying to keep their dinner out of the dirt as they laughed.

Amberle finally smiled and, shaking her head, resumed eating her new favorite meat on a stick.

After everyone had eaten and cleaned up, the boys rolled themselves in their blankets and lay on their backs, staring at the canopy of stars beyond the tree branches that swayed high above. Amberle lay swaddled in her giant coat, using Keaton's sweatshirt as a pillow.

"What would life be like," Cooper asked, staring at the night sky with his hands laced behind his head, "if we had a guitar?" The other boys sighed at the thought.

"What would life be like," Tyler answered, "if we could surf every day?" Cooper and Keaton moaned as if being tortured.

"What would life be like," Keaton asked, "if we could have dessert every night?" Cooper threw a small stick at Keaton's head and missed, but they both laughed. "Now it's your turn," Keaton told Amberle, turning his head to look at her through the dying flames.

"My turn for what?"

"It's kind of like a game," he explained. "You start by asking 'what would life be like.' Tyler started it a long time ago. He said it would help put us in a good state before going to sleep."

Amberle shifted, getting comfortable, and stared at the stars overhead. "What would life be like," she asked, "if we really lived it?"

Tyler turned his head and stared at the girl through the fading fire, but she was already closing her eyes to go to sleep. He watched her intensely for a minute, then closed his eyes and did the same.

Amberle had only been asleep for an hour when she found herself suddenly awake, sitting up. She sat next to the dying embers of the fire, listening. The forest was silent as well. Too silent. She listened and it came again - the dry snap of a twig breaking.

Amberle crawled around the remains of the fire toward Tyler's sleeping form and put a hand on his shoulder. He sat up quickly, looking around.

"What is it?" he whispered.

"Somebody is coming!" she whispered back.

Tyler gave Keaton and Cooper a quick shake and they both sat up, blinking the sleep from their eyes.

"Pack," he whispered hoarsely, rolling his blanket.

The other two were up in an instant, rolling blankets and stuffing them into their backpacks. A moment later all four were huddled together, listening. Another snap came from far away to the south, then another one from the east that was much closer. Then another sound reached them, a soft moaning sound like wind moving through the trees.

Amberle shuddered and clutched Keaton's arm. "It's them!" she whispered. "It's the workers!"

Cooper and Tyler looked at each other.

"Zombies!"

 FOUR

Tyler took a quick look around, his blue eyes scanning the forest. Two moons were out, and though Jupiter had already set, the moons reflected the orange-red glare from the planet, shedding a rosy light that sifted down through the shelter of branches overhead.

"The boards!" he whispered as loud he dared.

The three boys shouldered their packs and the boards opened as they dropped them, everyone wincing at the noise they made.

As Keaton helped Amberle onto his board Tyler turned to her, scowling angrily, as if he were trying to come to a decision. It didn't take long.

"Which way?" he hissed.

Amberle bit her bottom lip, trying to remember the plans she had seen for the woodland and worried about what would happen if she were wrong.

"North!" she whispered.

Tyler nodded and guided his board north through the trees, the others following close behind.

Though everyone was tense, the ride was smooth and peaceful for nearly five minutes. They rode quietly, weaving between the trees in the rubicund light of the darkened forest.

Then a howl shattered the silence behind them, angry and mournful. The little group stopped, gathering close as they looked back in the direction they had come, the boards bobbing gently but keeping off the ground.

"I think they found our trail," Tyler said softly. The group cringed as another howl went up, this one to their right, and closer. It was answered by another even closer, but to their left.

"They're trying to surround us," Coop said.

Amberle nodded. "Programmers are methodical."

They waited, bodies taut, listening in the direction they were headed. When nothing but silence ensued, Tyler moved his board forward and the others followed. They kept their course careful and steady until a cry went up right behind them.

"Go!" Tyler shouted and each of them leaned forward as far as they could, driving the boards as fast as they would go. Branches slapped at them and Amberle clutched Keaton, burying her face in his pack. Tyler knew that it was dangerous to speed through a wooded area in the dark, but he would rather risk a collision than being eaten alive.

They drove on, putting distance between them and their pursuers until Tyler came a hair's breadth to crashing into a dark wall that rose up in the night before him. He pushed with his back leg, driving it down so hard that he carved a wide arc into the forest floor, shouting a warning to the others as he pulled up short, his right arm a centimeter from a cliff of rock that rose up over forty feet into the night sky.

The others pulled up next to him, braking hard, bobbing on their boards as they eyed the wall of the cliff that stretched as far as they could see in both directions.

"What do we do?" Keaton asked. "Which way do we go?"

He was answered by cries of hate and hunger that came from directly behind them, as well as to their right and left, though much farther away.

"West," Tyler said. "They sound farther back on that side."

Amberle quickly shook her head. "It goes to a box canyon. They'll have us trapped."

"They have us trapped now," Coop informed her, smiling at

the girl despite their predicament.

Four pairs of eyes darted this way and that as everyone searched for an escape while the cries and howls grew closer. Amberle stepped down from Keaton's board and her eyes became soft and unfocused as they trailed across the face of the cliff.

"It's like broken code," she said, her tone full of soft surprise.

"What?"

"Go up," she whispered. "Up the wall," she said louder as the boys turned to her. "I don't think they can climb. We can."

"That wall must be forty feet high, or more!" Tyler told her, stepping off his board to stare up the cliff.

"It is," she agreed without looking at him. Her eyes were on the small divots and uneven protuberances that staggered up the rock wall. "But we can climb it."

"We can't climb that..." Tyler argued. "It goes straight up! And those ledges, what ledges there are, won't hold us. We're too heavy!"

Amberle looked at his lean form, trying to gauge his weight against the size of the small shelves in the earthen wall and shook her head. "You can't be!"

"We are!" Tyler shouted, growing angry as the cries of the zombies rose behind them. The waif with pink springy hair in the enormous coat leaned menacingly toward the man-sized human.

"I could do it."

Tyler's jaw clenched but before he could argue, she grabbed his arm and pushed him towards the wall. He grabbed his board as it collapsed in on itself, letting her momentum propel him towards the face of the cliff. She turned his shoulders so he was facing the wall and grabbed his right hand and thrust it into a small space between two rocks close enough together to scrape the skin off his knuckles.

"Now," she ordered, "put your left foot here." she pointed to a thin ledge of rock and Tyler, shaking his head, turned his toes out and put the inner edge of his boot on the ledge. "Now reach up and grab that ledge on your left!"

"That can't be more than..." Tyler started when the girl pushed him, heaving on his body with all she could while the cries of the undead echoed behind them. He swung his left arm up and caught the ridge with his fingertips. To his surprise the ledge held.

"Now bring your right foot up," the girl ordered.

Tyler did so, the toe of his right boot scrambling and finding the ledge on its own. It held for a second and then crumbled. His foot, suspended in the suddenly empty air, searched frantically for a toehold before he lost his balance and dropped to the ground, landing heavily but on both feet.

He whirled on the girl. "I told you!" he hissed. "We're too heavy!"

Amberle's lips disappeared into a thin line as she shook her head, frustrated, then her eyes opened wide as she looked at him. "Ugh! *You're* not too heavy, it's your pack! Take it off!"

"We can't leave our packs!" Tyler whispered hoarsely. "We need everything in them!"

"Do you have any rope?"

"I do," Cooper said, dropping his own pack from his back and opening it.

"Take the rope up," she told Tyler, "and you can pull the packs up."

Tyler shook his head. "We should head east," he argued.

The words had just left his lips when a cry rose from the east. It was answered by another cry from the west and one to the south. Four pairs of eyes tracked the sounds as they died into echoes.

"We can do this," Amberle said, her voice soft. "But we need to do it quickly."

Coop held out the coil of rope to Tyler. Without taking his chilling stare off of the girl, Tyler slipped his pack from his shoulders and let it fall. He took the rope and thrust his arm through the coil all the way to his shoulder. He went to the wall and started to climb.

Moving cautiously, he rose almost two meters before he was stuck.

"On your right," Amberle called as quietly as she could. "Don't reach out so far! The ledge is straight above your right shoulder."

Tyler, clinging to the rock face, ran his right hand straight up, feeling his way till his fingers found purchase.

"Now with your right foot, same thing - straight up."

Another cry went up in the forest, a triumphant howl calling to the others.

"They must have found our camp," Keaton whispered. Cooper nodded, his eyes on his brother as he clung to the face of the cliff. He was high enough now that Coop knew a fall would mean a broken leg. Or worse.

"No!" Amberle called to Tyler, searching for a handhold on his right. "Not so high! Down a little, and stretch more!" Tyler did so and found the handhold. Amberle kept scanning the wall, ordering directions from the forest floor as the wails of the undead grew louder.

Though he felt oversized and clumsy, the rest of the climb went quickly as Tyler got the hang of it, waiting for instructions when he was unable to see or feel out the next move on his own.

After three long and exhausting minutes he reached the top and pulled the rest of his body up and over the edge.

Without stopping to catch his breath, Tyler wrapped one end of the rope around his wrist and dropped the rest of its length to the ground where Cooper snatched it up. He slipped the end through a loop on Tyler's pack and tied a quick knot and gave the rope a tug.

Tyler hauled it up and dropped the rope again, pulling up Cooper's pack and then Keaton's.

"Follow him!" Amberle told Cooper as she grabbed him and propelled him towards the wall. She knew by the proximity of the cries that she wouldn't have time to coach them through it individually. She knew that there was a chance she might not make it herself. "You too," she ordered Keaton, giving him a push. "We don't have time to go one by one."

Cooper pressed himself against the face of the earthen cliff and started up, trying his best to follow the path that Tyler had taken. Amberle was quick to tell him where to place his hands or feet, and he only missed twice. Keaton followed, mirroring his every move as the eager moans closed in from all directions on the forest floor.

Amberle clapped her hands when Cooper finally reached the top, Keaton right behind him.

The bottom of Keaton's shoe disappeared over the ledge and was replaced by his face, next to Cooper's and Tyler's, peering down at Amberle as the zombies broke from the forest in a sickening wave.

The creatures, ones that had been people only a short time ago, were hideous. Their skin was gray and loose, as if their bodies had shrunk inside. In some places it hung off of their bones, as dirty and tattered and torn as their clothing. Their ragged skin was pocked with sores and showed wounds that would never heal. Seeing that most of their prey had escaped, they let out a collective wail of anger and anguish as dozens of dead eyes sought out the only one within reach.

They stumbled and lunged with astonishing speed as they closed the distance between the tree line and where the girl was trapped against the face of the cliff. The undead let out a hungry, victorious howl as they surged towards her, reaching with skeletal fingers that had sloughed off most of the decaying skin.

"Look out!" Keaton shouted, but Amberle was already moving.

The girl threw herself at the wall and began to scramble up the cliff with an uncanny haste. The zombies, however, seemed just as intent and - even though she was up almost five feet in two seconds - one lunged for her, made a grab at her foot, and caught it.

Amberle let out a yelp of surprise, trying to shake off the gray hand that clutched at her shoe with inhuman strength. Her hand started to slip, her fingers scraping the rock ledge she was holding as the hand on her foot began pulling her down. Other gray and rotted hands flailed wildly about, trying to grab her other leg.

There was a flash of red light as Coop shot the undead worker that had a hold of her right shoe. There was an awful crumping sound followed by a weak jerk - then she was free as the zombie, minus half of its head, fell to the ground.

The zombies tried scaling the cliff, some even trying to climb over each other in their eagerness to reach the girl, their moans loud and hungry. Only one managed to get close but as its fingers grazed the bottom of her maroon pant leg, the girl drew her foot up high and sent it back down, slamming it into the creature's face.

There was dull crack, like the sound of a rotten pumpkin splitting apart, and the hand fell away. It was all the time she needed. Nearly jumping from one handhold and foothold to the next without any pause, Amberle scurried up the face of the cliff like a squirrel scampering up a tree.

She reached the top and both Cooper and Tyler reached out to grab her by the arms and haul the rest of her body up over the edge of the cliff. The soil on the higher ground was surprisingly soft, and the vegetation much thicker than it had been below. Amberle rolled over onto her back, breathing heavily and looking at the stars.

They are there, she thought wildly, staring up at the burning points of light in the darkness. *Out there.*

Keaton was on his hands and knees, looking at her with wide eyes. "My God you can climb!" he said. "Where did you learn to do that?"

"I didn't know I could," Amberle admitted, still lying on her back and looking up through the trees dappled with rosy moonlight. Her heart was thudding riotously in her chest but it seemed to be slowing down.

"Did any of them bite you?" Cooper asked. "Scratch you?" He picked up her right foot and turned it back and forth,, examining her dark skin for any marks.

"Don't touch me!" Amberle yelled, kicking her foot out of his grasp. "And no, they didn't bite me."

Cooper looked dubious and leaned forward to examine her ankles in the moonlight, careful not to touch her.

"You look okay," he confirmed.

"I told you."

The boys edged to the cliff and peeked over. The girl rolled onto her stomach and joined them. A few crazed zombie workers were still trying to scale the cliff but they only succeeded in snapping off the tips of their fingers or toes. Or both. They wailed in frustration from below.

"There's more," Amberle whispered.

"What do you mean?" Tyler asked.

"I don't know how many programmers were working at the center," she told him, still looking over the edge, "but there weren't that many."

The bodies were in various stages of decay and had sustained injuries that looked fatal. Keaton saw that the chunks missing from most of the zombies had bite marks all around them.

"Well," Tyler said, "either GwenSeven gave that shot to more than just the programmers, or they've been attacking people and infecting them. Either way, let's get out of here." He and Cooper had already shouldered their packs. "We need to be gone by the time they find a way up."

"I don't think GwenSeven would do that," Amberle protested. "Plus, they can't get up the cliff."

"GwenSeven would absolutely do that," Tyler argued. "And besides, did you know how high the cliff would be from the plans stored in your little brain?"

"No."

"Then you don't know if there is a way up close by. You only know the terrain by the way it looks from above, not the rises and the falls." The girl sat up at and scowled at him as Keaton picked up his pack and threw it on his back - but she knew he was right.

Keaton held out a hand to Amberle and, surprisingly, she took it. He helped haul her to her feet. She grumbled under her breath but followed the boys across the top edge of the cliff and into the trees.

They went on foot this time, making their way deeper and deeper into the forest. When the moonlight had shifted from above them to lower in the sky to their left, and they heard no sounds of pursuit, Tyler signaled them to halt.

"We'll stop here," he said. Keaton and Cooper gratefully dropped their packs to the ground and Amberle fell unceremoniously to her butt. "We'll sleep in shifts," he told them. "I'll take first watch."

It was too risky to build a fire and, besides, they were too tired. They didn't even bother taking out blankets. Cooper curled up on the ground with part of his pack under his head. Keaton lay down next to him and, after a moment of indecision, the girl lay down close to Keaton. Just not quite close enough to touch. They were asleep in moments.

Tyler sat with his back against a tree watching the stars

move across the sky through the branches of the trees overhead. He strained his ears for hours, listening for the slightest noise, but no noise came.

Finally, when the position of the stars, along with the time on his watch, told him that the sun would likely be up in an hour, he gave Cooper a gentle shake.

Cooper sat up, blinking rapidly and looking around the forest.

"It's okay," Tyler said, "I haven't heard anything all night. Just let me sleep for an hour and then wake me up."

Cooper nodded and crawled over to sit against the tree, rubbing his face with his palms. He ran his short fingernails back and forth though his mass of dark hair, giving his scalp a satisfying scratch and gave his head a good shake to make sure he was well awake. Tyler took his place next to Keaton and fell instantly asleep. Cooper listened to the forest as the sky slowly began to lighten.

He checked his watch as the sun rose. Magnified by the artificial atmosphere put in place by GwenSeven, the distant sun threw its rays over the moon, its fingers of light reaching across the forest floor. It had been an hour. He didn't want to wake Tyler, knowing that he had taken watch throughout the whole night, but he also knew that Tyler wanted to get as far away from the zombies as they could. Coop couldn't agree more.

He put his hand on his brother's arm, waking him. Tyler sat up and looked around to find Cooper grinning at him.

"What?" he asked.

Coop jerked his head, motioning with his chin. Tyler followed his gaze to where Keaton was sleeping with his arm thrown over the girl. Tyler grinned and poked Keaton with the toe of his boot.

"Hey," he whispered. "Hey!"

Keaton stirred, waking the girl. They sat up at the same

time, the same look of surprise on their faces as Keaton quickly pulled his arm back. Amberle bit her bottom lip and looked away, embarrassed – but she didn't shout at him.

At least that's something, Tyler thought, shaking his head.

"Get out something for breakfast," he told Keaton before turning to Coop. "Let's take a look at the map," he suggested.

Cooper pulled out the map and shook it open while Keaton fished some cryo-dried oat bars out of his backpack. He handed one to Amberle without looking at her. She took it and held it for a moment, staring at him.

"Thanks for keeping me warm," she said.

"No problem," Keaton mumbled, blushing. He took two packaged oat bars over to Ty and Coop who were hunched over the map.

"Ask the girl," Cooper was saying. He took the silver packet from Keaton, opened it, and took a huge bite. Tyler sighed.

"Fine." He looked up, caught Amberle's attention, and motioned for her to join them. She came over, keeping a distance from Keaton. "Do you know where we are?" Tyler asked her.

Amberle shook her head. "No, but if I had a frame of reference to triangulate on our position," she said, "I could probably make a pretty good guess."

"Well, that way is east," Tyler told her, pointing. Then he dropped his hand to the map and pointed to the swath of green that floated above the map. "I think we came in the forest here," he said. "And then came up this way."

Amberle looked at the map, and then looked in the direction that Tyler had pointed. Jupiter was indeed on the rise in that direction, and it was especially bright behind them and to the left. She looked back at the map.

"Here," she said, pointing at a scalloped edge in the floating green. "This is where I think we are." She looked up and pointed to where she guessed was north. "If I'm right, that way will be the curve in the forest where it opens up to flat land again. Maybe scrub, maybe nothing at all."

Tyler and Cooper looked at each other. It was what they had thought as well.

"The pilot we met," Coop explained, "said that he had crossed a desert and it almost killed him. We hoped to go through the woodland as far as we could, and then cut across just a small part of the desert to the spaceport."

"I don't know if the zombies followed us," Tyler said, "or found us by accident, but they are milling around this forest looking for us now. We should probably get out as soon as we can." He looked at the girl. "Did you ever see the workers during the day after they had become zombies?"

Amberle shook her head. "Even when the soldiers came, the workers didn't come after them until the sun was going down."

Tyler nodded. "I hate taking us into the desert, but it's probably safer than staying in the forest. My biggest worry is having enough water."

"We all filled up last night," Keaton said.

"I know," Tyler said softly. "I just hope it's enough. If one of the boards break..." he trailed off, looking at the girl. She met his icy eyes with her own hazel ones.

"You can put Keaton on one of your boards and leave me."

Tyler cocked his head just a bit, surprised, but Keaton shook his head.

"We won't leave you," he insisted, reaching out to lay a reassuring hand on her knee.

"Don't touch me," she warned, though she kept her voice low and her eyes on Tyler. Keaton pulled his hand back, balling it into a fist and putting it on his lap.

Tyler sighed and looked back at the map. The holo paper was dark and nearly blank. Cooper gave it a shake and it went out completely. He shook it again, harder this time, and it sputtered back to life.

"Damn technology," he muttered. His blue-green eyes scanned the map and then flicked over to Amberle, a small smile set into his heart-shaped face. "Eleven times twenty-eight?"

The girl smiled. "Three hundred and eight. I thought I taught you that one already."

"You're still faster," he said, grinning. He looked at the map and his smile faded. "That's almost two hundred miles," he said, looking at Tyler. "I know that math at least. And that the boards only go about eight miles an hour."

"So about twenty-five hours?" Tyler asked, calculating out loud. "Two days, about thirteen hours of riding each, with what water we have?" Tyler rubbed at his temple. "I don't know."

"We can get water here," Amberle said, pointing at the map. "I think."

"There's no water holo there," Cooper said. Usually water was denoted by a blue patch of light hovering over the map.

"I know," the girl said. "It's an Easter Egg."

"A what?" all boys asked at once, turning to her.

"An Easter Egg," she explained, "is a hidden message, usually inside a computer program." She pointed to the map again. There was no floating hologram, but something was drawn onto the paper itself. "See this picture of a circle, with two smaller circles attached to it like ears?" The boys nodded. "It's a picture of a water molecule."

"So you think there is water there?" Tyler asked.

Amberle nodded. "I'm sure there is, or was, when the map was made. I'm not saying we can find it."

Cooper looked at his brother. "I think we should try."

Tyler thought for a moment and then nodded. "Let's get the hell out of here."

Without another word they gathered their few belongings and headed for the spot in the woods where it was growing brighter by the second from the reflected light of Jupiter. Ten minutes later they walked out of the line of the forest and stared out over the land that dropped away from them and spread out like an arid blight upon the moon.

Unlike the dry scrub-land they had left south of the forest, which had been littered with scraggly bushes and dry plants, this land was completely barren. The moonscape sloped down thirty meters from where they stood, and then stretched out as far as the eye could see; flat, hard-packed dirt, bleached and cracked by the sun and bereft of water. There wasn't a tree or bush in sight. The only movement was from the occasional whirls of gritty sand being kicked up by a dry wind that blew across the wasteland.

"Keaton, put on your goggles," Tyler instructed, his voice flat. Cooper was already fishing a pair of thick eyeshades out of a pocket on the side of his pack. The hover-boards opened as they dropped them while they each donned a pair of protective eyewear.

Coop and Tyler checked the map once more, along with the compass on Cooper's watch, as Keaton turned to the girl, apologetic.

"Don't worry," she told him before he could say anything. "You need to see where we're going. I'll just keep my eyes closed." Keaton nodded and helped her onto the board behind him.

Tyler took one last look at the forest before looking out across the parched horizon, measuring the danger behind them against the danger before them. Cooper pulled his heavy shades down over his eyes and grinned at everyone.

"Last one in the water is a barney," he told them, and dropped his board over the edge.

"What's a bar..." Amberle started and then yelped and grabbed onto Keaton as he launched their board forward, racing Cooper down the slope.

 FIVE

The boards sailed quickly over the flat ground, their progress only slowed by the need to maneuver through the continuous gusts of hot wind that would throw them off balance and pummel them with gritty sand. Amberle held on to Keaton, her face buried in his backpack.

The wind was hot and dry, even though it was still early, seeming to suck the moisture from their skin. Tyler had them stop after the first hour to drink a small amount of water. The boys peeled off their jackets and stuffed them in their packs.

Keaton looked at the girl, squatting on the ground to both stretch and rest her legs. "Do you want me to carry your jacket?" he asked. "I have a long-sleeved shirt you could wear instead."

Amberle shook her head and pulled the jacket tighter around her body, though the morning was already hot. "No thanks." Keaton offered her a drink from his canteen but she shook her head again. "That's okay, I'm not thirsty."

"We're making good time," Coop said. "Despite the wind, the ground is flat and smooth, even if it is dried to shit. We might make it to that water by noon, instead of four."

"That would be great," Tyler said. "Let's get going."

He had them stop and rest and drink a few sips of water every hour. The sun was scorching by midmorning. Each time they stopped Keaton offered Amberle some water and each time she shook her head.

"I'm fine."

Noon came and they took a longer break, though there was no water in sight. Cooper checked his map and his compass as they ate lunch.

"We should be there any time," he told the others. "If we're on course," he added cheerfully through a mouthful of cryo-dried spaghetti.

And if it's there, Amberle thought. All morning she had worried about what could happen if she was wrong. If they got lost, or ran out of water, they could all die, and it would be her fault. She had never felt such responsibility before. It made her hurt all the way to the pit of her stomach, which, at the moment, felt like a dry and shriveled walnut.

She remembered what Keaton had told her about Tyler: *He wasn't always this way. He feels responsible for us. Sometimes that's a heavy burden.*

Amberle looked over at the eldest brother and saw him looking back at her with his icy blue eyes. She turned the other way and saw that Keaton was holding out his canteen to her. She shook her head.

"No thanks."

"Come on," Keaton said. "Your lips are so chapped they're cracked. You should at least drink something."

Amberle was terribly thirsty but took the canteen only to appease him. She took enough to wet her mouth and let a few drops slide down her throat before handing it back.

Keaton gave her a dubious look but took the canteen and screwed the cap back on.

"Let's go," Tyler said. "No sense sitting out here and baking."

They stopped again at one, and again at two, but there was still no water in sight. The arid desert was as flat and empty as it had been all day. Amberle felt dry inside and out. Her tongue felt like a small withered stick, her eyes felt dirty and gritty and her skin itched all over. But she refused to drink Keaton's water and she refused to meet Tyler's stare.

Cooper looked back and forth from the map to his compass to the sun. "We have to be close," he said. "I'm sure we're on track, and I know we haven't passed it."

"Will you please have something to drink?" Keaton whispered to Amberle, but she shook her head.

"I'm not thirsty," she lied.

Keaton looked to Tyler for help but he only shrugged and gave the dark-skinned girl an appraising glance.

"Let's go then," Keaton said. Cooper looked at him, surprised, but Tyler gave him a small smile as he stepped on his board and pulled his goggles down over his eyes.

The others dusted off their pants and mounted their boards. Amberle tried not to groan as she climbed up behind Keaton. She buried her face in his backpack as they started, hiding her eyes from the blowing sand and the desiccated land she had opted for as their now imminent demise.

Only minutes later, however, she felt Keaton stop the board. She looked up, startled. He had come to a halt behind Coop and Tyler, who stood on their boards as they hovered above the ground, gesturing to an outcrop of rocks that rose out of the flat land ahead and to their right.

By the looks of it, the rocks were more than twice their height and set side by side. The east and west sides curved back to create a circle of stones. Farther back, on either side, was another curve of stones.

Keaton turned to Amberle, most of his face consumed by the huge goggles. "That's got to be it," he said grinning. Amberle felt a wave of relief wash through her. "Should we beat them there?"

Smiling, the girl nodded and Keaton leaned forward, driving the board as hard as he could.

Tyler shouted at him as he flew past but he heard Cooper laugh as both of them followed in immediate pursuit. Amberle squealed laughter and held tight to Keaton. Grinning, he pushed the board faster and headed for the gap in a wall of jumbled rocks the same color as the desert floor. He guessed the rocks had to be at least twenty feet high and lined up a hundred feet wide.

At the last second, good sense got the better of him and Keaton slowed down, not knowing what was on the other side. He figured that was what Tyler was probably yelling about behind them.

Carefully, he guided his board between a pair of stones over three times his height and confirmed that the wall of rocks was actually a ring of rocks. In the center was an expanse of green grass, small bushes with shiny leaves, and a waterfall.

The water fell from between a jumble of stones, but these were not the dry white rocks of the desert. These were gray and wet and covered with moss. The water fell from a height of twenty feet in a glassy sheet ten feet wide to crash into a pool of crystal-clear water.

Amberle jumped down off the board and fell to her knees in front of the pool as Tyler and Coop came shooting through the gap in the rocks only to stop short, carving arcs into the soft earth of the oasis they had found.

Tyler jumped off his board and, once he saw that Keaton was safe, looked at the girl. "Don't drink too much," he warned. "Go slow or it will make you sick."

"Alright," Amberle said, bringing a handful of the clear water to her small mouth. "But after you guys fill your canteens, I'm jumping in."

"Fair enough," Tyler said.

The boys, grateful to be out of the hot wind and in the cool, moist air of the oasis, filled their canteens and washed their faces and hands. Amberle took off her shoes and her heavy jacket and dove into the water. She came up grinning and Keaton splashed her.

"Now your clothes are all wet!" he said.

"I don't care!" she called back, laughing. "And you're all barneys, whatever that means!" She climbed out of the pool, squeezed water from her shirt, and lay on her back in the grass. Most of the water beaded on her hair and ran down her face. Her tightly coiled ringlets were soaked, but still perfectly formed springs of pink made darker by the water. She looked at the blue expanse of sky above, filled with a feeling of exhilaration she did not recognize.

Cooper laughed. "What is this place?" he asked.

"Like I told you before," Amberle said as she sat up and shook the water from her hair, "it's an Easter Egg. Something hidden, unless you know how to find it."

"Or find it by accident," Keaton said. Amberle nodded.

"That's how it usually happens."

"Where is the water coming from?" he asked, looking at the top of the waterfall.

The girl shrugged. "Where does it come from anywhere on the moon?" she asked. "There are only four natural sources, that are not saltwater but instead from the few forests, and they are pumped to all the settlements and waystations."

"Well," Keaton said, "this isn't a settlement or a forest. It's a waystation then?"

The girl shrugged again as she pulled on her shoes. "It must be." She put the jacket back on over her wet clothes.

"It's too quiet here," Tyler said. "Even though there's water, there aren't any animals."

"They'd never make it from the forest across all that desert," Cooper said, splashing more water on his face and scrubbing it clean. Droplets flew from the ends of his dark curls.

"I know," Tyler said. "Still, there's something weird about this place. I feel like...we're being watched."

The others, alarmed, sat still and looked around the small

clearing. There was nothing there, and nothing but the desert on the other side of the rocks. Except behind the waterfall. It was dark there, dark enough to be a cave.

They all stood up slowly, Tyler carefully pulling his crossbow from his pack.

As he did so, a figure materialized behind the glassy sheet of water and a young man stepped out from behind it. He was lean and muscular and stripped to the waist, wearing only a pair of baggy shorts and shoes without socks. His hair was a wild mass of brown curls and in one hand he held small round apple.

Amberle stared at him, mesmerized, as she stood up. Tentatively, she took a step towards him and, as if to answer, the young man stepped towards the girl, cocking his head as he looked at her. Keaton quickly stepped forward and placed himself between Amberle and the stranger.

"Who are you?" he demanded, though it was Tyler who usually spoke for them as a group.

The stranger pulled his sea-green eyes away from the girl and looked at Keaton, disinterested.

"I'm Bradley," he said as if Keaton should know. He took a bite of the crisp fruit he was holding and looked at Coop and Tyler with a similar disinterest before cocking his head back towards the girl. "Do I know you?" he asked.

He spoke slowly and his voice had a heavy accent. *British*, Amberle thought as she shook her head slowly, though she could not pull her gaze from him. He took another bite of the apple as he stared at her.

"What are you doing here?" he asked.

"We're on our way to the spaceport," Keaton told him.

"You don't mean the children any harm?" he asked, still looking at Amberle.

Keaton frowned. "Children?" he asked before Tyler stepped forward and waved at Keaton to be quiet.

"We don't mean harm to anyone," he told Bradley. "We're just passing through."

Bradley regarded him for a moment, looked back at the girl, and then shrugged. "Come on then," he said, turning and walking towards another gap in the back row of the giant stones.

The four who had traveled so far looked at each other, surprised, as Bradley continued walking as if he didn't care whether they followed or not. Tyler frowned and then scooped up his gear and followed him. The others grabbed their stuff and kept close behind.

Keaton looked at Amberle who was watching the muscles on Bradley's back shift as he moved. Bradley ate the piece of fruit down to the core and threw the remains back into the rocks as they left the oasis.

Tyler glanced back to see two other, smaller walls of rock that had been formed into rings against the larger circle of stones they had just left. He knew that, if seen from above, it would have looked just like the picture on Cooper's map. The one the girl said was the picture of a water molecule. He turned his gaze back around as they descended into dry grassland.

The grass was the same dusty color as the desert, each blade as thick as a finger and short, but got taller as they went along. Within five minutes the waving grass was as tall as the girl. Coop reckoned he could see over it, if he stood on his toes.

The four followed Bradley through the pale-colored grass that gradually shortened again to waist level. After ten more minutes of walking they could discern a tiny village in the distance.

Unlike the others they had seen, this village was intact with white-walled buildings roofed in thatch. Bradley led them under an arch made of white clay and into the settlement. The moment they entered, a cry went up and was answered immediately, echoing through the narrow streets.

The small group stood frozen, looking around as their guide turned to look at them, puzzled. Tyler glimpsed a tiled village square with a fountain at the center and rows of small houses in all directions separated by alleyways before those alleys suddenly became flooded with bodies, all moving in their direction.

"Coop!" he called out in warning, though his brother was already behind him, guarding his back. Keaton closed in with them, trying to pull Amberle into the protective triangle they were creating, but she was unfamiliar with the movements and actions that came so naturally to them. Keaton made a grab for her but as the wave of people collapsed upon the group they were separated.

Bombarded with bodies, Cooper was ready to draw his gun when Tyler started shouting.

"No!" he yelled. "It's kids! They're kids!"

He was right. They were being swarmed by a mob of people that only came up to their chins, if that. The children, ranging from what looked like four to fourteen, swarmed them, garbling in a tongue they could not understand, pulling excitedly at their clothes and packs.

Cooper and Tyler had pulled their weapons but now held them high out of reach. Keaton looked to his right where Amberle was being torn away as if by a riptide, hands grabbing and clutching at her, touching her dusky, dark skin and ringlets of pink hair. He caught a glimpse of her face, scrunched tight as if in pain before he heard her scream tear through the air.

Keaton lunged for her, pushing aside the bodies as gently as he could, struggling to reach her. But he was being pushed back even as she was being carried away. He heard her scream again and as he struggled to reach her Bradley pushed through the crowd, not as gently.

"Leave off!" the young man shouted, pushing the small bodies aside. He reached Amberle and scooped her up as she were an infant and, cradling her in his arms, made his way back to where the boys were being mobbed by the children.

"Follow me," Bradley told them with an expression of apologetic exasperation, carrying Amberle towards one of the white adobe houses. "Leave off!" he shouted again in annoyance at the children, shouldering them aside. An old man dressed in blue robes tied with a rope belt appeared in the doorway of the house.

The man smiled and beckoned to them, inviting them in. He was thin but not small, with tan skin, white hair, and a white beard. The children made a path for Bradley and the boys followed closely behind.

"Welcome, welcome!" the man exclaimed, clasping his hands together as Bradley led the party inside. "We never get visitors!"

Keaton looked him, abashed. "Maybe that's because you're in the middle of the desert!" he told him.

The man laughed and shooed away the children who were trying to follow the procession into the tiny house. The living room was barely big enough for the six of them, even though there were no furnishings, only some cushions and pillows on a floor covered with woven reeds. The tiny room was next to an even tinier kitchen with a wood-burning oven made of clay, a small sink, and a few cupboards covered by a thin curtain.

Bradley put Amberle down on top of a cushion and sat himself close by on a pillow facing her. He produced another apple and bit into it. Amberle's eyes followed his every move. So did Keaton's, as he stood protectively close.

"I am Hellas," the old man informed them.

"I'm Tyler," Tyler told him. "These are my brothers, Cooper and Keaton."

"You are all brothers?" he asked, his eyes falling on the girl. She shook her head, her gaze still fastened on Bradley.

"They can't all be brothers," she said quietly, her eyes never leaving the young man close to her. "Not entirely. Not enough patterns. Or time between."

Cooper stared at her in surprise. It was true. Tyler had a different mother than he and Keaton. Plus, he was only four months older than Cooper. Though her words were cryptic, the boys knew what she meant. But not how she could have known.

Tyler scowled at her before looking back to Hellas. "We picked her up along the way," he explained.

Hellas laughed. "The short story," he said. "I understand. Please," the old man said to the boys, smiling and spreading his hands towards the room. "Sit down. You must be tired and thirsty!" He stuck his head back through the door they had come through and shouted in an unfamiliar language.

"Thank you," Tyler said, finding a cushion to sit on and motioning to the other boys to do the same.

Keaton wanted to sit between Bradley and Amberle, but the half-dressed young man sat on the cushion across from her and sitting between them would be awkward. Instead he sat at her side, so close that their hips were touching. She didn't say a word, she just kept staring at Bradley.

Tyler and Cooper sat down on his other side and Hellas sat on a cushion facing them, next to the shirtless Bradley.

Two girls came into the house, one carrying a clay pitcher, the other with a tray of small cups that she handed out to everyone except Bradley. The girl with the pitcher went to each one in turn, filling their cups with water.

"To our guests!" Hellas exclaimed with a smile, holding up his cup for a second to toast and then drinking from it. Amberle looked at Keaton, who - like Cooper - was looking at Tyler. Ty raised his cup and took a drink.

"Thank you," he told the man. He looked at Coop and nodded. Cooper and Keaton, then Amberle, drank from their cups.

"How long have you been traveling?" Hellas asked Tyler.

"A long time."

Hellas nodded sagely and stroked his white beard. "That is as true as can be. It must be! There are no other settlements for leagues and leagues in any direction. Where are you headed?"

Tyler paused, deciding how much he should tell about their plans, then sighed. It was always easiest for him to be honest.

"We are headed for the spaceport. We hope to acquire passage off the moon in any way we can."

Again the man nodded. "A wise choice," he said solemnly, then laughed when he saw the look of surprise on Tyler's face. "I may be old," he said, still laughing, "but I am not a fool!" he sighed and shook his head. "This moon will be abandoned, if it hasn't been already, and that's if we are lucky!"

"And if we're not lucky?" Cooper asked.

The man gave him a solemn look. "Then it will be destroyed. Or wiped clean for them to start anew."

"GwenSeven," Tyler said, his tone more bitter than ever.

Hellas shrugged. "Perhaps. Perhaps not."

"How could there be any question?" Tyler asked.

"It's hard to see all sides, when you are on the ground," Hellas said. Tyler scowled at this, but did not disagree.

"How did you come to be here with all these kids?" Cooper asked.

"Like all colonies on this moon," Hellas said, "the people were here as an experiment, voluntarily of course." He gave Tyler a wink. Ty drained his cup but said nothing.

"What was the experiment?" Cooper asked.

"An anti-aging drug," Hellas told him. "The adults were given the drug; the children were given an immunization."

Amberle tore her eyes away from Bradley just long enough to glance at Hellas. She saw Tyler looking at her and she turned her attention back to Bradley.

"Whether the drugs and the immunizations were mixed up on accident or on purpose," Hellas continued, "we will probably never know. Needless to say, it was the children that were given anti-aging treatment. Except it didn't just stop wrinkles and halt the maturation of their faces, which I believe was the intent, but halted the maturation of their bodies and minds as well."

"When was this?" Cooper asked.

"Eight years ago."

Coop gave a low whistle. None of the kids he had seen outside looked older than the girl but, if they had been teenagers at the time of the experiment, they must actually be in their early twenties.

"What happened to the parents?" Tyler asked.

"When the scientists came to run some tests, the parents refused to let them see the children, much less take them away. The scientists returned with soldiers and I took the children into a hidden tunnel the parents had dug. When I ventured out, a few days later, the soldiers were gone. So were the parents."

Tyler looked at the girls as they came back from the kitchen. They looked no more than twelve years old, but in actuality they were almost his own age. "Do they know?" he asked softly.

"They know that their parents are gone but, like I said, they are still children. They hope they will return."

"GwenSeven," Tyler cursed between clenched teeth. The old man shrugged and motioned to the girls.

"Like I said," he remarked as the girls refilled the cups, "perhaps. Perhaps not."

Tyler stared at him, incredulous. "How could it be anyone else but them? They have been behind this from the start. Behind everything greedy and careless and cruel." He looked at Amberle and the jacket she wore. The old man shrugged again.

"Things are not always what they seem," he said, following Tyler's gaze.

"They seldom are," Amberle murmured in agreement.

The old man, his eyes, blue and bright, fastened upon the patch. The stitching at the bottom had come loose.

"Bradley," Hellas said.

The young man's shaggy brown head turned towards Hellas, who spoke a few quick words that no one in their small group could understand but, as soon as he finished, Bradley leaned forward and reached for Amberle.

Keaton was between them in an instant.

Bradley's dark brows drew together in confusion and he looked past him at Amberle. "What the 'ell is wrong wit 'im?" he asked. Amberle looked into his sea-green eyes.

"He wants to keep me safe," she told him.

"He won't hurt her," Hellas told Tyler who, after a pause, nodded.

"Keaton."

Keaton's whole body seemed to tighten, then he moved away. Bradley glanced at him as if he were crazy and then looked back at the girl. Reaching out, he grabbed the G7 emblem that had been sewn on the coat, and ripped it off with one quick motion.

Keeping his eyes locked onto Amberle's, he took a bite of his apple and sat back on his cushion, handing the patch to Hellas. Keaton could not keep from glaring at Bradley, but Cooper and Tyler were staring at the place where the patch had been.

Embroidered onto the jacket itself was another logo, this one a diamond filled with three capital letters - IGC.

Cooper, his lagoon-colored eyes ever full of mirth, looked at his brother. Tyler turned his blue-eyed gaze to Hellas.

"It can't be," he whispered.

"Of course it can," Hellas admonished.

He smiled and placed a hand on Tyler's knee. "But you must be hungry," he said. "Let's get you all fed."

 SIX

The girls who had served them water began moving around the small house, preparing an early dinner as Hellas told the visitors about their village. Keaton's mouth began to water as the smell of bread baking in the stone oven filled the air. He wasn't the only one.

Amberle pulled her gaze from Bradley long enough to glance into the kitchen. Her stomach rumbled loudly and she put her hand over it, embarrassed but smiling as she glanced at Keaton. Keaton looked back at her, his expression flat. Amberle cocked her head, puzzled.

"What's wrong?"

Keaton pressed his lips together, wanting to keep silent, but couldn't.

"Why do you keep staring at him?" he whispered.

"Who?"

Keaton's dark blonde brows came together. "Who?" he asked dramatically. "Him!" he hissed quietly, darting a glance at Bradley who had begun to eat another apple but seemed to be listening to the conversation between Hellas and the older boys.

Though Keaton was nearing the end of his teenage years, he had never suffered the normal teenage angst of insecurity. Being around Amberle, however, seemed to bring a lot of emotions out of him that he didn't know he had. The current one was not pleasant. It made him feel hollow, lonely, and angry.

Amberle turned her dark face back to the young man with his shaggy brown curls and sea-green eyes and for a moment Keaton didn't think she was going to answer him. Then she leaned close to Keaton, surprising him. She put her mouth close to his ear and he froze, listening.

"I don't think he's real," she whispered.

Keaton's brows shot up. "Really?" he asked, looking at the shirtless young man.

"Shhh!" Amberle hissed. Bradley glanced at them and bit into his apple before looking back to the older boys, still engaged in conversation.

"What makes you think that?" he asked, quieter. Amberle turned her face back towards his ear, leaning close again.

"Lots of things. The way he acts, for one, and he is definitely out of place here. Also, I think he keeps eating the same apple."

"How could he eat the same apple twice?" Keaton whispered.

"Because the apple is not real either. It's something he's making."

"How can you tell?"

Amberle shook her head as if she didn't know how to explain. "I know patterns," she said.

Keaton wasn't sure if she meant patterns of behavior, patterns on the apple, or what. He looked closely at the apple and saw that it did have interesting markings. It was red and gold, but one side had a rather large patch of gold that looked like a starburst.

The girls in the kitchen put out plates of fresh bread, butter, cheeses and fruits on the countertop. Even the older boys couldn't help but stare and Cooper laughed as his stomach rumbled loudly.

Hellas smiled. "Let's have something to eat, shall we?"

Everyone moved quickly towards the small space that

was the kitchen where the girls handed out plates and the visitors loaded theirs with food and sat back in the living room, balancing the plates on their laps.

"Oh god," Keaton said in between bites. "I can't remember the last time we had real bread."

"Mmhmm," Amberle agreed, buttering another piece.

"After we eat," Hellas said, "the girls can sing for you if you like. Maybe Bradley will play the guitar."

Three heads looked up as one. Keaton's blue-green eyes darted between his brothers. Tyler wet his lips with his tongue but stayed silent.

"You have a guitar?" Cooper asked.

Hellas nodded. "We do, but Bradley is the only one who knows how to play really well. He has been teaching some of the children. Do any of you boys play?"

Tyler nodded. "We all do."

"Really? Well then you must play for us when we are done, if you would like."

Cooper started eating faster until Ty elbowed him in the ribs, but for the first time since Amberle had known them, the eldest of the group could not stop smiling. Till his gaze fell on Amberle, then his smile disappeared. Reactive in nature, Amberle glared back at him, still chewing a mouthful of bread.

Though they were savoring the meal, the boys finished quickly, eager to be done. Amberle reluctantly handed her plate to the girl who was gathering them as Hellas motioned for Bradley to get going.

"Let's go outside," he suggested. "It should be lovely out by now, there is more room, and everyone can enjoy."

The group rose, bumping into each other in the small space as they were herded outside. Hellas was right. They emerged into the courtyard under a lavender sky and a fresh breeze cooled their faces as they crossed over a mosaic of tiles and sat on the dusty steps next to the bubbling fountain.

Other children began pouring into the courtyard as the word spread, sitting down on steps to the other houses or on the flat stones that paved the village square.

"Careful you don't touch the girl," Tyler warned a boy that was getting close to Amberle.

"I'm normal!" she told Tyler, moving away from him to sit on the tiles near the steps of the fountain, then turning on the boy as he bumped into her. "Don't touch me!" she shouted at him.

She could hear Tyler laugh but refused to look at him. Thankfully, Bradley was picking his way through the growing crowd as they seated themselves, holding a hollow instrument of light, polished wood over his head.

Keaton moved to sit next to Amberle as Bradley handed the guitar to Cooper. Coop looked at the instrument, grinning, then sighed and handed it to Tyler.

"But I'm next," he said, emphatic. Tyler nodded as he accepted the guitar and settled down with it across his knees. He turned some knobs at the top and plucked at the strings, tuning it.

"Bradley!" Amberle called. "Sit next to me." She patted the spot to her left, glaring at the boy who had bumped into her. Bradley pushed the boy a bit farther away and sat down next to her.

Keaton, despite Amberle's doubts about him being real, saw Bradley's naked arm brush against her shoulder and felt his own body tighten as he saw her shiver, but she didn't say anything, much less yell at him for touching her.

Then Tyler played a chord, and then another, and the murmuring children became silent. Keaton felt the music thrum in his soul, the way it always did, as he saw Bradley bite into another apple with a patch of gold on its side that looked like a starburst.

"Keaton!" Cooper called, making him look up. Tyler motioned with his head and Keaton stood and moved to sit next to him on the steps to the fountain, with Coop on Tyler's other side. The chords became a melody that Keaton recognized.

Amberle saw Tyler glance at her and then look away, a sly smile tucked into the corner of his mouth as Keaton took a deep breath and began to sing. It took the girl a moment to notice, her angst was so fixed on the blonde young man playing the guitar, but as the sound of Keaton's voice filled her ears, her eyes turned towards him as if being drawn by a magnet.

Keaton saw her staring at him and he looked away, but looked back after a few seconds. Amberle was still watching him, transfixed. Keaton looked away again, trying to focus on the other people in the crowd as he sang.

There were a few close to his own age but Bradley was definitely the oldest. Lots of smaller children, but no one younger than what Keaton would guess as four or five. His eyes drifted to Amberle again, her brown and green eyes still staring at him in wonder. He looked away again, smiling as he sang and when he finished the song Hellas and all of the children clapped, many of them cheering as well.

Keaton bowed his head at them as Tyler started a new song, and then another and another. Sometimes Cooper would sing, sometimes Tyler, sometimes Keaton, and sometimes they would all sing together. Everyone stayed as the skies darkened, clapping wildly after each song.

When they finished, all the children wanted to talk to the boys but Hellas told them to go back to their houses and Bradley shooed most of them off, though some of the smaller and sleepier ones he carried to their beds.

Amberle walked up to Keaton and, for the first time since he had known her, she seemed shy. Almost in awe of him.

"I didn't know you could do that," she said.

"What?" Keaton asked. "Sing?" Amberle nodded, looking

at him as if she was just seeing him for the first time. Keaton shrugged. "We used to sing a lot, back when we lived on the coast."

"Will you tell me about it?"

Keaton smiled. "Sure."

They returned to the small adobe house that belonged to Hellas and the boys pulled their blankets from their packs. Bradley brought a pillow and a blanket for Amberle, which she accepted without giving him so much as a glance.

Keaton grinned and looked around at the walls of the house as he shook out his blanket. "What would life be like," he asked as he laid it on the ground, "if we had a pet?"

"You already do, Keaton," Tyler told him, smiling as he put his blanket of the floor next to the wall.

"I'm normal!" Amberle shouted at him, knowing what he meant. He and Cooper giggled wildly like drunk children as she dropped her pillow down next to Keaton's.

Keaton gave them a glare of exasperation and then wrapped himself in his blanket.

"Being here reminds me of when we lived in a house," he told Amberle. "We had a cat then, but there were lots of other cats in our neighborhood. Did you ever live in a house?" The room had gotten dark but he could see her narrow face as it nodded and he could see the glimmer of a smile.

"Kind of. It was a podment. Do you know what that is?"

Keaton nodded. He wanted to ask her about her parents, but it made him think of his own. He worried about them, and hoped they were alive. He pushed the thoughts away.

"Tell me what it was like."

"I remember a red front door, and I remember how cramped it was inside. Even then I preferred to be there rather than be outside, or with other people. I was probably jacked in too much. I remember more of what I saw on my acrylic, than I remember my parents."

It was too dark for Keaton to tell if there were tears in her eyes, but he thought there were. He wanted to touch her, but instead he reached out and touched the small pillow Bradley had given her. She smiled and put the tips of her fingers on the edge of his blanket. They fell asleep that way.

◕◖

Hellas and the boys looked over Cooper's map the next morning during breakfast, discussing the best route to the spaceport.

"Bradley can probably fix that glitch for you," Hellas remarked as the holographic light flickered out for the second time. "He has all kinds of electronic equipment."

"Does he have a computer?" Amberle asked, sarcastically joking as she ate a biscuit with butter.

"Yes."

The girl's head snapped up and she swallowed a large bite without chewing it. "What kind?"

Hellas shrugged and Amberle looked at Bradley, expectant. Keaton was glad that the young man had finally found a shirt. It was a loose, white linen shirt with strings at the neck that hung down, untied. Keaton thought it was better than nothing.

"ML 80."

"Does it have a PR jack?"

Bradley shook his head.

"Is it a G7?"

Bradley nodded.

"Then I can make one. Can I use it?"

Bradley shrugged. "Sure. Follow me." He looked at Cooper

and motioned with his shaggy head of hair. "Come on, I'll fix your map."

"You should go too," Hellas told Tyler. "You might find something that you need as well."

"The wizard has gifts for all of us?" Tyler asked with a wry smile. Hellas laughed and clapped him on the back.

"Sometimes. Sometimes you already have the gift and just don't know it," Hellas said with a wink.

Bradley led the group outside, then into another small adobe house and into the kitchen. This house was even smaller than the one they were just in, but this one had a door in the kitchen that led to a cellar underneath. Bradley opened the door and started down a steep flight of stairs with Amberle and the others following close behind.

When they reached the bottom of the stairs Amberle could see that they were in a room that was even bigger than the entire house upstairs, but it was a mess. There were shelves against the walls with tables and desks in the middle and all of them were covered with electronics of some kind, some whole but most taken apart.

There were stripped monitors, broken keyboards, jumbles of wires, speakers and transmitters, LED light cubes and circuit boards. And there, on a dented metal desk towards the far side of the room, was a GwenSeven hard drive and a DubBlack wireless glass monitor.

Amberle's hazel eyes opened a bit wider and Keaton saw the fingers on her right hand begin to twitch.

She walked to the desk and leaned around the monitor, craning her neck to see the entire hard drive behind it. Her hand reached out and touched a round, almost flat nub on the casing. She straightened and turned back to the group, her eyes seeking out the young man with shaggy brown hair and sea-green eyes.

"I need a flat blade and a Phillips," she told Bradley who

frowned, not understanding. Tyler suppressed a smile as he saw Amberle's temper rise. "A blunt knife and screwdriver," she instructed impatiently. Bradley nodded and went to a worktable where he retrieved both items and took them to the girl. Curious, Keaton edged closer so that he could watch, putting himself between Amberle and Bradley.

Amberle took what looked like a short butter knife and wedged it under what appeared to be a flat plastic button on the box behind the monitor. She popped the piece of plastic off, exposing a small screw underneath. Using the other tool that Bradley had brought her, she removed the screw and then stuck the knife into a seam and levered off a square of plastic. She stuck two slender fingers inside the open square and pulled out a nest of wires.

The girl turned and, finding herself nearly face to face with everyone in the small group that had slowly gathered close around her, sought out Bradley. She opened her mouth to speak but, before she could, he handed her a small pair of clippers. Amberle accepted them with a smile before turning back to her task.

She separated two wires from the rest; one green with white spots and the other one all yellow. She cut the wires and pulled them farther out of the console before she peeled back an inch of their colored, rubber casings. Then she reached into an inner pocket of her enormous jacket and pulled out the glove she had brought with her from the compound along with a mated chip.

She wound a length of exposed wire around the chip before laying it down next to the monitor and put on the glove - a thin membrane of black silicone that fit over only her thumb and index finger. Finally, she pulled an air cushion under her rear end and sat down in front of the desk as the monitor sprang to life.

The group of boys and the old man edged in even closer, watching as she manipulated the images on the screen by simply moving her gloved finger over the desk, sometimes giving it a tap.

Keaton looked at Amberle's face as the images on the screen changed. Her lips were parted and the green in her brown eyes glowed. The image on the monitor disappeared, leaving behind green numbers on a black background.

The girl's mouth opened a bit wider as she sighed and Keaton saw that it wasn't every number, just an endless stream of ones and zeroes in glowing green.

"It's just numbers," Cooper said, though he sounded as amused as he was surprised.

A quick breath escaped the girl. "Yeah," she said, "but it's not the numbers that are important." All eyes turned to look at her but she kept her own gaze fixed on the glass screen. "It's the spaces in between."

Everyone looked back up to the monitor where the ones and zeroes dropped like spiders, but that was all that everyone else could see. After two minutes of the unending stream of the same two numbers, Coop straightened and looked at Bradley.

"Can you fix our map?" he asked. Bradley regarded Cooper for a moment then nodded.

"Come 'ere," he said, motioning with his shaggy his head as he waked towards a workbench. Coop and Ty followed him while Hellas and Keaton stayed to watch Amberle look at the glowing numbers on the screen.

"What do you see?" Keaton whispered. Amberle took a deep breath and a smile played at the corners of her small mouth.

"Pictures, videos, music. Things to make you laugh or cry. Stories. Everyone's story. Seeds sprouting from dark soil. Stars burning, dying in space. Everything. So much is out there..." the girl trailed off, her mouth still slightly open.

"You see all that?" Keaton asked, staring at the numbers and scrutinizing the spaces between them.

Amberle nodded. "But this link," she murmured, "I've never jacked into anything like it. He's hotwired into a system I've never seen before."

Keaton watched her for another minute before turning his attention to the others at the workbench, though he stayed by her side.

Bradley turned out to be quite the wiz. He filled Tyler's torch and tweaked it to run more efficiently before he started on Cooper's map. He was looking for another tool when one of the girls from the village came quickly down the cellar stairs, ran to where Hellas was watching Amberle, and tugged on his sleeve.

The old man leaned down as she whispered hurriedly into his ear and then he straightened, anxious, as he looked around at the others in the room. After a second of hesitation, he motioned to the girl and the two of them hurried back up the stairs. They were back only minutes later.

"Bradley!" Hellas called out. "Boys!" Bradley immediately stopped what he was doing with the map and went to Hellas.

Coop and Tyler, though confused, did the same. Keaton saw the commotion and, giving Amberle a reluctant glance but knowing that she was absorbed in the monitor, followed. Hellas leaned down to talk to Bradley and the boys leaned in to listen, making a huddle of conspirators.

"Someone has come to the village," Hellas told them.

"Really?" Bradley asked, surprised. "I ain't picked up any life readings."

Hellas looked at him, his white brows drawn down and together. "Jena said that a man came to the oasis. She said that he had skin that was gray and decayed...and that he smelled like a grave."

Hellas watched Bradley's face as Tyler and Cooper and Keaton all glanced anxiously at each other.

"Was he one of the dead that walks?" Bradley asked.

Hellas, his face grim, nodded. "I think it he might be."

"Did he hurt anyone?"

Hellas shook s head. "No."

"Did he say anything?"

Hellas looked at the girl and she nodded. She looked to be about twelve years old, wearing a blue and white plaid dress, her hair done in two long braids. She looked up at the old man with large brown eyes.

"He said to surrender the girl. If we don't, his entire tribe will be here at nightfall, and they will kill us all."

"The girl?" Bradley asked. "Which one? There mus' be fifty!"

The three brothers looked at each other and then, as one, they looked across the room at the girl who had joined them, her normally dusky face lit with an eerie green glow by the monitor.

"What do you want to do?" Hellas asked them softly.

As the boys turned back to him, Cooper wrapped a hand around Keaton's arm in a silent warning for him to keep quiet. Tyler frowned, then glanced back at the girl and sighed before fixing his blue eyes on Hellas.

"We're not going to give her up to those monsters," he said. "But we don't want to endanger you or the children. Any suggestions?"

Hellas nodded. "We will give you the supplies you need and send you on your way, quickly. We can hide in the tunnels until they are gone. They will not survive out here without food, if they can survive at all in the desert."

Tyler smiled him. "Thank you."

The man nodded once and then turned to the girl with braids and began giving orders in their language. The girl nodded and was off like a shot. Bradley moved back to the worktable to finish the repairs on the map while the boys hurried to gather their belongings. They were back within minutes as all of the children began to file into the basement as well.

Bradley handed the map to Cooper and then opened a secret door in the cellar behind a wall of shelves that led to the tunnels. The children began filing in and Tyler looked at Keaton, nodding towards Amberle. Keaton took a deep breath and knelt beside the girl who was still staring at the monitor as the ones and zeroes shifted and dropped.

"Amberle?" he ventured, his voice soft. "We need to go." Amberle didn't move and seemed only vaguely aware of his presence.

"I found her," she whispered. "Right here. There, I mean. Right there. Why didn't I ever see her before?"

"I don't know," Keaton said, "but we can't stay here. We have to go."

More children were filing down the stairs and into the tunnel. Some of them handed the boys gifts - bags of water, fresh bread or cheese wrapped in a thin cloth. As the last of them came down the stairs Keaton saw Tyler glance at him. He ran his tongue across his lips and turned back to Amberle.

"Amberle," he said, louder this time, "we have to go."

"There she is," Amberle replied, moving her gloved finger just a bit. "Oh my god, she's right there!"

Keaton looked at Cooper, not knowing what to do.

"It is time to go," Hellas announced as the last child entered the tunnel. He looked at the girl, mesmerized in front of the glowing monitor, before his eyes went to Keaton who gave him a helpless shrug. The old man's eyes flicked to Bradley.

Without a word, the young man moved towards the girl and, reaching behind the glass screen, pulled her chip from the wire and then pulled the girl from her seat.

Disconnected from the computer, Amberle looked like she had been thrown into a cold lake. Bradley picked her up and headed for the stairs as she stared about, her eyes wide and wild. Her tight curls trembled from the rage that began to pour out of her.

"No!" she shouted. "Put me down!" When Bradley's only response was to head up the stairs, she pounded her dark fists against his chest. "Let me GO!"

Bradley carried her up the stairs and waited for the others before heading from the house towards the far end of the village with the girl struggling to get out of his grasp.

"Put me DOWN!" she wailed.

"Hush!" Bradley told her. "Do you want to let the undead know where you are?"

Amberle was immediately quiet and became still enough that Bradley put her back down on her feet. She wiped tears from her face and snatched her chip from his hand.

"I was so close!" she accused, pulling the glove from her finger and thumb. She stuffed her items back into her jacket as Hellas and the brothers gathered close. Hellas put a reassuring hand on her shoulder and she shrugged it off, angry. He didn't seem to notice.

"Did you find what you were looking for?" he asked.

Amberle scowled at him, but finally gave him a reluctant nod. "Kind of."

"Hope?"

Amberle's mouth dropped open and the old man smiled. He reached out and touched a finger to the middle of her chest and this time she didn't move.

"Hope," he said, "is inside."

She nodded, her mouth still open, and Hellas turned to the boys as Cooper opened his map and gave it a shake. It flared to life in brilliant color. Bradley had not only fixed it, but had improved it as well.

"Wow," Keaton said.

"I know, right?" Coop agreed. Even Tyler looked impressed for a single second before his blue eyes lifted and began to scour the horizon.

"This is the spaceport," Hellas said, pointing to the map. Cooper nodded.

"We thought so, but we weren't able to tell before. Not for sure anyway."

"You might be able to make it there without stopping," Hellas told him. "But I wouldn't advise it unless you have no choice." He pointed to a spot on the map where a holograph image of a stepped pyramid surrounded by a jungle hovered over the paper. "There is water here," he said. "You can hunt and it will be a cool reprieve from the desert."

Cooper nodded as he studied the images that floated above the map. "And it would be a straight shot from there," he agreed. "It's not that far from the port." Grinning, he closed the map and held out a hand to Hellas. The old man shook it enthusiastically and then shook hands with Tyler and Keaton. They all looked at Bradley, wanting to thank him as well, but his back was towards them as his sea-green eyes watched the village.

"Be careful," he warned as if sensing their gaze. "Nothing friendly has come through that port for twenty-eight turns."

The boys nodded as though he could see them and dropped and opened their boards as Hellas turned to Amberle.

"Remember," he told her. "Hope is found within." The girl gave him a doubtful look and then held out her slim hand, which the old man grasped with gnarled fingers. "You will find your Faith there, too," he added and then laughed as she stared at him, clearly startled.

"We need to get back," Bradley said, a second before the wind kicked up - carrying the desperate and lonely sound of voices moaning in unison. Chill bumps rose on everyone's arms at the sound.

"And we need to get out of here," Coop agreed, stepping onto his board.

"Thank you," Amberle told Hellas who gave her a warm nod. She turned to find Keaton on his board with his goggles on, holding out a hand to help her up. She climbed up behind him as the wind gusted again, blowing sand along with the eerie moans which, to Amberle, sounded hungry. "Thanks Bradley," she added.

The young man nodded without turning around as the group began to slide away as one, heading north once again.

The girl held on to Keaton and buried her face in his pack as the board moved beneath them, carrying them away.

 SEVEN

The four rode across the desert, the far but blinding sun reflecting off the white, gritty sand. They stopped for a late lunch, taking shelter from the wind next to a group of large rocks.

Amberle took off her coat and sat on it.

"You should leave that on," Tyler told her.

"But I'm hot!"

"Just because your skin is dark doesn't mean it can't burn."

The girl rocked her head all the way back and sighed. "Fine." She shook out the coat and draped it over her shoulders like a cape while Cooper handed out pieces of bread and cheese.

"Let's eat these while they're still good," he said.

Though the cheese had gotten warm it was still as good as the fresh baked bread they had gotten from the village.

"Why do you think those zombies are after you?" Cooper asked Amberle.

"What makes you think they are after me?" she asked with a frown as she tore off a piece of bread with her small teeth.

The boys exchanged glances.

"She was on the computer when that girl brought the message," Tyler reminded him.

"They're after me?" she asked, surprised. Coop nodded and Amberle chewed her bread as she thought about it. Finally, she shrugged. "I have no idea."

"Were you working on the same thing as the other programmers?" Tyler asked.

The girl froze for a second, then shook her head. "I was on a private assignment."

"Well," Coop said, tearing off a hunk of bread and pointing the remaining crust at the girl, "you know what zombies like?" Amberle shook her head of pink hair and took a bite from her cheese. Cooper grinned around the bread in his mouth. "Brains."

Amberle's dusky face went a shade paler, turning her skin the color of ash. Tyler laughed.

"That means that, under that mass of rosy curls, there's something in that tiny head of yours that they want."

"I don't have a tiny head!" Amberle shouted. If she didn't like her bread so much she would have thrown it at him. "I'm normal!" Ty and Coop both laughed and Keaton had to press his lips together to keep from laughing. Amberle glared at them before giving Tyler a sly smile. "If they are really after brains, they obviously don't want anything from you."

Keaton and Cooper both hooted laughter and Tyler shook his blonde head though he was chuckling.

"Hilarious," he said.

They finished eating, brushed the crumbs from their hands, and drank a bit of water from the canteens.

"We should be there by sunset," Cooper said as he checked the compass on his watch. He glanced over to see Tyler looking back in the direction they had come. He followed his gaze to see a very small but distinct smudge on the horizon. "What would life be like," he murmured, "if we had a pair of binoculars?"

Tyler turned his blue eyes to him and grinned. "We'd have a lot less surprises," he said. "That's for sure."

Cooper nodded his agreement and stepped onto his hover board, grinning as he pulled his shades down over his eyes.

"Where's the fun in that?" he asked. Tyler shook his head and stepped onto his own board. Keaton and Amberle were already waiting, watching him.

"Let's go," he said, leading the way.

They kept to their course, following the sun. Just as it began to set, they could see their destination ahead and to the left. They adjusted their course slightly, driving on and angling west.

As dusk settled over the moon they reached the forest, dismounted and collapsed the boards. This time everyone moaned and stretched, even Tyler. It had been a long day of riding and they hadn't stopped for many breaks. Amberle accepted a drink of water from Keaton's canteen.

"Thank you," she said, handing it back to him. Together, they looked at Ty and Coop who were staring back in the direction they had come.

"Do you think they could be following us?" Tyler asked. Cooper shrugged, knowing he was talking about the zombies.

"Normally I wouldn't think so. But I also wouldn't have thought they could have crossed the first part of the desert, and they did." Tyler nodded, looking back with a crease between his brows. "They did most of that at night, though," Cooper added.

"And they might have holed up close to the village for most of today," Tyler mused. "And be starting out again now that night is coming."

Cooper didn't want to agree, but he knew Tyler was right. He nodded. "Do you think we got enough of a head start?" he asked.

"Possibly. But let's go as far as we can before we camp."

"I hear you on that one," Cooper agreed, taking out his map as Tyler turned to the girl.

"What do you know about this place?" he asked. He

expected her to glare at him and argue, but instead she closed her eyes.

"The forest is ovoid in shape. About ten kilometers by twenty kilometers. There are lots of waterways, and a temple in the northeast quadrant." She opened her eyes to find Tyler giving her a small smile, though it disappeared as soon as she looked at him.

"What kind of temple?" Cooper asked. "I don't see it on the map which, by the way, is working better than ever." Bradley had worked nothing short of a miracle, in his opinion. The paper of the map was clearly marked and holographic images of trees and streams, even the swirling sands of the desert they had just left, floated above it in perfect clarity.

"I'm not sure," Amberle said. "I just remember it from the blueprints. There was a triangle marked 'temple' on the far side of the forest, though this looks like more of a jungle to me."

"A triangle?" Cooper asked. "There is a pyramid holo on the map. Maybe that's it."

"Maybe it's a church," Keaton suggested. "Maybe it'll be a safe place."

"Maybe," Tyler muttered, looking at the forest. It was the densest patch of vegetation they had been in so far. Amberle was right - it did look more like a jungle than a forest, with heavy vines hanging from the trees, crisscrossing above every path. Personally, he was convinced that there were no more safe places on the moon, but it was not something he wanted to share with Keaton.

"Well," Cooper said cheerfully as he adjusted the pack on his back, "let's see if we can make it there to camp. It's the same direction as the spaceport, and maybe it will be safe enough that we can sleep under shelter."

"It's worth a try," Tyler agreed. "We can hunt along the way, hopefully." He adjusted his own pack on his shoulders and led the way into the jungle of trees as the others followed.

Two hours later, hunting along the way, they broke through the ever-thickening mass of verge to a clearing. The open ground was covered with uneven patches of grass and in the center rose a behemoth of stepped gray stone blocks wearing an erratic cloak of moss and lichen and draped with vines.

The size of it rendered the entire group speechless for a moment and when they finally spoke it was in hushed voices.

"Holy shit," Keaton whispered, looking up and up. "That thing is huge."

"How big do you think that is?" Cooper asked softly. He craned his neck to one side and then the other, trying to see where the sides ended.

"Two hundred and twenty-eight meters by two hundred and twenty-eight meters at the base," Amberle whispered back. "One hundred and forty-eight meters high."

Whether it was because she had been right on so many other things, her uncanny memory or mathematic ability, or the sheer size of the edifice, no one questioned her.

Cooper whistled as he looked up the giant steps of the weatherworn wall of rock that rose up out of the jungle like a mountain of granite.

There was a single opening they could see, a dark gap hewed into the stones that glared at them like an empty eye socket. The sky above was full dark now except for the ruddy glow from Jupiter and the white throw of stars that shone like chips of ice in the otherwise black sky.

"Is it a pyramid?" Tyler asked. Amberle shrugged.

"I think you can also call it a ziggurat. The remains of the first colony are on the other side, which is why it is so close to the spaceport. The colonists were Greco-Mayan, and this place was built as a tribute to the earthling hero from Greek mythology that defeated the Minotaur. It's a labyrinth inside, miles of mazes. The only danger is getting lost inside and never getting out. Other than that, it should be perfectly safe."

Tyler snorted. "Do you ever hear yourself talk?"

Amberle threw him a dark look that he ignored.

"It may be safe," Coop said, quietly, "but it sure doesn't look inviting."

"I don't want to sleep in there," Keaton said.

"We'll camp outside," Tyler assured them, still looking at the mossy stone giant in the clearing.

"Can we have a fire?" Keaton asked. They had shot three animals on their trek through the jungle forest - two oversized sqarbs and one fat quora - but he wasn't about to eat them raw. Tyler nodded.

"Yeah," he said, "but let's go back into the trees a few yards." Everyone nodded in agreement and backed into the trees, only stopping when the temple was out of view.

Amberle got the fire started as the boys cleaned and skewered the animals they had brought down. They ate the last of the cheese as their dinner cooked over the fire.

"What would life be like," Cooper started, "if we lived in a big city?"

Tyler laughed. "You would hate it," he said. "What would life be like," he asked, "if we lived in the Outer Banks, and slept on white sand beaches?"

Cooper grinned. "Life would be pretty awesome."

Keaton tossed a piece of cheese in the air towards Cooper. Coop caught the cheese in his mouth and Keaton tossed him a piece of bread.

"You're more of pet than I am," Amberle muttered, watching them. Cooper grinned at her, chewing the bread as Tyler took their dinner off the fire. "What would life be like," she said, helping Tyler divide up their dinner, "if we could move as fast as our thoughts?"

Cooper accepted half of a still-sizzling quora from her, his dark eyes wide. "Do you mean move as fast as the speed of thought, or faster – like, you think you are on the other side of the moon and suddenly you are there?"

The girl laughed, something he had never heard before. "Either one," she said, handing a crispy sqarb to Keaton.

"Then we would be off of this moon," Tyler said, "living on a beach, and eating toasted marshmallows instead of toasted jungle rodents."

"What's a marshmallow?" Amberle asked. "A rodent from the marsh?"

Keaton laughed. "No," he said. "It's like a fluffy ball of sugar, but it's better when you toast it over a fire. Even better if you squish it between sweet crackers with a piece of chocolate."

"That does sound pretty good," Amberle agreed. "Have you ever had ice cream?"

"No."

"Yes, you have," Cooper corrected. "You were probably just too young to remember."

"Then it's almost the same thing," Keaton argued before turning his attention back to Amberle. "What is it?"

"It's a dessert made of sweet, frozen milk. Sometimes filled with cookies or chocolate or candy. It's amazing!"

"It sounds like it," Keaton agreed. "Did they have it at that center, where you were working?"

Amberle shook her head of pink coils. "No, I've only had it once. It was delivered to our pod on my sixteenth birthday. There were two different kinds, and they were in a special box to keep it cold. We thought it had been sent to the wrong place, because we never ordered it, but it had a card - a *paper* card - that said 'Happy Birthday,' so I argued that it had to be for me."

"Was the card signed?" Cooper asked.

Amberle's small shoulders lifted under her heavy jacket. "Only with an initial. J."

They finished their dinner, each one lost in their own

thoughts, before they rolled themselves into their blankets next to the fire. Amberle put a hand over her mouth as she yawned.

"What would life be like," Tyler asked, "if nothing ever stood in the way of your dreams? If nothing stopped you?"

"Nothing ever does," Amberle replied, sleepy and quiet. "You only stop yourself." She got the feeling that Tyler was staring at her through the flames, but she didn't turn her head to look.

Keaton carefully reached out and touched the corner of the girl's pillow. Smiling, the girl reached out and touched the edge of his blanket before she closed her eyes.

ೞೞ

When Amberle opened her eyes again she was sitting up. There were chill bumps on her arms and the tiny curls of hair on the back of her neck were standing up.

She looked across the glowing remains of the fire to see Tyler sitting up as well. Even Keaton and Cooper were propped up on their elbows, still and listening. It was so quiet that if everyone else hadn't been sitting up, Amberle would have thought she was imagining things.

Then the wind shifted and it came again, a low and lonely moaning.

"Is it the wind?" Amberle asked, hopeful.

"It's not the wind," Tyler answered, his voice tight. "Hurry, let's get out of here."

They packed their things and Coop moved to kick dirt over their fire but Ty put a hand on him and Cooper froze, watching and listening. Tyler peered through the flames at Amberle.

"If they're close, and it sounds like they are, our best shot to lose them would be inside the temple, wouldn't it?"

The girl nodded. "Probably."

"Can you navigate us through it?"

The girl nodded again, her hair bouncing. Tyler took three short, heavy sticks from near the fire, turned Keaton around, and stuffed them in his pack. Then he carefully took two more sticks from the fire that were burning on one end, handed one to Cooper, and then kicked dirt over the remains of the fire, extinguishing it.

"Let's go," he said. He turned and led the group through the jungle-forest, picking his way carefully but as quickly as he could. Before long they were back in the clearing, the temple rising before them into the night. Pausing only briefly, the group made their way across the open ground to the darkened doorway. Amberle faced the door with the others.

"What direction are we facing?" she asked.

Cooper checked the compass on his watch. "North."

Tyler handed her his torch and she led the way, the darkness swallowing them up as they entered. Inside, the torchlight flickered off walls of stone blocks dripping with moisture. The girl did not hesitate to lead them straight ahead, taking the first corridor that opened on their right. She led them on, taking a second left and then another right.

"I'm lost already," Keaton whispered to her.

She gave him a small smile, leading them on, taking turns seemingly at random but never hesitating. Finally, they came to a four-way intersection in the hall. Straight ahead, the floor began sloping down. To the left was a stone stairway going up and on the right was a stone stairway leading down.

Amberle grinned and started up the stairs with Keaton right behind her and Ty and Coop bringing up the rear. When they reached the top, the hallway was surprisingly wider and branched left and right. A heavy wooden door blocked the way straight ahead of them.

There were iron brackets on either side of the door but they were empty, leaving the door unbarred. Amberle pushed on it and it swung open ponderously but smoothly. There were brackets on the other side as well, also empty. Cautiously, the group entered a large chamber with more doors along the walls, some open and some closed.

"Does anybody need to rest?" she asked. Though they were all breathing heavily from climbing the stairs, they all shook their heads. Amberle nodded, looked at the wall to their right, and chose the third door from the left. Keaton pushed it open for her and she led the way.

The hallways twisted and turned. There were dozens of doorways in each passage. Some had actual doors on them and some were just empty sockets. All led to darkness.

They went up stairs and down ramps. Through corridors that smelled of must and damp. They continued that way for another hour.

Finally, they stopped after another flight of stairs to catch their breath.

"Are we almost through?" Cooper asked. The girl shook her head and took a drink from Keaton's canteen before handing it back to him with a grateful smile.

"Only about halfway," she said.

"Only halfway?" Coop asked. He gave Tyler a dubious look and Amberle sighed.

"The way through is never straight," she said by way of an explanation.

"Are you sure you're not lost?" Tyler asked. Amberle nodded.

"I'm sure. We go left here, then on our right will be a wooden door to another chamber."

"You better be right," he warned. Amberle was about to sarcastically ask him what he thought he was going to do if she wasn't but Cooper interjected.

"Well," he said, "at least we're hopefully succeeding in throwing those damn zombies off our trail."

Tyler grunted as he adjusted his pack and the girl rolled her eyes and started down the left corridor. A dozen yards later there was a wooden door on their right side, this one barred. Amberle gave Tyler a triumphant smile, which he ignored as he lifted the heavy wooden bar from the brackets and leaned it against the wall before he pushed the door open.

It swung open easily to expose another large chamber where an enormous Golgoth stood only a few paces away. It seemed as startled to see them as they were to see it, its black eyes full of hate and murder.

The Golgoth was humanoid, in the fact that it had two arms and stood on two legs, but the creature was grossly huge. Over seven feet tall with a barrel-like torso, bulging arms, and a misshapen head that sat directly on the monster's broad shoulders. Each leg was thicker around the thigh than Keaton was at the chest. It was covered with skin so red and shiny that it could be mistaken for body armor except that it was knobby and bumpy as if plagued by warts.

It carried a weapon that was actually many weapons - a pistol, a trazon, a laser rifle, and a photon launcher - all fused together and nearly the size of the girl.

Though the boys had never seen a live Golgoth before, they knew what it was and moved without hesitation. Cooper had pulled out the laser pistol and had it raised and aimed before Tyler had even unslung the crossbow from his back, but the creature was faster.

It swatted Cooper's gun aside with a massive hand and fired a hot round into the young man's right leg, only inches above the knee. Coop screamed in surprise and pain and fell forward as Tyler brought his bow up to his shoulder to fire. The creature whirled at him, raising its own weapon but, as it moved for Tyler, Amberle stepped forward and to the left, brought her knee to her chest at an angle and slammed her foot down on the joint in the creature's leg.

The Golgoth roared in pain as it went down on its ruined

knee, shaking the stone walls with its howls. Tyler shot a bolt deep into one of its black eyes and the sound cut off abruptly, answered only by echoes. It fell forward without ceremony and landed with a cracking sound as its head hit the floor.

Tyler looked around frantically to make sure there weren't any more of the creatures and then pushed his way between Amberle and Keaton who were already hovering over Cooper. He took one look at Coop's leg and grabbed Keaton and spun him around and opened his pack.

Tyler pulled two shirts from Keaton's pack and was on his knees beside his brother in the blink of an eye. He wrapped his hands around the lower part of Cooper's thigh, feeling around with his fingers. Coop arched his back, grinding his teeth together to keep from crying out.

"You're lucky," Ty told him. Despite the pain, Cooper gave a short bark of laughter.

"Seriously?" he asked.

"Yes," Tyler said, ripping each shirt into strips. "The bullet went clean through and cauterized most of its trail and, though you're still bleeding, it's not from your artery."

"Lucky me," Cooper hissed though his teeth, but when Tyler tried to bandage the wound he cried out and his leg jerked away.

"Wait!" Amberle whispered. She fished around the inner pocket of her jacket and pulled out a slim, plastic box. She opened it and offered it to Tyler, who quickly scanned the contents of the field kit and selected a small syringe.

"You really are lucky," Ty muttered as he stabbed the needle into Cooper's thigh and pressed the plunger.

Coop's head rocked back almost immediately in relief.

"Thank you," he whispered.

Tyler pulled out the syringe and tossed it aside and then tied the strips of cloth above, below, and around the wound. He opened his mouth to speak but snapped it shut as they all froze, then turned their heads as they heard a sound from the corridor behind them.

The moaning was far away, but clear and haunting as it carried through the stone walls of the temple.

"They're inside," Keaton breathed.

Ty's face snapped back to Coop.

"Can you walk?"

Cooper glared at him though his blue-green eyes still brimmed with humor. "Do I have a choice?"

Tyler grinned at him and shook his head. He jerked his head towards the laser pistol on the floor across the room and Keaton ran to retrieve it. He checked the safety and stuffed it down the waistband of his pants. Tyler handed his crossbow to the girl and picked up the Golgoth's giant weapon and slung it over his shoulder. Then he glanced meaningfully at Keaton who nodded solemnly.

Together, they hooked their hands under Cooper's arms and hauled him to his feet. Coop draped his arms over their shoulders and squeezed his eyes shut but didn't make a sound. He did his best to walk on his own, but it wasn't much.

Amberle held the torch high and led the way wordlessly as they half carried and half dragged Cooper to the far end of the chamber. The girl cautiously peered around the corner of an open door and led the way once again. They made their way from one stone hallway to the next, though now they were going much slower.

"Thanks," Tyler said, darting his blue eyes at Amberle.

"For what?"

"For giving me a crucial second."

"How did you know what to do?" Keaton asked.

Clips of martial arts movies, instruction, memories that she was not sure were her own, flashed through her mind. "I don't know," she said. "It just seemed like what I should do."

They carried on in silence for a while before Tyler spoke. "That was a Golgoth," he said, "wasn't it?"

Amberle nodded. "I think so."

"I didn't think they traveled alone."

"They don't," Amberle said, choosing yet another doorway without pause. "They travel in platoons, though even those are always part of a much larger company. It must have gotten lost."

"Can't imagine how that could happen," Cooper remarked with his normal joviality, at least as near to it as he could muster.

Keaton laughed at his brother's humor, though he was already sweating from having to support so much of his weight.

"So there's more of them around somewhere," Tyler said. "A lot more."

"The spaceport is close to here," Cooper grunted as they moved him along. "Maybe they are there, and the one we found had wandered off."

"It's a likely explanation," Tyler agreed. The girl shook her head as she turned right down yet another stone corridor. Her springy pink curls looked tarnished and dull in the dim light of torches.

"But this is still an IGC system," she argued. "They wouldn't let a Golgoth ship into this galaxy, much less land on one of its moons. Do you have any idea how close we are, galactically speaking, to the nexus of human civilization?"

"Maybe the IGC is up to more than just sewing patches on their field jackets," Tyler replied with undisguised acerbity.

The moaning wafting through the halls behind them became a duet, then a chorus.

"It's not just one, the one that talked to the village girl," Cooper said, breathing heavily. "It's a group. They're here. And they're gaining on us."

No one answered him, they just kept going. Amberle directed them through the twists and turns of the corridor. After an hour, Keaton began to sag under his brother's weight and then finally faltered, bringing the group to a halt.

"Give me your pack, Keaton," Amberle demanded. He unshouldered it and handed it over without a word before giving Cooper his support again. Both he and Tyler were sweating and breathing hard. Coop's face was a tight mask of pain as the morphine shot burned up with his exertion to stay upright and moving.

"Which way?" Tyler asked. Amberle looked up and realized they were stopped next to a doorway. She cocked her head, examining the mark carved high in the wall.

"Through the door," she said.

So it went.

Through twists and turns until the chorus of moans went up behind them, becoming wails of hunger and need. Quickly, as quick as they were able, they went left through a doorway into the passage beyond, moving with purpose and determination. It was not enough.

Whatever was chasing them, was gaining. Before long they could hear the echoes of shuffling feet and the grunts of the undead as they jostled one another in the corridors. The four knew that in mere minutes they would feel the foul breath of the zombies caressing their necks. It was only moments later, pushing with all that they had, that the small group came to stop next to another doorway.

This opening had a thick stone door and was secured by a heavy bar of oak. Cooper's body sagged between a drained Tyler and an exhausted Keaton. Tyler looked questioningly at the girl. She put her hands on her hips, trying to catch her breath, as she looked at the door and then nodded.

"Through there," she said.

Tyler used his free arm to lift the oak bar, pushing it all the way up until it was vertical, resting it in the iron bracket. He pushed the door open and the group stumbled through.

"We need to take a breather," Ty instructed as he and Keaton lowered Coop to the ground.

"We can't," Keaton puffed out, though he was glad for the rest, however short. "They're too close!"

"I can walk," Cooper said, staring at Tyler with steadfast determination. Ty knelt down and grasped Coop by the sides of his head with his strong hands, looking into his eyes.

"You just worry about holding it together," he told him. "Hang in there. You'll be as good as new."

Coop nodded as well as he could between Tyler's big hands. Ty looked at him, his blue eyes intense, for a moment longer and then he let him go and stood up. He messed Keaton's hair.

"Take care of him," he instructed. "Give him some water. I need to talk to the girl."

Keaton nodded and sank down beside his brother as Tyler looked at Amberle and jerked his head towards the door. She followed him, noticing another heavy bar leaning against the inner wall as she adjusted Keaton's pack on her back. She still carried Tyler's crossbow.

They stepped into the doorway and Ty leaned close to her. She instinctively wanted to pull back but made herself keep still. Sounds came drifting from the corridors that were close. Very close.

"We're not going to make it like this," Tyler told her. "Someone needs to lead them away."

Amberle kept his gaze for a second and then nodded. Blowing out a quick breath of determination, she began to unshoulder Keaton's pack but Tyler put a hand on her arm, shaking his head as a soft chuckle escaped his lips.

"Not you," he said. "Me." Amberle stared at him, surprised

and confused. "Get them out," he instructed, "and get them to the airfield. Coop knows enough about circuitry. With your help, you two can rewire a motherboard and get a craft working. Use the homing device to get the hell out of here and back to a real civilization."

Amberle stared at him, her brown and green eyes opened wide in her dusky face. "Why?" she whispered.

"Because they need..."

Amberle shook her head vehemently, her coils of hair going wild. "No! I mean, why would you save me? You don't even like me."

Tyler's expression softened and he reached out and touched her on the chin. "That doesn't mean you're not worth saving," he told her.

The sound of the moans came echoing from around the last bend of the corridor and they both froze.

"Tyler!" Coop hissed, hearing the same. Amberle watched Tyler look right and left, ready to run. Coop, as if sensing something wrong, pushed himself up onto his elbows. "Ty?" he called.

Tyler glanced at him, his brows drawn together in concern. He straightened, taking a step back from the girl and into the hall. He was ready to bolt when she grabbed him tightly by the arm.

"Wait!"

He looked at her as the sounds grew louder but she had her eyes squeezed shut. Inside the chamber, Cooper pushed himself into a sitting position.

"Ty?" he called, louder this time.

"Straight," Amberle commanded, her eyes still closed tight. "Then left, left, left. Always left until you see the mirror. Then go right through it, it's only water. Take the left-hand slope down all the way to the bottom." She opened her eyes and Tyler nodded. He wasn't sure what she meant but the sounds of the pursuers were almost upon them.

"Take care of them," he commanded. She met his eyes.

"I will," she promised.

"TY!" Cooper shouted, struggling to stand. Tyler glanced quickly at his brothers then pushed Amberle back through the door and swung it shut. There was a heavy thump as he dropped the bar into the iron brackets on the other side.

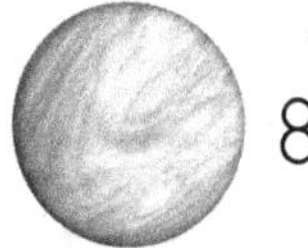 8

"TYLER!" Coop shouted, lunging for the door despite his injured leg.

Keaton made a grab for his shoulders but missed, sending them both crashing to the floor. Amberle was there in a second, helping Keaton to his feet and then hoisting up Cooper on one side.

"Bar the door on this side," she told Keaton.

He ran for the door and hefted the heavy bar up and settled it down into the brackets as Cooper struggled against the girl.

"Let me go!" he yelled. *"Tyler!"*

"He's gone!" she told him, "And we can't stay. We'll see him on the other side," she assured, hoping she was right.

Only seconds after Keaton had dropped the bar into place, the moans became louder, a cacophony of torment on the other side of the stone walls. The three that were left huddled together on the stone floor, frozen, listening to the shuffling of feet as they stopped on the other side of the door. The moans were replaced by grunts and groaning, along with the sound of the bar on the far side of the door being lifted and dropped to the ground with a crash.

Three pairs of eyes watched the door shake as the zombies fought to break through from the other side. The door shook again as it was hit, the bar jumping in its brackets before thumping back down. Suddenly, there was a shout from the other side and, though it was muffled, they all recognized the voice.

"Ty!!!!" Cooper managed to get out before Amberle clamped dark fingers over his mouth.

Coop struggled to take her hand away but the girl was surprisingly strong and it didn't matter anyway. The sounds on the other side of the door disappeared as the zombies followed the shout deeper into the temple. Cooper let out a groan and sagged to the floor.

"We need to get out of here," Amberle whispered. "They can't get through the door but other passages lead to this one." Keaton nodded. He looked at Cooper, who simply shook his head. "Do you want another shot for the pain?" Amberle asked quietly.

Coop frowned at her. "I want Tyler back," he said. "We shouldn't have split up. We should go after him."

"Someone had to lead them away," Amberle argued. "Or they would have gotten us all. Look how close it was just now." Cooper looked away and she put a hand on his chest. "I told him how to get out," she assured him.

"Did you tell him how not to get swarmed by a herd of zombies?" he demanded angrily, tears standing in his blue-green eyes. "I'll never forgive him for leaving like that!" he said, his voice cracking.

Amberle licked her small lips and looked at the dark hallways before fixing her eyes on Keaton, not knowing what to do or say. Keaton frowned and looked at his brother.

"Stop being an asshole!" he told him. The girl's eyes opened wide in surprise and Cooper looked as if he had been slapped. Apparently he had never seen Keaton in his current state. "Tyler is a survivor," Keaton continued, his blue-green eyes intense. "If he knows the way out, he'll find it. Besides, he has that weapon. It could take out a whole army of zombies."

"You think so?" Coop whispered, hoping.

"I know so," Keaton told him. "And if he shows up at that spaceport and we don't, he'll be pissed."

Coop considered his words for a second and nodded. "Alright. Let's go."

Amberle, still wearing Keaton's pack, slid her arm behind Cooper, propping him up on her thin frame as best she could while Keaton put on his brother's pack and wedged his shoulder under Cooper's other arm.

At first, Cooper just hung between them and a sob escaped his lips for the first time. Amberle glanced across his back at Keaton who pressed his lips together and shook his head. They waited in silence until Coop finally put his feet underneath himself, pushing forward as best he could.

Though smaller, Amberle and Keaton managed to hold him up and guide him through one dark tunnel after another. And another.

The time became endless, nameless in the darkness. It became a matter of putting one foot in front of another and then doing it again. And again. And again. Finally, when it seemed like all three were going to collapse and let fate take them where they fell, Amberle realized that the rectangle at the end of the downward sloping hallway was midnight blue, and studded with stars.

She felt her knees buckle with relief and struggled to keep her feet only because she was supporting half of Cooper's weight as well. The three staggered down the sloping corridor and sank into a heap when they reached the opening. Amberle and Keaton slipped out from under Cooper with a sigh of relief and propped him up against the wall. They dropped their packs and saw that his leg was bleeding badly.

"Probably from being on it so much," Keaton muttered as he pulled out another shirt and bound it around his brother's leg. Keaton gave him another shot from the field kit to kill the pain and then he and Amberle edged over to the open doorway.

At first glance through the door they could tell they were back to ground level. They stuck their heads out of the opening for a look around the outside base of the temple and stared around in shock.

"Oh my God," Keaton whispered, his voice cracking and catching in his throat. "We're back where we started." Amberle felt a wave of panic and shook her head.

"No," she whispered, clutching his arm. "Look, the trees are much closer to the temple on this side. But they're thinner. You can almost see right through them."

Keaton's eyes darted around, following her words, and he sighed as he looked up. "You're right. In fact, I think it's getting lighter on the other side of the temple."

Amberle nodded. "It's probably only an hour before dawn." She pulled her head back inside and looked at Keaton. "What do you think?" she asked. "Should we make a run for it?"

Keaton knelt on the stone floor, considering, as Cooper turned his face to him. It was drawn and pale in the muted light from the stars.

"Did you see Ty?" he asked, hopeful.

Keaton frowned. "No." Cooper turned his face away, dejected. "But that doesn't mean he's not out there," Keaton added. "Or right behind us." When Cooper didn't respond, Keaton turned back to Amberle. "Not yet," he told her. "Tyler said that the sunlight stops the zombies, or at least slows them down a lot. We could use an hour of rest, especially Coop, and any help that the sun might bring."

Amberle nodded and settled down with her back against the wall, realizing that she still carried Tyler's crossbow in one hand. Keaton sat down between her and his brother. There was a moment of silence before Keaton gave his head a slight turn in her direction.

"I know you think differently than most people," he said quietly. "So tell me what you think of that Golgoth we found. Not as a species, but why it would be here."

The girl looked down at the weapon in her lap that had killed the creature, already loaded with another bolt, though she had no idea how to use it.

Or do I? she wondered absently. Images wafted through her mind of similar weapons, being loaded, being wound, being triggered.

"From what I have read," she said, her voice soft, "of Galactic Law, they are eliminated without question if found trying to infiltrate any system of the IGC. They are the only known enemies of what we call civilization."

"And their galaxy is even farther away than Andromeda."

Amberle nodded, realizing that they were shoulder to shoulder. And that it didn't bother her. "And this system is too far in without them just happening by unnoticed."

"So basically," Keaton said, "there is no way they would be here without an actual invitation from the IGC."

"Or someone high up in the organization is turning a blind eye. And offering them concealment."

"And these are the same people," Keaton continued, "the same organization that has been operating here under the guise of the GwenSeven Corporation. Running experiments on some drop of a moon in the outer quadrants, and either killing or contaminating the survivors that don't turn out as expected?"

"It seems that way," Amberle whispered, staring at the wall of cut stones only a few feet in front of her.

"What would life be like," he said bitterly, "if the universe wasn't filed with money-grubbing whores?"

"What would life be like," Cooper said, choking on his words, "if we didn't always lose the ones we loved?" Keaton looked at his brother, who turned his tear-streaked face away towards the wall.

"It wouldn't be life at all," the girl answered quietly, staring straight ahead. "Just some crazy dream."

Keaton grimaced and shook his head. Everything was

starting to feel like it was a dream. A bad one. "Let's get some sleep," he suggested.

Cooper's body shuddered and Amberle closed her eyes and let her head drop down to Keaton's shoulder for the short hour of rest before sunrise. Keaton stayed awake the whole time, listening to the darkness while watching the light in the universe grow bright.

When he finally stirred, the girl woke immediately, looking around quickly before standing up and stretching her back. Cooper let out a groan and they both knelt close to examine his leg which had swollen horribly. The bleeding had stopped but the wound was crusty and stiff.

"I don't think I can move it," Cooper said quietly.

"Don't worry," Keaton told him, "you won't have to. Not much, anyway." He pulled out Cooper's map and shook it open. "Are we going to come out of this place on the side you expected?" he asked the girl.

She nodded and pointed at the map. "We're right here. On the north side."

"The port isn't far from here," Keaton said, "maybe three miles. We might even be able to see it once we get through the trees."

He closed the map and stuck it into his pack. Then he reached into Cooper's jacket and pulled out his chunk of hover board. Keaton dropped it and, after it had opened, he turned it over and made an adjustment to the controls underneath. When he flipped it back over, it hovered waist high instead of knee high.

"Help me get him on this," he told Amberle, who moved without question to help him heft Cooper up and get him next to his board. "Sit on it," Keaton instructed. "Like you're waiting for a wave." Cooper was able to get his butt down but couldn't bend his leg at the knee. Keaton grabbed the cuff of brother's pants and hauled his wounded leg onto the board and then did the same with the other leg so that Cooper sat with both his legs straight out in front of him.

"I feel stupid," he complained.

"Does it hurt?" Keaton asked.

Coop shook his head. "No. The painkiller is still working."

"Then feel stupid," Keaton said. He put on his brother's pack and dropped his own board. Amberle put the crossbow on the outside of Keaton's pack before she put it on. "Can you guide your board?" he asked Cooper, "or do you need me to tow you?"

"I can guide it," Cooper said, sullen. He obviously didn't like his brother's new demeanor any more than he liked losing Tyler.

Responsibility is a heavy burden, Amberle thought. *But it's one someone takes without question when it comes to someone they care about.* The realization made her feel strange inside. The girl looked at Cooper and decided that she hated seeing him the way he was. He was always the cheerful one, always optimistic. It just wasn't normal to be so morose, not for him anyway.

"They won't get him," she said, laying a hand on his arm.

"You really think so?" he asked, doubtful. Amberle nodded quickly. "And you think he will find his way out?" Coop asked. "He won't get trapped in there forever?"

"I'm sure of it," Amberle said, realizing that for the first time in her life she was lying to save someone's feelings. Cooper gave her a small smile, a glimmer of his former self. Amberle smiled back and then climbed on the back of Keaton's board as he led them out of the narrow tunnel beneath the temple and out into the dawn.

They went slowly since Cooper was not used to controlling the board while sitting on it, cruising silently through the trees as Amberle continued to look behind for any pursuers while Coop kept looking around for Tyler.

They left the jungle-forest and all were glad to see rolling grasslands on the other side instead of desert. They angled east, the small knolls continuing to rise up and up until the three reached the top of a line of high hills.

Amberle and Keaton stepped down from his board and crawled to the crest to look over. The hill dropped away at a steep angle on the other side, going down down down - all the way down to a flat area where the acres of grass gave way to acres of concrete.

On the concrete were a few small buildings made of corrugated steel and, beyond those, waited a number of spacecraft. Jets and transports of all sizes sat patiently, quiet and still.

"It looks deserted," Keaton said.

"Thank God," Amberle replied. "Can the boards make it down this steep slope?"

"They can, but we'd have to cut hard to slow down. Coop can't do that while he's sitting down."

"Leave me here," Cooper said.

"Shut up," Keaton told him. "We're not leaving you."

"Then we should wait for Ty," Coop insisted.

"For how long?" Amberle asked.

"For as long as it takes!"

Keaton bit his lip and frowned, thinking. "Let's go down to the port and see if we can rig a jet. It will give Tyler time to find us, and we'll be ready when he gets there." He looked at his brother. "Good enough?"

Coop nodded. "Good enough."

Keaton collapsed his board and with Amberle's help they were able to guide Cooper's board over the crest of the hill. Holding tight to keep Coop from toppling over and to stop the board from shooting down the steep incline, Keaton and the girl carefully edged their way down the hill.

"I feel like a sitting duck out here," Amberle said through her teeth, one hand grasping the board and the other holding onto Coop by the sleeve of his jacket.

"I'm the sitting duck," Cooper muttered.

"Yeah," Keaton said, "and if anyone comes out of one of those building down there, I'm going to turn you into a sitting missile."

Cooper grinned at him. "I'm okay with that."

"I think," Amberle said, digging her feet into the hill with each step to keep from slipping down, "that if someone hasn't come out and shot us yet, we're good."

Keaton grunted in agreement, struggling not to slip while keeping Cooper upright. A half-hour later they were at the bottom - sweaty and tired. Amberle and Keaton sat on the grass to rest, sharing water from Keaton's canteen as they looked at the four structures a hundred yards away.

The buildings were set two by two so that the four of them made a square with a kind of courtyard in the very middle. Keaton took a drink and handed the canteen to Cooper, still sitting on his board.

"Do we go around?" Keaton asked, "or straight through?"

"Straight through," Cooper answered. "Check for a control room as we go through, and a kitchen or a cafeteria, look for supplies - anything we can use."

Keaton nodded in agreement and took the canteen from Coop and put it into the pack that Amberle was wearing. "Alright," he said, "let's get going, but let's go quietly. This place is already making me nervous."

Amberle stood up, adjusted the pack on her back, and helped him guide Cooper's board the last hundred yards to the waiting airfield and the buildings that guarded them.

Once there, they headed for the opening between the first two buildings. The steel structures had Plexiglas windows and the three looked in as they went past. The one on the right looked like a control room with a huge square hole in the floor with stairs leading down.

"Do you think there might be weapons down there?" Keaton asked softly. Cooper shook his head.

"It's not a military base. Probably just a bomb or storm shelter." A glance into the building on the other side showed the same.

"I hope one of the others is a cafeteria," Amberle said as they entered the courtyard. Keaton smiled at her and saw that she was leaning away from Coop, craning her neck to see something.

"What is it?" he asked.

"A craft," Amberle replied, "on the other side of these buildings. It's small, but big enough for us - and it's long range. We should..." Her sentence cut off as they heard a noise behind them and the two spun around, Cooper turning his head as far as it would go to see the commotion.

Hundreds of huge, red bodies were pouring out of the building behind them like ants from an anthill and lining up in ranks. Their humanoid forms looked insectile from the red, armor-like plates that covered their bodies. They moved quickly, methodically. All of them were armed.

"Good call on going right through," Keaton muttered.

"My bad," Cooper chirped.

The Golgoths came running out in an orderly fashion. Two platoons formed up facing the three young humans while another platoon split to flank them. Keaton tried to push the girl behind him but she stayed by his side.

"Can we make it to the craft?" he asked.

The girl shook her pink curls. "No."

"What can we do?"

Tears filled her brown and green eyes. "Nothing," she said. "There's too many of them and they're..." she trailed off as the first shots were fired, filling the air with heat and noise as they ricocheted around the courtyard.

The girl fell to her knees and Keaton threw himself in front of his brother just as he realized that the shots were not coming from the Golgoths, but from between them.

A split second later the swarm of massive red bodies were driven apart and flung to the sides by a creature that came crashing through their ranks. A creature with blonde hair and blazing blue eyes and death in his wake.

"Ty!" Cooper shouted as the young man came careening by on his board, followed by a wave of crazed, decaying bodies.

Go!" Tyler shouted as the wave of zombies collapsed on the broken formations of the aliens. "Go, go, go!"

Keaton and Amberle turned and ran for the tarmac, pushing Cooper's board between them as they followed Tyler towards the group of waiting spacecraft. In the crook of his right arm and supported with his left hand, he held the massive weapon they had taken from the Golgoth they had killed in the temple.

The sound behind them was horrible, screams and moaning along with sounds of munching and tearing, punctuated by occasional shots and more alien screams.

"That one!" Amberle shouted, pointing to a square craft with a pointed nose and lined with windows.

Tyler was there first, jumping from his board before it had even stopped and pulling the hatches on the doorway. He pushed the girl through first, and then he and Keaton got Cooper through the opening before they both climbed in and pulled the door shut. Cooper grabbed Ty, giving him a bone-crushing hug before letting him go.

"I see you managed to stay alive without me," Tyler said, grinning. Coop laughed and followed Tyler's gaze to the windows. They could glimpse the carnage in the courtyard between the buildings as the zombies and the Golgoths tore each other to pieces.

"Let's get out of here before any of them come after us," Amberle suggested.

"No kidding," Tyler said, turning to Keaton. "Get him as comfortable as you can," he instructed, glancing at Coop before fixing his blue eyes on the girl. "Let's see if we can get this thing moving."

Her hazel eyes glimmered. "Let's go!"

The two made their way past rows of cushioned seats and a galley and entered the cockpit. The cabin was small, with four swivel chairs bolted to the floor and every inch of the space, other than the expansive window in the front, was covered with dials, switches, readouts, screens, levers, and controls.

Tyler whistled. "I knew it wouldn't be simple, but this looks a lot more complicated than I had imagined," he said. "Where do we start?"

"Find anything that looks like a keyboard," the girl said, pulling off her huge jacket and throwing it on one of the chairs. "They are always wired to the mainframe computer on any craft." She fished her glove and chip out of an inner pocket and sat heavily down into another chair.

"Right here," Tyler said, pointing to the keypad that was set into the console at knee level.

Amberle spotted the button for main power and pressed it. Nothing happened. She glanced around the small cabin before her eyes fell on the first aid pack.

"There," she said, pointing. "Open the hatch above the kit."

Ty opened the hatch and saw a switch that was labeled "Emergency Power." He flipped it and looked up and grinned as the lights in the cabin came on. The girl was tapping furiously on the keypad as he retook his seat.

"Can you fly this thing from the computer?" he asked.

Amberle laughed. "I don't think so. But I can find out how *you* can fly it. Make sure Keaton and Coop are strapped in."

Tyler ducked back into the passenger cabin. Keaton not only had them both strapped in, but he had propped Cooper's leg and had him comfortable. His lagoon-colored eyes looked up as he rummaged through his pack for some food. He gave Tyler a broad smile and a thumbs up. Ty went back into the cockpit where Amberle was fastening a length of safety webbing over her lap. He sat down and did the same.

She looked at the screen and then motioned to a row of twelve metal switches, tipped with red plastic. "Flip all of those up," she instructed, "and then press the green button to the right."

Tyler did so and they both heard all of the engines begin to fire.

"Next," she said, "the three big levers to the left, pull them all down."

Tyler pulled the levers and the space craft gave a small jerk before it began rolling smoothly forward. He followed all of the girl's instructions as she tapped the keyboard and read from the screen. Half a minute later, the craft shot forward, throwing them back hard into their seats.

"Pull the blue lever!" she cried. As soon as he did, there was a furious jolt and the transport shot up, hurtling into the sky. Wisps of clouds flew past the windows. The craft streaked through the thin atmosphere and seconds later burst into the dazzling star-filled black of space.

A stunned silence filled the cabin as they stared.

"It's so beautiful," Tyler whispered.

Amberle nodded, watching with wide eyes. She felt as if she were floating. Seeing the pink coils of her hair drifting around her face she realized she *was* floating, held down only by her safety webbing.

"Hit that switch by your knee," she said.

Tyler flipped the switch and they both sank back into their seats. Together they peered out into the star-studded darkness until she finally turned her attention back to the keypad and monitor.

"I'm going to try and reach my contact," she told him.

Ty nodded, still staring at the glittering night that had engulfed them. After a few moments a voice came from a speaker on the control dash.

"This is MadDawg7," the voice said. "Please identify yourself."

"This is Amberle Nine Eight."

"You're kidding," the voice replied.

"No, I'm not. Do you need my security number?"

"No," the voice said, laughing quietly. "I just hadn't heard from you in a while. Are you okay?"

Amberle laughed quietly herself. "Yeah, I guess."

"Where are you?"

"I have no idea. But I am on a transport craft. We just launched from the Elba moon. I can probably find…"

"No need, I see you. Sit tight, I'm sending someone to bring you in."

The girl sat back, relaxing in the chair as she looked at Tyler, who was smiling at her. She shifted under his gaze.

"Where will you go?" she asked.

"Callisto," he said, looking back through the enormous windshield. "We have family there. How about you?"

Amberle shrugged. "Back to work, I guess." She smiled at him. "But I'm going to ask for a better office this time."

Tyler laughed and undid his safety webbing. He stood and dipped down to give the girl a quick kiss on the cheek, making her dusky skin blush a shade darker. "Thanks," he told her earnestly, and then ducked back into the main cabin.

When the door to the cockpit opened again a minute later, it was Keaton who came through.

"Wow," he said, looking out into the sparkling black as he took the seat next to Amberle.

She grinned, watching in silence with him. After a few minutes he cleared his throat and Amberle looked at him, though he kept his eyes forward.

"Tyler said you're going back to work."

"Yes."

It was quiet for another minute before he cleared his throat again. "What would life be like," he asked softly, still looking at the stars, "if you stayed with us?"

The girl raised her hand, hesitated, and then reached out and grasped Keaton's, entwining their fingers. Keaton looked at her, surprised.

"I think life would be great," she told him. "But first I have to finish this job. I don't know how long it will take."

Keaton grinned at her as the voice returned from the console.

"Amberle?"

"Yes?"

"I have a pilot en route. He should be there within the hour."

"Thank you," Amberle said and then nixed the com.

"Will you come find us when you are done?" Keaton asked.

"Will you make me one of those marshmallow things?"

Keaton exhaled a chuckle. "Absolutely. Will you find me some ice cream?"

Amberle laughed and looked at his hand in hers, the difference in size of their fingers, the shape of their nails, the contrast in the colors of their skin. She took a moment to marvel at the progress she had made then looked at him and have him a broad smile.

"You can count on it."

In the early years of what became known as First Contact, around 2650, the elves brought with them a race of dragons that had been slowly dying, their numbers dwindling to near extinction. After years of experimentation, the humans were able to save them by replacing most of their organs with machines, gradually transforming them into living starships.

By the year 3200, the Dragons become the most powerful force in the Intergalactic military. They have the ability to travel through both space and time at any speed, and have unmatched weaponry. Their children, hatched from eggs, are called Fledglings. The humans and elves, chosen by the Fledglings themselves to be their pilots, are called Jordans.

PART II

The Jordan

NINE

The girl stood in front of a great curved glass wall and looked out into the black of night. Jupiter, closer than she had ever seen it, dominated the right half of that all-encompassing star-studded darkness. It gave off a pinkish glow, making Amberle reach up and touch the springs of her hair in a distracted manner.

My pink must be faded to almost nothing by now, she thought absently. *Maybe I'll dye it purple, next. Or braid it.*

"Please sit down," the woman invited, waking the girl from her reverie. Amberle blinked her hazel eyes and turned around. The woman was of average height and had a rather average face. The only aspect of her that Amberle found remarkable was her eyes. Not just that they were a mixture of brown and gold, but that they perfectly matched the color of the woman's long, straight hair.

The woman known to the universe as Faith de Rossi was wearing white pants and a white blouse with gold buttons. She wore a heavy gold chain necklace and a few links of the same size and type of chain hung from her ears. There was a wide gold bracelet around one of her wrists and a large ring with three golden stones on the index finger of her right hand. The same hand held a white ceramic mug, its rim laser engraved with a concentric circle of repeating G7 logos. The other hand - the one with the bracelet - was extended towards a couch.

The floor of the living room was a great expanse of three-inch thick and diamond hard polished black granite, topped with plush white sofas that sat upon thick rugs of white fur.

Smooth white leather chairs flanked the sofas and stood in pairs about the room.

To the left of the living room was a dining room with a doorway that led to what the girl supposed was the kitchen. Against the wall that separated the kitchen from where they were now was a cocktail bar and to their right was a hallway that led to doors that were open to darkened rooms. Behind the living room was a raised foyer of the same black granite floor with a round elevator in the center. Around the elevator was a spiral staircase that led up on one side and down on the other.

Amberle left the curved wall of glass to settle her thin frame on the edge of one of the sofas.

"Sherpla?" she asked, glancing down at the rug.

The woman gave a small start, surprised. "Yes," she said, a smile drawing out across her face. "How did you know?"

Amberle shrugged, though it was only out of habit. She knew because she had read about Sherpla on the Galactic Web. "I just know that the fur does not stain or wear like it would from a.." she paused as she searched for the right words, "a real animal?"

Faith wanted very much to know what the girl's definition was of real, or how she knew about an animal that had been cloned before cloning was banned. Instead, she handed her the mug she had been holding. "Here, drink this. It will warm you up."

"Thank you," Amberle said, accepting the steaming mug and breathing in the sweet smell of sugared cocoa. "I like hot chocolate."

"I know," Faith whispered.

Amberle took an experimental sip and smiled. The chocolate was rich and thick and did indeed warm her as it went down. She felt a foreign, yet sudden, stab of responsibility and her eyes went to the woman.

"My friends?" Amberle queried.

"Are being cared for on Callisto," Faith assured her. "They will be taken care of for the rest of their days - which they seem to want to spend on the beaches of Europa," she finished with a smile.

Amberle's smile mirrored Faith's. "They like to surf," she told the de Rossi woman. "Keaton wants to teach me how..." her voice trailed off, as did her smile.

"You are free to join them any time you wish," Faith offered, but her smile faded as well, and she had gone as taut as the girl had been only a moment ago. She did not want her to go. Despite the fact that the girl was trembling with a fading case of cyber sickness and it made her feel guilty as hell, Faith wanted her back in front of a monitor and jacked into the Web. But she was not about to press her. Not yet.

"No," Amberle said, her hangdog expression awash with her own feelings of guilt. "I would rather keep working."

Faith smiled broadly, a deep breath expanding her lungs and filling her with elation. The girl's hazel eyes brightened over the lip of the mug and she lowered it quickly.

"Maybe," she suggested, "I could go visit them after I finish out our contract."

"I think that is a fine idea," Faith agreed as she accepted a flute of champagne from a young woman in a tailored brown jacket and skirt, her brown hair pulled back into a smooth tail. Amberle watched the young woman and the way her brown eyes moved fractionally behind her black-framed glasses. She knew the left lens had a micro monitor and felt a sharp pang of envy.

"Thank you Penny," Faith told her PA. "Is Mari preparing a room for our guest?"

"Yes," Penny affirmed. "And I ordered her some new clothes."

"Thank you," Faith said. "And Charity?"

"Is on her way. Her ship was in line to orbit the city. She should be in her shuttle by now, and arrive here any minute."

Faith nodded and forced herself into the white wing chair that faced the girl. She did not want to sit. She wanted to pace. She wanted desperately to question the girl about her missing sisters, but knew it was better to wait for Charity. Her brown and gold eyes followed Penny to the bar and watched her PA retrieve a glass from a cabinet and fill the ice bucket from the mini freeze in preparation for Charity. Her tawny gaze went back to the girl.

"That might be soon," she said, picking up their conversation where they left off, "if your calculations are correct."

"They are," Amberle assured her. "But I was thinking about the other job offer you had for me." Her guarded eyes went to Penny as the PA left the bar and headed for the kitchen. Ms. de Rossi had already cautioned her not to speak of her work to anyone or in front of anyone other than herself or sister, Charity. Faith's own eyes were round with surprise.

"You found the Fledgling?" she asked, leaning forward and keeping her voice low even though she had already disabled the security microphones on the center floor. The girl nodded and gave her a lopsided smile.

"She found *me*, actually."

Faith's tawny eyes grew wider.

"How?"

"The same way you did."

"The advertisement?"

The girl chuckled softly as she nodded, her spirals of coiled hair bobbing. Faith straightened and took a sip of champagne as she thought. She had been looking for her twin, the true Faith de Rossi, for a long time. Faith had been missing along with their sister, Hope, for almost a hundred years. It was Gwendolyn de Rossi, who now sat next to Amberle. She had been posing as her twin, Faith, and had been searching for her - as well as Hope - ever since.

She had started with high-priced private detectives, some of whom even referred to themselves as WebGods - claiming to be omniscient regarding everything on the Galactic Web. She had told them, of course, that she was looking for her sister, Hope, as well as her biodentical dyer. It mattered little. They found bupkis.

It was late one lonely night that she was perusing the Callisto Classifieds that she came upon the ad.

I can find anyone it announced with immodest simplicity.

Bemused and intrigued, and also a little drunk, Ms. de Rossi had sent a secure message to the link attached to the ad.

Find my sister. Name your price.

The response had come - not on the next business day but only a minute later - which was late on a Saturday night, making Faith wonder where the person actually was. What surprised her even more was the response itself.

Most galactic PI's asked the same questions.

Physical description?

Last known whereabouts?

Any idea where she might have gone?

The questions were so stupid that Gwen thought she would have better luck flying around in a space dinghy with an old-fashioned pair of binoculars and looking herself. Instead, the reply had been: *Send me things she wrote. Copies of IMs, emails, whatever. As many as you can.*

Even more intriguing was that the person did not want to be paid in money or credits but in compute hardware and software. Ms. de Rossi immediately set up a vid conference call on a secure net. The surprises just kept coming, along with a good deal of suspicious doubt when she saw that the investigator was a girl in her late teens with a snub of a nose and springy coils of hair that were decidedly pink.

The only thing that kept her from cutting the line was the look in the girl's eyes. They were a hazel brown-green, light compared to her dark skin, but intense and under a pair of feathery brows that seemed always on the verge of a scowl. Despite her young age, those eyes seemed to hold no trace of childhood. Gwen had only seen eyes like that on one other person - her biodentical twin. The look of carefree innocence had left her gaze, she guessed, about the time they turned eleven. It sobered her immediately.

"Why the mail and messages?" the supposed Faith de Rossi had asked the girl straightaway. "Other detectives have gone over them, looking for any clue about what they had been planning..." she trailed off as the girl shook her pink hair.

"I'm not looking for where they were going, I'm looking for where they are."

The statement was so simple that it made Gwen feel like a fool.

"And how will you do that?" she asked.

"The way people communicate, especially in the way they write, is always unique. Better than a poker tell but not quite a fingerprint, more like a signature. Either way, they all have specific markings. I'll feed whatever you give me into a program I wrote. After that, it's a lot of searching and cross-referencing."

"Mmmhmm." It sounded simple enough. Too simple. Gwen suspected she was being had. "I'm sending you a small variety of things I've written. I'd like you to tell me what you see."

The girl shrugged as the woman who had identified herself as Faith de Rossi tapped a key on her ghostpad, sending her three different items that Faith had written shortly before she had left in search of Hope. Other messages had popped up on the mainframe periodically after their disappearance, prewritten instructions for Gwen that she had shared only with

Charity and decided to still keep private.

Gold and brown eyes had watched the girl's face shift to the right and her body move back as she typed on whatever compute or pad she was using. The girl's hazel eyes moved as they read and then flicked back to the woman known as Faith.

"One of these is signed Faith de Rossi," the girl said.

"And?" the de Rossi woman challenged. "You said the way people write is like a signature, a tell. What can you tell me by looking at them?"

"I can tell you didn't write any of these," the girl said softly.

Gwen had felt the skin all over her body prickle with gooseflesh and her only response was stunned silence. She knew she should laugh and play it off as if she had been trying to trick her from the beginning as some sort of test. Instead, she moistened her lips with her tongue.

"Find my sister. Name your price," she said and for the first time it occurred to her how fortuitous it was to have stumbled upon this girl. The price most people would be naming would not only be astronomical, which Faith - the old and the new - could handle, but it would be the price of a bribe rather than a business deal.

The velvet night sky encased the villa of Faith de Rossi, spattered with stars and aglow with the light reflecting off the largest gas giant in the system.

The girl smiled as she lowered the mug and rested it on the thigh of her pants. The pants had once been maroon in color and certainly had seen better days. "Yeah," she said. "The advertisement."

The woman who was now Faith de Rossi blinked owlishly. "I would not have thought of a Fledgling Dragon to be reading the Callisto Classifieds."

The girl laughed, her small white teeth flashing in her dark face. "Is that a polite way of saying you think I'm full of shit?"

There was another laugh from the foyer making Faith look up and the girl turn in her seat to see they were no longer alone in the room. Far from it.

A woman with white blonde hair wearing a cocktail dress that looked like a slice of moonlight stood on the circular platform by the elevator. The fabric of her silver dress shimmered and her slim shoulders were draped with a white fur stole.

"Faith wouldn't say shit if she had a mouth full of it!" The beautiful socialite shrugged off the stole and it was quickly caught by one of the two assistants that flanked her. Charity de Rossi waved the assistant away. "Find the kitchen, you two," she instructed and then smiled broadly at Penny, already standing by to hand her a glass of her current favorite cocktail before the PA escorted the other personal assistants from the room.

Charity glanced over her other shoulder to see Geary, Faith's head of security, standing behind her own bodyguard. "You can go upstairs," she informed them before turning back to the living room, her smile returning. Faith had risen from her chair, her lips pressed into a tight line that was turned up at the corners. The girl was looking at her as if she were a space-corgi.

"Sister!" Charity called out, flowing into the room to embrace Faith.

"Charity, you look amazing!" Faith returned as they exchanged cheek kisses. Once the pleasantries were done, Charity turned to the girl, her green eyes blazing with excitement.

"And you must be Amberle!" she gushed.

Amberle nodded, wary, but the woman did not reach out to embrace her or even shake her hand. Faith had already warned her. "And you are Charity de Rossi," she stated, matter of fact.

Charity's head tipped back, exposing a neck that was

smooth and white as she laughed. "I was the last time I looked in a mirror!" she exclaimed as she let her head drop back down, her green eyes glittering. Still, she looked at Faith with an edge of nervousness.

"It's fine," Faith assured her, indicating that the microphones had been temporarily decommissioned for the privacy of her present company.

Still, Charity glanced about. The center of Faith's villa was huge, the living room alone was a stretch of polished darkness that showcased another stretch of darkness - outer space broken by the great glob of Jupiter looming high in the upper right side of the glass wall. She didn't like it. She never had. It made her feel too exposed.

"Maybe we could.." she started as she quickly considered options she knew to be limited. Obviously not a bedroom and she was discomfited even more by the pool area than she was the living room. "Speak in your office?" Charity suggested.

She certainly did not prefer offices, office meetings, or anything of the sort - but at least they would be behind closed doors. That offered her some comfort. Faith shrugged.

"Certainly. Are you hungry?" Charity frowned and flapped a hand at the suggestion. Faith looked at Amberle and the girl gave her a crooked smile.

"Not especially, but I could eat."

Faith brought her wrist close to her lips and spoke into the gold cuff that was fastened there. "Penny," she instructed, "please have cook prepare a..a..hamburger. And some julienned potatoes and bring them to my office. A carbonated cola as well."

There was an affirmative answer from the gold cuff and the de Rossi woman moved her tawny eyes back to Amberle. "Let's go into my office," she said, holding out a hand to show the way as the girl nodded and rose to follow the two sisters. They led her, their expensive heels clacking on the black marble, across the living space and up a few steps and slightly to the right through an open door made of dark and heavy wood.

Once they were through, Faith closed the door behind them. Charity sighed in relief as she crossed the room and kicked off her shoes before sinking down into a chair covered in distressed leather. Amberle sighed as well, in hunger.

The room was an immaculate span of polished metal and burnished wood, deep chairs and gleaming compute surfaces but what caught her attention was the compute monitor. The trace of a ghost pad she could see on the desktop. There was a barely detectable hum coming from the unseen hard drives, making her blood tingle, calling to her. She felt like a derma junkie, spying a derma pin still glistening with promise. She wet her lips with her tongue.

"Please," Faith intoned, holding a hand out towards the huge leather chair next to Charity, inviting her to sit. Amberle lowered herself down, trying not to look at the chair behind the desk. Faith sat on the sofa and turned to face the girl, her expression somber.

"First, I would like to say how sorry I am about what happened on that moon. I had no idea that those tests were going to be run nor what was happening on the other side. At the time, it seemed like a good place to hide that had a lot of access for equipment that you needed."

The girl gave her a bit of a smile. "Thanks, but don't worry about it. Everything turned out okay and I met some really good people."

She had grown close to the boys, Keaton in particular, and it was the first time she could remember making friends. It was a rare occurrence for her.

Amberle felt a pang of remorse for leaving them on Callisto but she knew that Ms. de Rossi had more work for her. Work that Amberle was interested in. What was she supposed to do if she stayed with them? The only surfing she did was on the

Web. She already had another job lined up, and had promised Keaton she would go visit just as soon as she was done.

She liked Keaton. And Cooper. She had never met anyone so optimistic. Even Tyler, who had finally been warming up to her.

The thought of them, of the last time she had seen them, her gave her a jolt. Mostly it was the image of Cooper, waving at her from a chair. His leg had been propped up in front of him, held tight in an air cast, but his smile had been as wide and bright as ever.

"There's something else," Amberle said abruptly. "Something important I need to tell you."

The sisters glanced at each other worriedly, slowly lowering their drinks as they looked back at the girl.

"I told you about the...workers," she said, swallowing. She looked at Charity, who gave her a nod, silently telling her she was aware of what had happened. Faith had informed her sister about the computer programmers that had been given an experimental drug that had turned them into flesh-eating zombies. "And about the children that had also been given something, something that was keeping them children..." This time both women nodded solemnly. Faith had assured the girl that GwenSeven had nothing to do with it. Why would they? They already had anti-aging drugs that worked perfectly. Amberle took a deep breath. "What I haven't told you, yet, is that there were Golgoths on that moon."

Faith jerked, almost spilling her champagne, but Charity's green eyes narrowed in disbelief.

"That can't be," she said.

"It is," Amberle affirmed.

"They are not allowed to be even within a light year of the seven systems," Charity argued. "Certainly not *here*. In the Jovian system!"

"Are you sure it was a Golgoth you saw?" Faith asked softly, though she was beyond doubting the girl at this point. She knew what a Sherpla was for Pete's sake.

Amberle nodded. "And not just one. I'm guessing it was an entire company. And that's only what I saw. I don't know if there were more, somewhere else."

A silence followed that was gently broken as the door was pushed open by the ample backside of Mari, Faith's housekeeper. The rest of her body followed, carrying a tray with food and drink for the girl. She thumbed a switch on the side of the tray and it obediently hovered where it was placed. She was followed by Bowe, an assistant to the cook, who had brought in a bottle of champagne and a bottle of Varti.

"Why, thank you!" the sisters chimed in unison as he topped off their glasses. He left both bottles on a nearby bar cart, carefully placing the champagne in a magnetic chilling tube.

Mari put down utensils and condiments in front of the girl on the floating tray. "I hope you find everything to your liking, Cook did the best with what she had on short notice."

"I'm sure it will be fine," Amberle said with a smile. "I found I could eat just about anything."

And she had certainly done so on the zombie-ridden moon she had so recently left, including ground roots, leaves, and rodents roasted on sticks in forests. Still, Mari watched her nervously until the girl picked up the burger and took a large bite.

"Delicious," the girl said, smiling around her mouth full of food. A smile of satisfaction crossed the housekeeper's face and she departed, followed by Bowe who closed the door behind him.

The silence swam back into the room.

"Who?" Charity finally asked her sister. "Do you think it could.."

But Faith cut her off with a subtle slash of her hand and nearly imperceptible shake of her head, silently shelving the discussion for another time. She looked instead at Amberle.

"Is it really all right?" she asked, indicating the hamburger.

The girl nodded vigorously. "I don't really pay much attention to food," she said, "unless it's something sweet."

Charity, taking Faith's cue, took a deep breath, regaining her composure. "Your eyes keep going to the desk," she murmured with a smile. "Do you see something sweet over there?"

The girl's dusky face took on a look that was both knowing and smiling at once. "I can tell you have some really high-tech equipment there. I'd be lying if I said my hands weren't itching to go exploring."

"Feel free," Charity encouraged, her blonde brows high as she gestured towards the compute equipment with the drink in her hand. Amberle looked at Faith, hopeful.

"Be my guest," Faith told her, also extending a hand in the direction of the desktop computer.

The girl dropped what was left of the meat sandwich, which was most if it, back onto the plate and pushed the hover tray away from her body. She snagged the napkin as she stood up and wiped the skin of her dark hands meticulously as she made her way to the chair behind the desk. She sat down carefully, almost reverently, and turned on the computer. Her fingers hovered above the ghostpad. They twitched with anticipation as she looked up and smiled at her employers.

Her hazel eyes reflected the glow from the compute screen, turning them a luminous green.

"What do you want to know?" she asked.

"Where is Faith?" they both said synchronously. "And Hope," they added, also in unison.

"I'm quite certain I've found Hope," she assured them as she pulled a small flap of black latex from a pocket in her maroon pants and slipped it over the thumb and index finger of her right hand.

The sisters watched with bated breath as she expertly connected her mini glove to the compute and got to work. The fingers of her left hand danced over the keypad while her other hand moved entire sections of the screen to display in the air to her right. Only moments later, the same hand pulled up and back, the fingers splayed wide.

The tension was palpable as the sisters looked on in anxious anticipation.

From the desk sprang a globe of yellow light, swathed with green and gold and coddled in wisps of white.

Amberle sat back, an expression of triumph lighting her young face, dark skin framed by her faded pink coils of hair.

Charity froze, her expression hard and cold.

Faith sighed and sat back in her chair, feeling disappointed and ashamed.

It's my fault, she thought. *The girl is obviously sick. Yet I pushed her.* She took a sip from her glass and closed her eyes.

Amberle's expression fell, seeing the obvious disappointment on their faces. "It's Venus," she said.

Charity took a drink from her own glass and Faith simply blinked at the girl, feeling as if she had sustained a physical blow.

"What?" Amberle asked. "You wanted to know where they are. I can't say for sure regarding...the other Faith - not yet anyway since there are no electronic transmissions there. But this is where Hope is." The girl stood up and walked around the desk, examining the globe. "I can't pinpoint her exact location, no yet anyway, but I could with the right equipment."

Faith looked at the floor, feeling guilt-ridden and sick and disheartened. She had no words.

Charity did.

"*Venus,*" she told the girl, her tone as hard as her features, "is the one planet in the Solar System that is not inhabited. It has *never* been inhabited."

"It's where she is," Amberle said softly.

"Venus?" Charity demanded, her voice rising. "Are you serious?"

The young woman bit her lip, awash with an unexplainable anxiety that bordered on terror but was saved from answering by a low chuckle that turned everyone's head.

"It's not Venus," a voice said from the doorway.

A young man with skin the color of caramel stood there, lean yet heavily muscled under a simple yet snug cotton shirt and trousers. His hazel eyes were dark, topped with thick black brows and a head of jet-black hair.

Jasyn stared at the globe of light, a smirk curving up one side of his full lips. "It's a mirror of Venus."

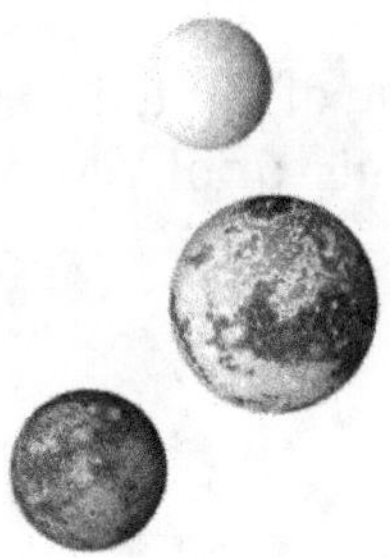

 ONE ZERO

The young man leaned casually against the doorframe, his crossed arms showing round biceps and shoulders. He had a straight, sharp jawline with a slightly pointed chin that had the barest hint of a dimple. His eyes were of the darkest hazel and unnervingly intense.

Amberle's mouth had dropped open at the sight of him. His build and his face were so breathtaking that it was frightening. She shrank back, using the compute monitor as cover.

Faith stood frozen, as if a dangerous animal had caught their scent and had paused at the entrance to their den.

Only Charity smiled. "Jasyn, please come in." The raven-haired man straightened, uncrossed his arms and took a few steps into the room, still staring at the hologram of Venus that floated in brilliant hues of orange and red and gold above the desk. "Ahem," Charity said, delicately clearing her throat to get his attention. "The door, please," she murmured when he looked at her.

The young man, Jasyn, momentarily mesmerized by the globe of light, shook off the feeling. He put a strong hand on the heavy door, which had eased open just enough to let him slip through, and silently pushed it closed.

His eyes went to the young woman behind the desk and she shrank back a little more. "Can you pull up an orrery?" he asked her. "Not the entire system," he added. "Just from the sun to the Earth."

Amberle perked back up instantly once she could be of use.

She leaned forward and her fingers danced across the plane of the desk.

Suddenly, the hologram of Venus was thrust to the side so quickly that both Faith and Charity jerked back in surprise. The entire far side of the office, and the office was quite large, was lit up by a swirling globe of golden light so great that they could not see the edges. Between the hologram of the sun and the one of Venus floated another three-dimensional sphere. Mercury, tiny compared to the sun, floated like a gray marble. Venus came next and then Earth, a beautiful globe of blue and green surrounded by a caul of white clouds.

Jasyn stepped between the two planets and grinned triumphantly at the two sisters, much in the same manner Amberle had done only moments ago. The young woman watched, wide-eyed, to see if the reception would be different this time.

Faith's countenance was stoic and tight lipped while Charity's held the suggestion of amusement.

"I'm not sure what I am supposed to be seeing," she drawled. "Why don't you enlighten us, darling?" She took a sip of her drink and smiled encouragingly.

Jasyn looked surprised. "Are you serious?" He looked at Faith but her expression had not changed. "Look at how close these are!" he told them. All eyes went to the holographic spheres floating in the office and the sisters blinked at them. Jasyn's dark brows went up as no one offered any revelation. "Look at the color, and at the sizes of Earth and Venus!" All eyes now moved across the glowing orrery but again neither sister did anything but blink and wait for further clues.

"The dimensions are to scale," Amberle offered.

"Exactly!" Jasyn exclaimed, making her jump slightly. But when she had nothing else to add the young man stuck out his bottom lip and blew a burst of air over his face. Then he snapped his fingers, struck by an idea. "Keep this system here," he told her, "and project on it the same model and scale of Venus as it was a hundred and fifty years ago."

Amberle leaned forward once more and again her fingers thrummed over the top of the desk. There was a pulse of light and she sat back, her eyes darting over the spheres of light and color. Initially, she thought nothing had changed.

Jasyn's smile broadened once again and he waited for them to see. A moment later it hit them all at once.

Both sisters were on their feet, Faith letting out a strangled cry as her free hand went to her mouth. Charity leaned back in an effort to take it all in, her green eyes staring and her mouth open. Amberle's fingers twitched.

"Holy shit," she whispered.

Faith moved precariously around the globe in front of her, as if afraid to disturb it. The gold-colored sphere was turning gently, rotating on an unseen axis. Inside the holographic image of Venus was a duplicate of the planet, about half the size and slowly rotating in the opposite direction.

"This can't be real," Faith murmured.

"What is real?" Jasyn asked, his voice flat.

Faith gave him a cold glare before turning her eyes back to the image in front of her. "I mean, is it just a mirage?"

"Well," Jasyn said, "a mirage is an optical illusion. This is a physical one."

"To what purpose?" Charity asked, swirling her cocktail as she regained her composure. "And how did you know?"

"I've become wary of mirrors," Jasyn told her, his voice as cold and hard as ice.

Charity shrugged but Faith looked away from him in dismay and back at the planets. "It's spinning too fast," she mused aloud and glanced at the image of Earth before staring once again at Venus. "It's going about the same speed the Earth is."

Amberle looked at the computer in front of her and then

stood up and sidled around the desk. She went around Venus and stood next to Faith, looking inside. Finding what she sought, she pushed her gloved finger through the projection of the outer gases, and touched the globe inside.

"I traced the genetic code you gave me and got a hit." Her hand moved under the projection of noxious clouds. "Here." The outer orb was slightly larger than her own head, and the place where she touched was a continent just above the southern hemisphere. "Traces of Hope are here."

Tears filled Faith's brown and gold eyes and her hand came up to cover her mouth.

"Do you mean,'" she whispered between her fingers, "her... remains?"

Jasyn stepped up behind her and grasped her shoulders gently but firmly.

"Oh no!" Amberle said. "There is someone alive there with the genetic code you gave me. It's just that the transmission is off – fuzzy."

Faith's body sagged with relief, supported by Jasyn's strong hands.

Charity stood and retrieved the bottle of Varti. "So you are now telling us that there are life forms on Venus? Where nothing has lived, ever?" She shook her white-blonde hair in disbelief as she refilled her glass and then sat on the arm of one of the large leather chairs.

Jasyn released Faith and moved towards the desk. Amberle edged away from him and shrugged at Charity.

"There is plenty of life there," she told her.

Faith frowned. "That planet is notorious for being uninhabitable. It is too hot, has too much pressure, and the atmosphere is mostly carbon dioxide." She looked at Charity but was met with blonde brows raised high over green eyes.

"You're not asking me, are you?"

Faith's frown deepened in exasperation and she looked at Jasyn for help. His handsome face was split with a grin that showed perfectly made teeth.

"Humans, and elves, have been terraforming less hospitable worlds for centuries," he reminded her, leaning back against the desk.

"And that is what you think happened?" she asked. "That it was terraformed? That someone… that they.." her voice softened and trailed off as she comprehended the possibilities, and the probability.

The room became silent.

Charity's green eyes flicked back and forth between Faith and Jasyn. "Are you telling me they succeeded?" she asked, incredulous. "Those crazy Zenarchist monks terraformed Venus and the elves simply covered their tracks?"

Jasyn shrugged, the muscles of his shoulders bunching under the snug shirt. "It *was* what they were trying to do," he told her.

Charity tipped back her white blonde head and laughed. And laughed. Amberle thought she sounded a little bit crazy. Her brown and green eyes sought out Faith who was staring raptly at the image of Venus.

"I don't understand," the young programmer said.

Faith turned to her. "How much history do you know?" she asked.

Amberle blew a burst of air through pursed lips and made her way back to her cooling hamburger. "Mostly just what I've read online. I wasn't very good in school. I dropped out early and took Galactic Web classes to graduate."

In truth, Amberle had hated school. Not the learning, though it was taught at an incredibly boring speed. It was the other kids. Middle school had been the worst. Amberle was teased by everyone about practically everything, and none of it she could understand.

They made fun of her dark skin, though every kid in her neighborhood had skin in varying shades of black and tan. She was teased for being poor, though most had less than her. She was ridiculed for being smart by a sea of people she saw as idiots, a conundrum she could not get her head around.

When Amberle was only twelve she had begged her parents to drop out and finish her schooling on the Web but they refused. It wasn't until years later, when they saw she could make money from all her time spent jacked into a computer, that they finally relented. Extra income, even a little, helped ease the pressure on their small family.

She took a bite of the burger and waited for Faith to explain.

"You know about our company?" she asked.

Amberle looked at her as if she were crazy. "GwenSeven?" she asked after she finished chewing her food. "Of course. Everybody does. You guys make everything, including people." Her eyes flicked to Jasyn and back to Faith.

Charity chuckled and took a sip from her drink, but a slight line formed between Faith's brows. She had not told the girl that Jasyn was a construct. But it seemed the girl knew. She would ask her later.

For now, the elder de Rossi woman gathered her thoughts and nodded before taking a sip of champagne. "Yes. Well, some years before the rebellion, we were approached by the Elves of Titan. They wanted to leave known civilization and start over on a terraformed planet or moon, away from technology and war."

"Wait," Amberle said, lowering her sandwich. "The same elves that blew up in the explosion that wiped out life on Earth?"

"Well," Faith replied, "no one is quite sure what happened. But, for the lack of better knowledge, it is certainly a possibility."

"It was never proven that the explosion affected Earth,"

Jasyn added from where he leaned against the desk. "Or if it was a coincidental but unrelated incident."

"Either way," Faith continued, "Venus was where the elves were headed, though no one knew that except the elves...and very few others."

Amberle's hazel eyes went between the two women and the gorgeous construct. "Present company being the very few others?" she asked.

Faith nodded. "The expedition of elves disappeared at the time of the explosion, leading everyone to believe they had been evaporated by the blast."

"Our sisters as well," Charity added, again swirling her drink, making the ice clink in the glass.

"But I never thought they were dead," Faith said softly. "I refused to think it."

The girl's eyes drifted back to the two images of Venus, one inside the other. "That's what he meant," she whispered. "It makes sense, now."

"Who?" Faith asked. "What makes sense?"

"Hellas," Amberle said softly. "A man I met on the Elba moon, where I was starting my work for you. He told me that Hope was within."

A small whimpering sound came from Faith and she cleared her throat to cover it. "And you said you could pinpoint her once you got closer?"

"Yes," the girl agreed. "I'll need a UPG, a Universal Positioning Guide. Then I could program.." she left her sentence unfinished as Faith turned and circled behind the huge desk. She opened a drawer and pulled out a box small enough to fit in the palm of her hand. She walked back around the desk and handed it to the girl.

"Use this when you get closer. It might help."

Amberle switched on the box to see a holographic grid. It

was filled with numbers - galactic coordinates. The planets were clearly marked. Two blips of red, one faint and one slightly darker hovered in the image. The faded one hovered close to Earth. The brighter one inside of Venus.

"You had this the whole time?" the girl asked, incredulous. "Why didn't you just use it?"

Faith shrugged as she went to the bar cart and refilled her champagne glass. "For one, I thought it was broken."

"I'm not surprised. This thing has to be a hundred years old!"

Faith shrugged again. "Plus, there should not be more than one dot." She walked back to the girl and leaned forward, touching the grid image and then moving it across the galaxy. Then, placing a thumb and forefinger over the hologram, spread them apart, zooming in. Amberle could now see Mars as well as Jupiter. In the image, close to Jupiter, were two bright blips - one gold and one green.

Amberle's eyes went up and flicked between the sisters, noticing the similarity of their rings for the first time. And the differences, in the colors of the stones. "You and Charity," she said, glancing back down at the lights in the holo.

Faith nodded. "Hope's beacon had become two beacons, one barely there and both of them where no person was to be found. It was better to think that the tracking device, or the homing mechanism, or the transmission itself had been corrupted somehow - rather than think that something terrible had happened to her."

"And Faith?" Amberle ventured. "Did she not have a similar tracking device?"

Faith held up her hand, showcasing the set of rings there.

"Ah!" The young woman sat down and resumed eating her hamburger, thinking. After a moment, she swallowed. "So, now that we know where at least one of them is, what are you going to do?"

"Go after her," Faith and Charity said in unison.

"How?" Amberle asked. "I know enough to know that nothing, other than a probe, can get through the atmosphere on Venus."

Faith looked at her sister in despair, then at Jasyn. His dark eyes softened. "I think a Dragon could go through it without any trouble whatsoever."

The corners of Faith's lips turned up, but her expression was forlorn. "I do not consider many things beyond my reach these days," she replied, "but a Dragon could be tricky." Her eyes took on a faraway look, turning back to the fiery orb as she murmured quietly to herself. "Actually, if I took it to a certain party in the IGC I'm sure they would...but do we want keep this to ourselves, and how long would the IGC take.. could a Dragon..."

"We definitely want to keep this to ourselves," Charity answered. "And not just because we promised the elves secrecy."

"Could a Fledgling do it?" Amberle asked.

Jasyn shrugged. "If a Dragon could, I think a Fledgling could manage just as well."

Charity's green eyes flicked up to meet Faith's tawny gaze.

"Do you think she would?" Faith asked.

"I cannot say," Charity replied. "I am not sure if she is ready to leave the IGC. But I definitely think she is questioning, wavering."

"Are you talking about Noel?" Jasyn demanded, emotion in his voice for the first time since entering the room. "The one that shot me?"

Both sisters ignored him.

"She's not sure what to think or whom to trust," Charity finished.

Jasyn grunted in agreement and was ignored again.

"We can ask her, though I do not think she is ready," Faith confessed.

"What then?" Charity asked. "Hatch the eggs and fly them ourselves?"

Faith smiled. "An intriguing idea."

"I was joking."

"I know." Faith turned and let her eyes rest on the young woman, who was less than delicately sticking fried potatoes into her mouth. "I'm wondering if there is another Fledgling that might help us."

Amberle nodded as she licked salt from the tips of her fingers. It was what she had been considering as well. "I think Verdana would do anything for us if we find Jade."

Jasyn dipped his chin and looked from Faith to the girl and then back again. "You're talking about the Fledgling that disappeared and the dead Jordan?"

Faith gave him a nod and took a sip from her glass. "Amberle has found the Fledgling."

Jasyn and Charity regarded the young woman with no small amount of surprise.

"She, Verdana I mean, wants Jade back," the girl informed them.

"His body?" Charity asked.

Amberle gave her a nod and swallowed. "Yes. But what she wants even more, and would probably be easier for us to get, is Jade alive."

Charity planted an elbow on her knee and her glass moved back and forth in front of her face like a charmed snake as she smirked at the girl. "And just where are you going to find a living Jordan who has been dead for half a year?"

"Not where," Jasyn corrected. "When."

Amberle grinned. "Exactly."

"Wait, wait, wait, wait," Charity said, leaning forward. Her green eyes narrowed as she thought. "Are you talking about... going back in time to get the Jordan?"

Jasyn nodded. Charity's face scrunched in puzzlement.

"That's ridiculous," she said. "If you can use the Fledgling to go back in time, why don't you just go back and talk Hope out of leaving? And Faith?"

"For one thing," Faith said, "no one was ever able to talk Hope out of anything. Faith wasn't very different in that aspect."

Charity harrumphed. "I'll give you that," she agreed.

"Plus," Jasyn added, "time can be tricky. And messing with it can be dangerous. Otherwise, the IGC would already be manipulating it to their own ends."

Amberle narrowed her eyes at him. "Dangerous how?" she asked. She wasn't afraid, just curious.

"If we go back into our past, we run the risk of changing our future, which would alter our current reality."

Amberle laughed at her own feeling of confusion and then, glancing at Charity, laughed harder at the woman's expression of absolute perplexity. On her perfect face, the look was comical.

"I think he means," Faith said, "if it was safe to do, the IGC would be doing it. They could use a Dragon to go back and change anything. They could crush the rebellion before it even starts."

"I see," Charity said, sipping her drink as she thought it over.

Jasyn smiled. "I don't think it would be safe for any of us three to go. We could run into our former selves, or even someone who has known us. God only knows what it would do to our future, or the future in general. Though I'm no expert in physics, I think there is a good chance we could end up in a time loop, a temporal paradox, or possibly even rip the fabric of time."

Charity sighed. "You lost me again on that one," she said. "But I have a hard time believing it is as terrifying as you make it sound."

"If you could go back a hundred years," Faith proposed, her voice soft, "what would you do?"

"I would try to warn my former self," Charity answered immediately.

"Which would change the past and affect everything that happened after that moment," Faith affirmed. "Even the smallest act could ripple out to continuously disturb the entire universe. Good or bad, we couldn't know."

"Which," Jasyn added, "makes Amberle perfect for this. If she goes back far enough, even her parents would not have been born yet. Her altering anything would likely have little or no repercussions to her future."

"What about the Jordan?" Amberle ventured. "What will happen to him? To his own future?"

Faith pressed her lips together and shook her head slowly, almost in apology.

Charity identified the look and understood that Faith did not care much about the life of the Jordan, past or future, as much as she cared about getting their sisters back. Charity knew, because she felt the same way.

"He might be able to prevent his early, untimely death," she offered the girl.

Amberle looked at each of them in turn. What they were asking went a lot farther than programming or hacking. This was involvement on another level, more than just a job. She took a moment to measure herself and see if she was up to such thing. She blew a gust of air through puffed cheeks.

"And," Faith added as if sensing her thoughts, "our original contract still stands. Any hardware, software, money, credits...

you name it."

The young woman nodded, a small smile gracing her lips at the reminder. She thought of the glasses she had seen Faith's PA wearing and her smile widened.

Or I could skip the glasses and go straight to orbital implants, she thought. The idea made her entire body tingle.

"I'll reach out to Verdana," she said.

Faith gave her a warm smile. "Thank you. Though I think it could wait until morning. How about a shower and some fresh clothes?" She knew the girl had been through hell, and there was no knowing the last time she had slept, yet the disappointment on not getting back behind the compute screen was clear on her face. "And maybe some dessert," she added.

Amberle brightened instantly. "I think that sounds great."

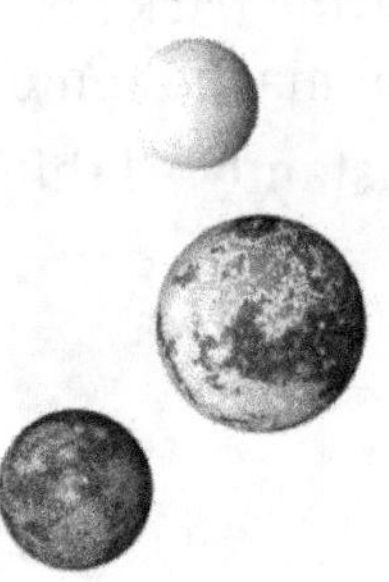

# ONE ONE

Verdana flew low over the watery planet-moon. The waters were dark and choppy, the wind whipping furiously.

The Fledgling Dragon hardly noticed. She was nineteen meters in length and matte silver. As light and shadows shifted on her surface the color changed and shimmered to a glowing and glistening green, as if her silver skin had been dusted with crushed emeralds when caught by the rays of the magnified sun. The effect had given the Green Fledgling the nickname of the Emerald Fledgling, but Jade had named her Verdana.

Jade, the green-eyed elf she had chosen as her Jordan.

Jade, ever-cheerful, compassionate, and mischievous.

Her Jordan, who was now dead.

Verdana was sick with emotions she did not know Dragons could endure, but she was very young herself. The foremost and most dominant feeling that flooded her was grief. The Otherlings, the race of beings created by the humans and elves that they called *Chimera*, had captured her Jordan, her darling Jade, and now he was gone.

The Fledgling had fled the universe in terror, traveling on the fringes of the parallels in hopes of finding his soul. She had not returned to her mother Dragon, nor to her brothers, for the other emotion she was racked with was shame. Shame that she had not protected her Jordan.

There was a communication motherboard installed by the humankind and she had it running constantly, searching for any trace of him or someone who knew where he could be found.

Most of her time was spent trying to decipher the words. The Fledglings could understand speech, but mostly communicated with their Jordans with images and feelings.

Verdana undertook the arduous process of teaching herself to listen and read.

Months later, she was monitoring every communications broadcast in the civilized galaxies. More months went by and she neither saw nor heard anything of Jade.

Then one day, she came upon a public communique in the Jupiter system from a human who said they could find anyone.

Find Jade, she had sent. A request had been made for copies of the Green Jordan's past communications, which Verdana had plenty of, along with plenty of suspicion.

Who are you? Verdana had asked.

The human had given her name and, after prodding by the Fledgling, her citizen identification number. Verdana thought of it as a serial number, and ran it through her network. She saw everything there was about her in a blink, including her age. It was a shock. Verdana had known Jade was young, but even he had been over a hundred years older than this, this fledgling human.

Girl, she had corrected mentally. *Fledgling females are called girls, by both humans and elves.*

Are you.. the girl had asked, a brief pause as she typed...*the Green Fledgling?*

Verdana was shocked again that the fledgling human had ascertained as much, and so quickly. Hope flickered in the starfire that served as her heart.

Yes, she answered immediately. *Find Jade.*

I will need to research him a bit, and you too. Verdana saw the words in her inner coms as the girl typed them onto whatever device she was using. *I am leaving on another assignment tomorrow. I will contact you as soon as I am done.*

Verdana felt herself flooded with desperation. Here was her first step forward, and it was already slipping away.

How will you find me?

The words popped up on her c-board in a steady stream and Verdana processed them as quickly as they appeared.

My compute is already tracking you, from this message relay. I take the micro-c with me wherever I go. Don't worry, this important to me, too.

Despite her young age, something about the human girl tugged at the Fledgling's heart, making that hope inside her flare and ache.

Find Jade. I will do whatever I can for you.

The girl had cut the communiqué but Verdana had felt a measure of assent and agreement. Then she had waited with no human sense of time, since there was no day and no night in space to delineate days or weeks, but to the lonely Fledgling it felt like an eternity.

Verdana immersed herself back into the universe and went straight to the Jupiter system where she hid - in the planet itself. She flew slowly, almost lazily, two miles down into the gases of the giant planet - where no human or elfin made ship could go.

She spent days gliding through the noxious clouds, then weeks. More time passed, but she had no way to measure it.

Finally, a direct message lit up her communication board.

It was the girl.

And she already had a plan. It seemed exceedingly simple, except for one thing. The girl told her that she, Verdana, would need to be grown.

Why? Verdana asked, already fearful at the prospect.

Because, the girl had answered, *I will need to go with you to find Jade. Then we will need room for him.*

It made perfect sense, but it still made her nervous. She

wished the girl could just tell her where to find Jade, but even the young Fledgling knew that when she found him, communicating with him could prove difficult.

I can arrange it, the girl sent. *And arrange for an Engineer.*

Engineer.

Verdana knew the word. It was term used for the metallurgists that worked on Dragons, what she thought of as a doctor for Dragons.

Who? Verdana had demanded, fear tickling her. The girl had given the man's name and serial number, which Verdana checked immediately. She was assuaged that he truly was an Engineer, and one with whom she was not familiar. She did not want someone she knew, someone that had known her.

Known Jade.

Jade, so caring, so small and fragile.

Stealing herself against her fears, she replied, *Tell me where.*

If there were any way to get him back, she would do it.

She had found the Distant Shore quite easily, as anyone with the exact coordinates could. But there were few who had those numbers. Very few.

Now she flew over the choppy waters of the moon, approaching an island. A giant obsidian building with the towers stretching to the sky zoomed by on her port side. She circled the island and could both see and sense the opening she had been directed to by the girl. The Fledgling Dragon, her silver skin shimmering with an emerald glow, banked and dove.

She went straight for the opening, a black maw that had been bored from the black stone of the island, and then braked. Water spewed up from either side as she slowed, the spray of the sea going in all directions before it dissipated into mist. The last time she had been in an enclosed space it had not ended well. It had ended in disaster. The opening, dark and ominous, grew and grew even as she slowed her approach.

Then, at the final second, she balked entirely.

The last time she had been invited into a walled chamber she had been trapped. And her Jordan had died.

But that's why I am here, she thought as she flew skyward, once again racked with indecision.

A single word sprang up on her communications board.

Verdana? the girl asked.

For the first time, it occurred to the Fledging Dragon that she had never heard the voice of the fledgling human. So far, all communication with her had been through electronic keyboard transmissions. Suddenly, she knew how lonely she had become. Not just for Jade, but for any kind of connection.

The last of her indecision drew tight, like a thread being pulled in opposite directions, as she realized that it came down to trust.

Trust the girl, a voice said softly in her mind. It surprised the Fledgling and Verdana tried to decipher the voice and where it had come from. It might have come from her Mother Dragon - though the feeling she got was male, not female. One of her brothers, perhaps? It might have somehow come from Jade. The mere possibility was enough. The thread inside her snapped.

The Fledgling altered her course, banking sharply enough to tear the atmosphere which mended itself with mirage-like shimmer in her wake. She headed back toward the black edifice on the island and circled around to the cavern cut into the rock foundation on its rear side. Thinking only of her lost Jordan, she braked slightly and plunged into the darkness.

The darkness was complete, but it meant nothing to her. The tunnel was short and she could see clearly the flat rock of the landing platform. Air and water followed, sucked in with her speed and she slowed her approach, pushing out her legs and landing gently on the smooth and even floor of the cavern that had been fashioned into a hangar.

She took in everything at once as the torrent of wind and mist dissipated around her. There were desks and chairs along a curved wall, another aircraft not much bigger than the Fledgling, and smooth metal doors that led to the upper parts, undoubtedly to the building were the humans stayed.

There were people there, but only a few, which put her more at ease. One, a small dark-skinned human with pink hair that bobbed about her head, stepped forward and Verdana knew her immediately as her contact. Her hands were clasped in front of her chest and a wondering smile almost broke her small face in two. The human fledgling was barely as big as Jade had been, but she had the same youthful glow of compassion.

Girl, Verdana sent out in warm greeting without realizing what she was doing. Non-verbal communication was for Dragons, and their human-kin. But the girl laughed, delighted.

Amberle, she sent back. *My name is Amberle.*

Amberle, Verdana acknowledged, surprised and curious. The girl had not spoken aloud, but with her mind. It was something the Jordans on the Opal Dragon, after three years with their Fledglings, were just learning.

Amberle, Verdana repeated, her silver body emitting an emerald glow.

Amberle clapped her hands like a child and looked around at the others in the small group.

Charity de Rossi was there, of course, since it was her castle. She was casually dressed, for her, in a cream-colored skirt and jacket with matching heels. Her fingernails were the same cream color, and in one hand she held the long, slim stem of a vapor cigarette. The other hand held a glass of cut crystal that was half-full of black liquid.

Jasyn stood next to her in a charcoal-colored shirt that hugged his torso and gray pants that were comfortably loose. His expression was almost as dark as his hair and his muscled arms were folded over his broad chest. The girl stood between Charity and Faith, who was clothed similarly, for once, as her sister.

Nathan, an unusually tall and lanky Engineer with blonde hair and ginger-colored facial hair, stood just behind her left shoulder dressed in pearlescent coveralls. If Jasyn made Amberle apprehensive, the Engineer made her downright skittish.

The tension between Faith and Jasyn had been apparent from the beginning, and thick enough to be cut with a knife. Amberle was with them for a day in the villa in which time she had politely sequestered herself in Faith's office, telling them she was researching. And she was. Kind of.

Then she flew with them both to Charity's home - the Last Castle on the Distant Shore. At the castle she was introduced to the Engineer, who Amberle guessed to be almost seven feet tall.

If his height was not intimidating enough, he always moved his body close to hers. He spoke slowly, sensually, and he had a way of pinning her with his eyes. It made her want to squirm and she was pretty sure he knew it.

The strain between Faith and Jasyn was exponential when Nathan was around. Amberle wasn't surprised.

"My God," Charity murmured. "We have ourselves a Fledgling. Can you believe it?"

Faith laughed for the first time in weeks. "I can," she replied. "I just can't believe it took me this long."

"Well," Charity conceded, "it's not like they have them at the local market."

And edge of a smile found its way onto Jasyn's normally stoic face. "You have a local market?" he asked.

Charity blinked in surprise. "You know, I have no idea. Certainly not on the island. But we must get our...our..."

"Groceries?" Jasyn offered.

"Yes!" Charity agreed. "Our groceries, from somewhere."

"You do," Jasyn told her, "though I'm guessing it is from a Grow Ship via a private shuttle to the moon."

Faith laughed again. "You both guess right. No local market and no Fledglings in stock, not yet anyway." She sighed but her expression was pleased. "I certainly thought our first Dragon would be through our dear little sister. After all, she is a Jordan." She turned her tawny gaze to the girl. "We have Amberle to thank for this."

Amberle gave her a nervous, lopsided smile.

Jasyn's smile widened in spite of himself. The smile evaporated a second later when the tall blonde with the ginger-colored beard put his hands on Faith's shoulders and leaned down to speak softly in her ear.

"Would you like to stay and watch me work?" he asked Faith, giving her shoulders a gentle squeeze.

"Yes," she agreed, "I would. You don't mind?"

The Engineer gave her a lecherous smile. "Not at all," he said, keeping his face next to hers. Faith blushed while he kept the contact for a few more moments.

Charity's gaze slid to Jasyn. His dark hazel eyes blazed with murder but, other than that, he seemed under control.

"I might watch for a while as well," Charity announced, bringing her wrist to her mouth and speaking quietly into the silver bracelet there. When she was done, she looked at the dark-haired construct by her side. "Jasyn, darling, would you mind scooting a few of those seats over here?" she asked, pointing with her cigarette at a few high-backed leather air-chairs behind the desks that lined the left curved wall.

Jasyn dipped his dark head in acquiescence and moved away as Amberle turned to look at the rest of them, her expression bright.

"Is that okay?" she asked.

"Is what okay, dear?" Charity replied.

Amberle's look of excitement slowly crumpled. The enormous cave was silent save for the distant sound of waves, crashing on the rocks. "What Verdana asked," the girl said. "Is that okay?"

Charity glanced at Faith, who had kept her tawny eyes fixed on the girl.

"Did you guys hear her?" Amberle asked. The eyebrows of both sisters went up in surprise.

"She is speaking to you?" Faith asked. "You can hear her?"

Amberle nodded. "You can't?" she asked, feeling stupid. It was obvious by looking at them that she was the odd one out.

"It's not out of the ordinary," Nathan interjected, his hands still on Faith's shoulders though he had straightened to his abnormally tall height. "Fledglings often communicate through one person, usually their Jordan." He gave Faith's shoulders another squeeze, "I'm going to make sure all my metals are in order," he told her before moving off to the neatly stacked rods of lithium and titanium.

Amberle gave a sigh of relief at his words, though she was discomfited by the words from Verdana. Faith's scrutiny did not miss it.

"What is it?" she asked the girl after the Engineer had moved away.

"Verdana doesn't like him," Amberle admitted softly.

"Then she is a good judge of character," Jasyn said as he guided two of the chairs over for the de Rossi sisters.

"No thanks," Amberle said as he held the third one out for her. "I'm too fidgety to sit."

Jasyn nodded and there came a chime from the lift that led up to the castle. The doors opened and two butler droids floated out. One held a bottle of champagne glistening with condensation by one metal limb, a magnetic chill bucket with another, and four champagne glasses with a third. The other droid held an ice bucket, a silver tray topped with short glasses of heavy crystal, and a decanter of cut glass full of dark liquid.

They floated over to where the four waited and began preparing and pouring the drinks.

"What did she ask?" Faith asked Amberle, ignoring Jasyn's snide remark as she lowered herself down into a chair that bobbed slightly under her weight. "When you asked if it was okay."

"She wants to know if she can stay here," Amberle said before her expression turned a bit sheepish. "She hasn't come right out and said it, but I get the feeling she wants to stay hidden."

Charity gave a snort of laughter and then a small yelp of surprise as she sat in her own chair, a bit less gracefully than Faith, making it drop and then bounce so hard that it nearly tossed her out. The chair righted itself and the younger de Rossi quickly recovered and exchanged her empty glass for a fresh one full of liquor from one of the droids.

"Well," she breathed, settling into her seat, "how fortuitous!"

"We would be happy to oblige her," Faith said as she took a glass of champagne from the outstretched metal limb of a droid. Amberle smiled and turned back towards Verdana as Jasyn and the de Rossi sisters watched, intrigued that she was communicating silently with the Fledgling.

"Fortuitous indeed," Charity murmured as she sipped her drink. Nathan, having checked his materials, rejoined the group. Jasyn took a step closer to Faith's chair.

Amberle watched their silent exchange even as she had her own interchange with the Fledgling. She took a tentative step forward.

"Verdana wants to know if I can go inside," the young programmer told the Engineer, "while you work. Can I?"

"Certainly," he agreed. "At least, until I need to pressurize the cabin. Until then, I'm sure you'll be a great comfort to her."

Amberle smiled and trotted away towards the Fledgling, her coils of hair bouncing. As she neared Verdana, a small hole appeared in the silver skin and a silver ladder formed and slipped down against its side. Amberle felt like she might burst with excitement.

The young woman grabbed the first rung and hauled herself aloft, shimmying up the rest of the ladder and pulling herself up and into the temporary door that closed up once she was inside.

Amberle, grinning from ear to ear, looked around the small space as she felt the thrum of excitement around her.

Though she was not overly tall, she had to bend over to keep from hitting her head on the low ceiling. She found herself behind a single chair, obviously a pilot's chair, nooked into a cockpit that faced the clear eyes of the Fledgling Dragon.

"Whoooaah," Amberle whispered.

Sit down, Verdana encouraged.

"Really?" Amberle asked aloud.

Verdana glowed, inside and out. *Yes, really.* Something about the girl touched her starfire. The girl stepped forward and she slipped her slight frame into the lone seat.

Amberle's brown and green eyes slid over the console. Though the Fledgling looked like a military fighting jet on the outside, her dash was smooth and unmarred with the normal dials and digital screens of a fighter. Amberle's gaze moved over the dashboard of Dragonskin, sensing what was beneath - communications, connections, webs... knowledge. She sighed.

What, Verdana breached softly, *do they want to do to me?*

Amberle pressed her lips together. Her fingers twitched out of habit, as if ready to type, then she opened her mouth to speak as she realized it was not necessary to type anymore. Then it struck her that she hadn't been speaking aloud since the Fledgling had arrived.

They want to make you bigger, she thought, and immediately felt that Verdana had heard, and understood.

For Jade? Verdana asked.

Yesss, Amberle sent back hesitantly, *but also for their own ends.* She sensed now that Verdana was even less mature than she was. It gave her both a feeling of camaraderie and one of a need to protect the young Dragon. She could feel the tension around her.

What does that mean?

Amberle stuck out her bottom lip and sent a blast of air up and into her coral-colored spirals of hair. *I don't know,* she replied. *But I will do whatever I can to help.*

Around her, the Fledgling glowed.

From inside, the girl watched as bars and rods of different types of metal floated by outside. The Engineer, using only his mind to move the materials he needed, placed and melted the metals all over the Fledgling Dragon.

"Does it hurt?" Amberle asked aloud out of habit.

No, Verdana answered, and then sent the girl an image of a child putting on a coat. Amberle smiled in understanding. They sat in companionable silence for the entire morning, breaking it occasionally with questions and answers mostly sent by images and thoughts.

They took a break for lunch, for which Amberle was always eager and grateful. Then Amberle watched, from the outside, as the Engineer finished the growing. She kept up her mental conversation with Verdana. She reassured her as metals were melted around her body and the Engineer guided a droid inside to pressurize and grow the cabin.

At the end of the day, when it was obvious that things were wrapping up in the hangar, the others began preparing to go back upstairs, into the castle.

"We'll finish tomorrow," Nathan said, his hand raised as he guided the left-over metals into piles at the side of the hangar.

"She's not done?" Amberle asked, her hazel eyes sliding over the smooth and shiny (and much larger) Fledgling.

Nathan smiled as the metals seemingly organized themselves into neat rows. "She is done with her physical growing," he told the girl. "What come next is for us, or you - rather. She will be internally fitted with a galley, a bed, and a lavatory." There was also an upgraded weapons system to be put in, but he did not feel the need to mention that to the girl.

"Until then," Charity said, rising a little unsteadily to her feet, "it's time for dinner. And another cocktail or two."

The others smiled in agreement, except for Amberle.

"I'd like to stay here," she ventured softly, "if that is alright."

Verdana had not asked her to stay, but the girl could sense feelings of uneasiness and loneliness coming from the Fledgling. They were feelings she recognized. Feelings that she was well acquainted with.

"All night?" Charity asked, surprised. Amberle nodded.

"Why, of course," Faith told her. She turned her eyes to the dark-haired construct. "Jasyn can bring down some dinner for you. Blankets, an airbed, whatever you need."

"Yes," the Engineer said, stepping up behind Faith and putting his hands on her shoulders. He was so tall that he looked over the top of her head at the construct. "Maybe he can stay and keep you company."

Jasyn's expression darkened with fury and the air became so heavy with pressure that Amberle thought her ears might pop.

Danger, the Fledgling warned.

Yes, the young woman sent back, holding her own ground. *But not for us.*

"Charity can send a droid," Jasyn said through perfect,

clenched teeth. "Besides," he said, putting his glass down on a floating tray, "I promised Faith's security detail that I would make sure that she made it safely to her room tonight."

Faith would not be surprised in the least to find out that Geary, her head of security, did indeed make Jasyn promise to see her safely to her room. She knew, however, that it was just as likely that the construct did not want her alone with Nathan. And she did not miss how he had freed up both his hands.

"Of course," she agreed quickly, stepping away from the Engineer and looking at the girl with her eyebrows raised over her tawny eyes. "Is there anything in particular you would like?"

"Ice cream?" Amberle asked, hopeful.

Faith's lips pressed down to conceal her smile. "I was thinking of dinner."

"Ice cream?" Amberle asked again.

The corners of Faith's lips quirked up. She suddenly remembered another young girl, the only one she had ever really known. But she had been very different from Amberle. "I'll send down some spaghetti," she told her. The girl gave a her a resigned smile. "And some ice cream," she added, making the girl's face brighten. "What kind do you like?"

"Chocolate," Amberle answered immediately. "Or anything with chocolate. Or chocolate with anything in it."

Everyone was now smiling, everyone except Jasyn. His black stare was still fixed on the Engineer.

Faith gave the girl a nod and then turned and headed for the elevator that led back up to the castle. Jasyn fell into step right behind her, Charity and Nathan following. The two droids trailed behind, carrying empty bottles and dirty glasses.

Amberle sat down in one of the forgotten air chairs and carefully pulled her feet up onto the seat. She hugged her knees and looked thoughtfully at the newly grown Dragon Fledgling. She knew Verdana had cybernetic wiring and was somehow hooked into the Galactic Web, which was how she had seen the advertisement and made contact. Amberle now wondered how deep her connection was, and what her clearance might be.

Before even a few minutes had passed, there was a chime at the elevator and its doors opened. Two droids, Amberle could not tell if it was the same two from before or two entirely different ones, floated into the vast space of the cave.

One carried a platter with steam snaking from beneath the silver domes that rested there. Another limb held a tray topped with a carafe of lemonade along with a glass and a bucket of ice. Behind it drifted a metal box, its sides coated with frost. The other droid carried what appeared to be a much lighter load, holding only a metal disc in one limb and a small plastic package in another.

As they neared, the second droid dropped the disc. The circular piece of metal, about the size of a dinner plate, though much thicker, began to unfold over and over. Metal pieces snapped and clicked until there was a bed not much bigger than a cot. Amberle watched as a pad on the cot began to fill with air. While the mattress was inflating, the droid opened the plastic square - a pillow and blanket practically exploding into being as they were released from the compression cube.

Meanwhile, the other droid had expanded a table in front of the young woman and was carefully placing plates and utensils down for her. It set down a glass, poured it full of lemonade and then retreated back to where the elevator waited, leaving the frosted silver box behind. The second droid followed.

The young programmer pulled the table closer to her chair and lifted the silver domes off the plates and set them aside. There was enough spaghetti, meatballs, and garlic bread to feed three people. Amberle ate it all.

Completely stuffed, she leaned back in her chair. Listening to the sounds of the surf crashing on the rocks outside of the hangar, she looked at Verdana and knew that - in one way - she was still hungry. As if hearing her thoughts, a circle opened in the side of the Fledgling and, what looked like melting silver, formed itself into a set of stairs along the side.

Grinning, Amberle wiped her hands and hurried to the slender staircase. She climbed up and in and looked around, her eyes wide.

The first thing she noticed was that she could stand all the way up without bumping her head. She had seen how much bigger Verdana had become on the outside, but it seemed entirely different inside. So much empty space. Yet she could sense a feeling of pride coming from the Fledgling.

Amberle crept into the cockpit and slid into the pilot's chair. She marveled at the smooth expanse of Dragonskin and chuckled.

"I don't know what to do without a keyboard," she said softly. "Or at least a glove."

Three different types of keyboards rose up out of the smooth console before her, offering her choices. And her right thumb and index finger glowed silver, the same place where her silicone glove would normally go.

But, Verdana sent, *you can just tell me what you want.*

Amberle grinned again.

Then went to work.

Sometimes she spoke, sometimes she typed, sometimes she just let the Fledgling glean her thoughts.

All ways were seamless.

The young woman paused after two hours of being immersed in the Web only to go back into the cavern and open the silver box coated with ice crystals. As she had suspected, it was filled with different kinds of ice cream. She selected one, a lone bar dipped in chocolate, along with a pint-sized container of another. She grabbed a spoon off the table and, though she knew Verdana could keep her warm, she took the blanket off the makeshift bed.

Back inside, she finished both desserts while she read and watched and researched. Finally, when she felt she had learned enough of Jade, and what Verdana was capable of, she decided exactly where to go after the lost Jordan. And when.

Amberle was thinking of exploring more of what Verdana could do when she felt her seat moving underneath her.

What's happening? she asked. The chair was flattening, stretching out, and the girl realized it was becoming a bed.

You need to rest, Verdana replied.

But... Amberle started only to feel the Fledgling shush her.

For being so childlike, the young Dragon was being quite motherly.

Reluctantly, the young woman eased down with the newly formed bed and pulled the blanket over her. She wished she had the green jacket she had gotten on the Elba moon. But Faith had taken it and given it to someone to find out where it had come from.

Thinking of her jacket made her think of Keaton. She wondered where he might be and what he might be doing. She realized she missed him. She even missed Cooper and Ty, but she wished Keaton was there with her.

A small tendril of silver melted away from the bed, like the tail of a snake. It slipped up and, like a small and sparkling finger, touched the edge of the girl's blanket.

Amberle smiled and closed her eyes.

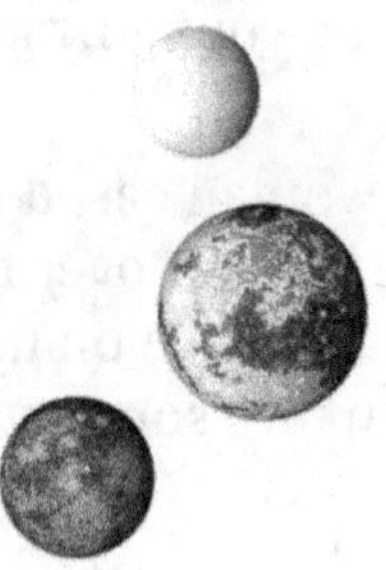

 ONE TWO

"That. Was. Amazing!" Jade exclaimed in three quick breaths. He tucked a lock of Sheila's brown hair behind her pointed ear and kissed her neck. "Let's do it again."

Sheila laughed, still panting and damp with sweat. She had slightly tilted brown eyes framed with dark lashes so thick they looked like butterfly wings. "You act like you're thirty years old," she teased.

Jade raised himself up on his hands and looked down at her face, cradled in the pillow. "Wellllll," he said, his own brown hair hanging down over green eyes that sparkled with mischief.

Color blossomed in Sheila's cheeks like a pair of scarlet roses. "Oh my god," she whispered, gathering the sheet in a small hand and trying to cover herself.

"I told you I was fifty because I knew you would think I was too young," Jade said quickly, "and when I saw you I thought you were the most beautiful woman I had ever seen."

Sheila's face softened. "You think I'm beautiful?" Jade nodded, his smile nearly splitting his face in two. Sheila, however, looked as if she were about to cry. "Thank you so much," she said, "I don't think my husband thinks so."

Jade's face went slack with shock. "You're married?" he gasped.

Sheila bit her bottom lip, caught in her own deception, and nodded. "I've only been married ten years, but my husband never looks at me anymore."

"Well," Jade said firmly as his surprise wore off, "if I was your husband I would tell you every day how beautiful you are. If I was staying in town, I would tell you myself."

"You're heading off to the college," Shelia realized aloud. "You and your friends."

The hamlet on the edge of the forest was small, but was often a meeting place and last stop before another day's journey to the city-town of Qrockett. The village had a large inn for just this reason and it had been in the tavern downstairs at the inn where Jade had met Shelia.

The young elf had gone to the bar to buy a round of ales when he saw a lovely elfin woman sitting on a stool, disconsolately sipping a glass of chilled wine. Jade left the mugs of ale on the table where his friends were sitting and then left, as his mates watched open-mouthed, with the pretty elfin lady.

Jade nodded at Sheila and was about to suggest again that they take advantage of what time they had when a door slammed downstairs. The pair in the bed froze.

"Is that your husband?" Jade whispered.

Shelia shook her head but pushed Jade off of her as she sat up to listen, her brown hair falling over her shoulders. "It's too early," she whispered back. "He's a woodcutter. He always works until dark."

Then a voice thundered from the first floor. "Sheila!" the voice boomed.

"It's him!" She exclaimed, her voice soft but fearful

Jade did not need to be told what to do. He rolled off the bed and was yanking his pants on a moment later.

"You don't have time!" Sheila hissed as she threw her dress over her head and pulled it down. "Get out the window!"

There was a clumping on the stairs and Sheila's name was shouted once again.

That sounds like one heavy elf, Jade thought as he threw the window open and crawled through the casement and dropped to the ground. His shirt came flying out after him and he caught in one hand as it was followed by one boot, which he also caught, and then the other, which nearly clunked him on the head.

He buttoned his pants and realized that she had not thrown out his belt. Considering the amount of shouting that was now coming from the bedroom, Jade decided to cut his losses. He looked around to find he was in an alley that was all but deserted save for a few refuse containers and some scrawny cats looking inside them for a meal.

Worried that an outraged face might make an appearance in the window at any moment, Jade pulled on his boots as he hopped down the alley and rounded the corner. He pulled his shirt on over his head as he hurried back up the street to the inn where he had left his friends.

Three young elves were standing outside of the tavern, the small table next to them holding empty ale glasses and a few coins. All three were over thirty years old, though looked no older than a human not yet twenty.

"Jade!" Kinneth hailed as he approached with an impish grin. The others turned, expressions of delighted shock on their elfin faces as the warm summer air filled with their nattering.

"Who was she?"

"Holy hell!"

"Did you...?"

"You didn't!"

"Crimmeny!"

"Her name is Sheila," Jade answered, his smile still so big it was starting to hurt his cheeks, not that he cared. "And, yes, I did." This was followed by more even more boisterous exclamations and denials. If it were true, it made Jade the first among them to lose their virginity.

"I knew you'd be the first!"

"I'm so jealous!"

"What was it like?"

They all waited with bated breath after this last question but as Jade opened his mouth to answer, their faces turned and their expressions fell. Jade followed their collective gaze to an elf that stood on the corner, fuming. He was so stout and stocky and muscled that if not for his pointed ears and smooth face he might have been mistaken for a human.

"Now, which one of you lads is missing a belt?" he thundered, holding up and shaking a slim piece of leather like he was throttling a garden snake.

There was a moment of frozen silence and then Jade bolted.

His friends, being true friends, ran with him.

Jade and Kinneth ran around the right side of inn while the other two ran to the left. The back of the inn bordered a forest and the four young elves met around back and dashed into the trees with the enraged woodcutter on their heels.

For an elf so stout, and presumably older, he ran surprisingly fast.

And if he is a woodcutter, Jade thought, *he knows these woods well. Still, I hardly believe he can catch us, and what a story this will be!* Jade almost laughed when he realized the man was right behind him. He dodged left and Kinneth and the others moved with perfect synchronicity, like fish in a school.

Like minnows, they turned in a flash, and all at once. Sometimes to the left, sometimes to the right. Separate bodies with one mind, they led a merry chase through the trees.

Jade knew he was safer with his friends and even safer staying in the woods - they had all been raised in a similar hamlet and could navigate most any forest with little trouble - but something inside was insisting that he leave them and the safety of the woods. Something was calling him east.

Something strong and insistent. Not so powerful that he felt he would be unable to resist it, but for some reason, he did not want to.

"Split up!" he shouted. His mates did so without question and with a precision that it was almost military. The boys had been friends since they were in knickers and it was not the first time they had been chased.

It was the first time, however, that it was by a jealous husband.

Ilin and Rame peeled away from one another while Kinnith turned tail and ran back in the direction they had come. Jade dashed right, cutting through the trees. As luck would have it, for Jade already held to the belief there were no such things as accidents, the woodcutter followed him.

As a sweat broke out on his forehead, Jade cleared the trees and burst into open grassland. He headed northeast, up the rise of a rolling hill. He felt the woodcutter was at last falling behind but something urged him to hurry.

Jade pushed his legs harder as he crested the grassy knoll, and then stopped cold in his tracks. It only took a few seconds for Sheila's husband to catch up with him. He still held Jade's belt as if planning on whipping him with it but his eyes caught sight of what had stopped the younger elf and he was ensnared in the same spell.

"Jesus, Mary, and Mikeal," the woodcutter whispered. The belt slipped from his hands, forgotten.

The knoll dipped down into a grassy meadow populated with wildflowers of white and yellow and purple. In its center was something that neither man nor nature could produce, yet something that they could possibly manage to do together.

For the most part, it looked like a mythical dragon. It had a reptilian snout, a long body atop four squat legs, and a long tail - over one hundred and twenty feet from nose to end.

But the hand of man was clearly visible. Rather than scales, the small Dragon had titanium skin that gave off a shimmer of green. Its wings were fixed rather than supple and foldable. Where eyes should have been were two huge blocks of diamond glass.

Jade?

The elf started with a jolt. It felt like a feather had slipped across the space between his ears.

Jade!

He did not recognize his name as a word but the feeling was clear and the small Dragon glowed brightly with a tearful exaltation that made Jade's throat close up. He watched as a small part of the Fledgling's skin melted away and a door appeared. A dark face surrounded by coils of pinkish hair appeared in the doorway and then withdrew.

Bright metal dripped out of the opening like quicksilver before forming into a narrow staircase, followed by a bottom (presumably belonging to the face he had just seen) and then the rest of a small person quickly descended to the meadow floor.

The person looked around and Jade saw that it was a girl, a human girl. Almost a woman, he guessed - by human standards. Even then, he figured she was probably close to ten years younger than he was.

She had brown skin and a wild head of curls that were a faded pink, more like coral in color. She wore military boots and trousers, and a t-shirt with a picture of a music group and what Jade thought might be a Golbi swear word. She stood on her toes and waved enthusiastically at Jade, and then beckoned him with the same arm.

That feeling swept across his mind again and this time it felt like a sigh.

The young elf took a deep breath, blew it out all at once, and looked over at Sheila's husband.

"Well," he chirped, "looks like my ride is here!" Then, and certainly without waiting for a reply, he ran down the knoll to where the young woman and the Fledgling were waiting.

The girl was bouncing up and down and clapping her hands and, as Jade got to her, for a moment it looked like she was going to hug him. She even leaned forward, her arms out, and then pulled back as if frightened and stuck her hands into her back pockets.

"Hi!" she greeted. "I'm Amberle."

"I'm Jade."

Amberle laughed. "You better be!"

Jade chuckled and looked around, glancing up at the glowing Fledgling before fastening his green eyes on her. "You were looking for me?"

"Yes. I was trying to be a little more discreet, but you actually found me first."

"That's crazy!"

It's about to get crazier, she thought.

Amberle laughed again and the sound made him smile. She had a nice laugh. And a nice face. Her light hazel eyes were a startling contrast to her dark skin.

"Well," she admitted, "it is, a little. But I could really use your help."

"*My* help?" Jade asked, perplexed. He was always willing to help when it was needed, he just couldn't believe that she was actually looking for him specifically.

"Yeah."

"Why me?" he asked out of sheer curiosity. The day was getting more interesting by the second, something he had not thought possible.

"I need you," Amberle explained, "to help me with the job I'm working on." She rocked back on the heels of her boots, trying not to appear as nervous as she felt.

Jade was nearly coming undone with the intrigue but did his best to bite back the million questions swimming through his brain and narrow them down.

"What do you need me to do?"

Amberle laughed again, softer this time. "I don't really know. Maybe nothing at all. But you would need to come with me..."

"In that Fledgling?"

Amberle nodded as she continued "... and I honestly couldn't say when you'd be back." *Or if you'd be back, she thought with a pang of guilt.*

Jade filled his lungs with a deep breath and looked up at the Fledgling Dragon before fixing his gaze back on the young woman. Though the elf was plenty young, he could read the implied danger in her eyes.

His brain felt like a hive of angry bees, but that was nothing new. He tried to slow his thoughts and weigh his options.

If he left, he would be leaving his mates without an explanation - to wonder and worry about him. He would almost certainly be late for his first day of college and very possibly be too late to start until the next semester. Also, climbing into a military vessel that could travel faster than the speed of light meant that he could literally disappear and never be seen again.

But how often are you offered a ride in a Fledgling Dragon? he thought. *And just in time to save your neck from a jealous husband?* Even at the young elfin age of thirty, Jade did not believe in accidents. A grin split his boyish face and his green eyes danced with excitement as he found words to voice only one question.

"What are we waiting for?" he asked.

Amberle rose up on her toes and clapped her hands as she gave a squeal of excitement. "Nothing! Let's go!"

She turned and shimmied up the steps like a squirrel. Jade followed and, just before going through the door, he turned and looked back. Kinnith, Ilin, and Rame had joined the woodcutter at the top of the grassy hill and stood staring with wide eyes and open mouths. Jade could not help but laugh. He threw them a quick wave before climbing inside, hoping that Sheila wouldn't be in too much trouble.

Behind him, the Fledgling sealed shut.

He looked around, his slightly slanted green eyes nearly round with amazement as he brushed back the lock of brown hair that had fallen over them.

The inside of the Fledgling was larger than he had imagined, and much larger than the first time Amberle had seen it.

Near the front, *the fore*, Jade corrected mentally, were two seats facing a smooth silver console under the great glass windows that were the eyes of the Fledgling. In the other direction, *aft*, Jade thought, was a tiny kitchen. Past it was a small sleeping area with a bed and a door that he guessed must lead to a washroom.

He turned back to where Amberle was slipping into one of the pilot seats. She turned and watched him, waiting. He walked forward to the cockpit of the Fledgling and took the other seat.

Jade Jade Jade Jade Jade

Jade gave Amberle a sheepish smile. "Can you feel that?" he asked.

Amberle returned the same smile. "Yeah," she said, not just feeling it, but hearing his name as well - clear as a bell. She found it curious that the elf could not. "It's Verdana. She's really happy to see you."

"Verdana," Jade said softly, his green eyes looking through the glass. "I like that." He shifted his gaze to Amberle. "It feels like she knows me."

Amberle's smile became a little lopsided. "Well, you're her Jordan. That's why we came to find you."

Jade's laugh was genuine. "You must have confused me with someone else. I couldn't even fly a crop duster." He laughed heartily again though he felt a jab of disappointment that his new adventure was about to end so abruptly.

"No? Well, maybe you could be one someday," she suggested.

Jade tilted his head and looked out the eyes of the Fledgling. "That's an intriguing idea. But I haven't even started college yet. Much less flight school and all the other schools Jordans go to. Plus, I seriously doubt I am military material."

"I think you could do it," Amberle said. "If you really wanted to." She smiled broadly. She had prepared a bit of a speech for him but liked this exchange better. It was almost like a game, or listening to someone read a story.

Jade considered the possibility and smiled himself. He ran his hand longingly over the smooth silver Dragonskin that covered the arm of his seat, sad that he would be leaving so soon. "I know this planet is on the outer edge of the galaxy, but I didn't know there even was a Green Fledgling. What Dragon did she come from?"

"The Opal Dragon."

Jade looked at her, surprised. "I know of the Opal Dragon, but if she had borne eggs, we would have heard of it - even out here in the sticks."

"Well," Amberle said, "it hasn't. Not in your time, not yet. But it will."

Jade frowned at her. "In my time? What are you talking about?" Then his expression fell into one of disbelief and slight disgust and a low chuckle came from his throat. "Please don't try to tell me you're from the future."

The girl gave him an exaggerated shrug, pulling her shoulders almost to her ears. "I know it sounds corny, and it's been in about a thousand holo movies..."

"Tens of thousands."

"...or tens of thousands, but I don't really know any other way to say it." Amberle glanced out the window to see that Jade's friends had been joined by others. All were gawking at the young Dragon in the meadow. "Uh, do you mind if we leave? I can explain it to you on the way."

"Sure."

A million questions once again went hammering through the young elf's mind. *Way to where? Will I ever come back? Are you really from the future?*

"Verdana," Amberle said, "get us out of here, please."

The Fledgling pulled her legs back into her body, turning herself back into a seamless vessel. She rose a hundred feet into the air and hovered.

"Xelsior University," Amberle replied in answer to her silent question.

"Hey!" Jade exclaimed, excited. "That's the college I'm going to! How did you.." The realization sank in as the Fledgling rose higher and banked north. "Because you're from the future," he said softly. "That's what you're going to tell me."

Amberle chuckled. "Yeah."

"But anyone could have found that out," he argued. "Everyone in my whole village knew."

"You don't believe me?"

"Would *you*?"

That had Amberle stumped. If someone told her they were from the future, would she believe them? Two months ago, absolutely not. Now, she was beginning to think that anything was possible.

"Can I ask..." Jade started but Amberle shook her head, making her curls bounce around her dusky face.

"Let me explain first, then you can ask me whatever you want. Otherwise you will just be confused. But," she added, "you'll have the coolest ride to school ever." If she could wink at him, she would have.

Jade laughed and looked out into the clouds that were now going by them in streams of white. "Okay," he agreed. "Go ahead."

Amberle drummed her dark fingers on the arm of the seat. "You know about GwenSeven?"

The young elf gave her a look of exasperation. "Just because we are in the Outer Banks, doesn't mean it's some Podunk moon."

"Podunk?" Amberle asked giggling.

Jade was not as amused. "Podunk," he repeated. "It means small, out-of-the-way, ignorant, unimportant..."

"I know what it means," Amberle said, still giggling, "I've just never heard anyone actually say it before."

Jade rolled his eyes and continued. "Of course I know of GwenSeven. The company to first perfectly manufacture people? Until almost two hundred years afterwards when some of those constructed beings started going berserk and began a rebellion?"

Amberle smiled and gave him a nod, remembering just a few weeks ago when Faith had asked her the same question. She guessed that, since they were young, older adults also assumed they were idiots.

"Yes, but it won't actually be classified as a rebellion for another seventy years or so."

"So the government is about as quick and efficient in the future as they are now?" Jade asked with a smirk.

"Yeah, pretty much."

The face of the young elf brightened and he sat up straight in his chair. "Is that why you need me? To help stop the rebellion?"

A chuckle slipped out from her lips and Amberle quickly put her hand over her mouth. "No, sorry. It doesn't really have anything to do with that." Then she saw his expression fade into disappointment and quickly said, "It's more of a rescue mission."

Jade lit up once again. "A rescue mission? That would be amazing! I would love to help!" He sat back in his seat and could have sworn the seat was hugging him. His head was spinning but he made it slow so he could sort out his thoughts. One idea struck him and he cast his green eyes at the girl, cocking his head. "You said before that I'm her Jordan?"

Amberle nodded slowly, steeling herself against the questions she knew would follow. Must follow.

"Then why don't you ask me to go on this rescue mission in...what do I call it? The future? Your time? Whenever that is?" He began guessing without waiting for an answer. "Can you not get through the right military channels? Will they not let me? Do I not want to?" He sucked in a breath before he continued. "Am I an asshole?" he breathed with an expression of disappointment and fear.

Amberle gave him a ghost of a smile and his countenance deflated like a popped balloon as suspicion hit him like a load of bricks. He felt the seat tighten around him, *really hugging him*, and he knew. "It's because I'm dead," he said, his voice completely flat. His green eyes looked at her, but all the joyous light had gone out of them. "That's why you have to come to the past to get me, isn't it? Because where you're from, *when you're from*, I'm dead."

"Yes," Amberle affirmed, her own voice barely above a whisper.

"How? When?" the young elf demanded, incredulous for merely a second before he swiftly held up a hand. "No, wait!" He blew a great breath of air out through pursed lips. "Don't tell me," he said softly. "It's better that I don't know."

Now it was his turn to drum his fingers on the arm of his seat as he thought.

Fuck! he shouted inwardly. *I'm going to die!*

The realization hit him again and he sagged in his seat. Then it hit him again and he almost laughed aloud. *Of course I am. Aren't we all?*

Still, it took him a minute to gather in his senses and his feelings, both of which were running wild.

Well, he deliberated after a moment, *the Opal Dragon doesn't even have eggs, much less Fledglings, so I know I've got some time.* His arched brows went up over his narrow green eyes and he smiled as his thoughts flicked back over the day. *I'm not going to die a virgin*, he realized with no small amount of satisfaction. *I'm not going to do anything crazy enough to die in school, or even flight school - should I decide to go.*

But he knew then and there that, deep inside, he had already decided.

The elf sighed as he contemplated his next thought. *This might not be my purpose for living, but it surely is part of my destiny.*

Then he felt his heart swell with pride and excitement at the notion that followed. *I'm going to be the Jordan of the Green Fledgling.*

"Can I ask just one question?" he implored.

Amberle nodded, her face somber. She expected him to ask about GwenSeven, or the war, or about his own life - or worse, death.

"In the future, do they finally make cars that can fly?"

Amberle chuckled, and then laughed. Really laughed. "They make those now," she told him, still laughing.

"Damn," the young elf muttered. "I've seen them in movies, but I didn't think they were real. I guess I really do live on a

Podunk moon."

"So...you'll come with me?"

Once again Jade drummed his fingers on the arm of his seat as he thought about it. Amberle noticed that they were slim, almost dainty.

"I will, but I want you to do something for me first."

"If you need me to prove that I'm from..." she started but he shook his head, his brown hair falling over his eyes. He pushed it from his face and swallowed, uncomfortable. He was not an elf that usually made demands. Especially ones that sounded childish, but that was something he could not help.

"I want to see my mother."

Amberle knew without looking that they were nearing his college and she silently instructed Verdana to pass over it as she considered his request.

It could mean trouble. If he told his mother she might try to talk him out of it. She would certainly denounce Amberle as crazy.

Verdana, however, was substantial proof to support any story. Plus, the young woman could see the yearning for adventure in the green eyes of the young elf.

"Alright," she acquiesced.

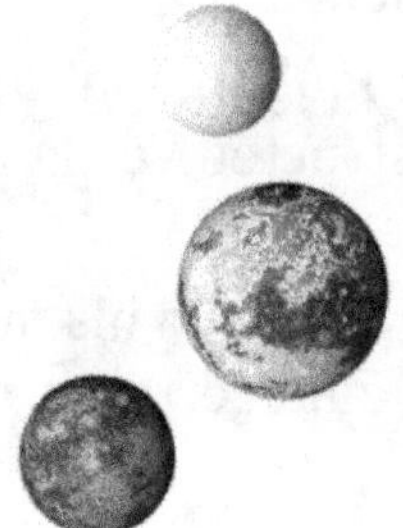

ONE THREE

"Should we head back to your village?" she asked.

"Yes," Jade answered. "No."

Amberle's feathery brows went up over her eyes of brown and green. The elf let out a shaky sigh.

"I should explain," he said and released another breath, this one deeper – more solemn. Amberle cocked her head, intrigued at his sudden change of demeanor. "My father died last year," he said quietly.

Amberle's face softened. "I'm sorry."

Jade accepted the condolence with a nod and continued. "It was hard for me, and even more so for my ma, though she managed to put on a smile every day – at least when I was around. I knew she was struggling and hiding her grief. I even offered to postpone going off to university for a few years but she wouldn't hear if it." The small elf pulled in another deep breath and let it out slowly. "I don't need to talk to her, in fact it is probably better that I don't. I just need to see her. To know she is alright."

Amberle nodded, understanding. "So I don't need to know just where you want to go, I need to know when."

Jade gave her a sheepish smile. "Yeah. Any suggestions?"

Amberle contemplated the question and then blew a stream of air from her lower lip that went over her face and fluffed her curls. "How long do elves typically grieve?" she asked. "A year? Two? Ten?"

Jade tried to laugh but no sound came out. He swallowed

it down, still feeling the grief and loss of his pa. "They never stop," he said, his voice soft and sad. "But we continue. We must." He drew another of those deep breaths and squared his shoulders. "How about if you take me to...your time - do you know where my village is?"

Though she truly did not know it off the top of her head, Amberle nodded. The knowledge was at her fingertips. Literally. She leaned forward and placed her hand against the smooth silver console, in this case conveying her wishes to the Fledgling better with feelings than words.

Verdana banked and the two seated in the cockpit shifted as they tilted, the port side lifting up as the starboard side dipped. Once she had them turned around, the Fledgling gained altitude at breakneck speed, streaking over the landscape far below. Then there was feeling of *rippling*, as if going through a wall of water.

Amberle had experienced it on her journey to find Jade. She assumed, correctly, that it was from crossing from his *when*, to hers.

This time, however, there was a jolt. Nothing traumatic, but enough for her to notice. It felt as if the Fledgling had hiccupped, or passed through a stroke of lightning. The hairs on the back of her neck rose up and an electrical current went sizzling down her spine. A frown creased her brow and she was about to ask Verdana about it when Jade spoke.

"Don't get too close to the village if you don't want to be seen," he advised.

Amberle came out of her distraction and looked out at the forest passing beneath them. "We don't," she agreed. "Bank east, V." She turned her face slightly towards the elf by her side but kept her green and brown eyes scanning the trees. "Any suggestions where we can hide a Fledgling Dragon and slip in unnoticed?"

Jade nodded. "Keep on this course. See those mountains?"

"I see hills."

"They're mountains."

Amberle's lips quirked up. "You really need to get off this moon and travel."

Jade's brows furrowed. "And you've seen so much in your, what - mighty eighteen years?"

Amberle laughed. "Actually, I'm nineteen – if you must know. And the years might not be many, but they have been mighty. I'm quite sure I've seen more than you." She glanced at Jade and saw he was still agitated. "Okay," she acquiesced, "we head for the mountains, and then what?"

Placated, the elf's usual smile returned and he looked at the approaching range. "Take us a little more east and then come down between the forest and the mountains. There's lots of caves there and we can leave her in one. No one ever goes there."

"Why?"

"They're haunted. Supposedly."

"But you've been there?"

"Plenty. Kids are always daring each other to go inside. I went the farthest of all of my friends," he said with obvious pride.

"Alright," the young woman agreed.

Verdana angled east as they neared the edge of the forest and then made a swooping turn to the west, flying low into the space between the woodland and the craggy ridge of jagged hills. As promised, the hills were pocked with caverns. Some were barely more than cracks, some were tremendous caves, choked with vegetation.

"V?" Amberle asked as the Fledgling slowed, cruising under the leafy canopy. "Is there any way you can tell if you'll fit in any of those?"

A feeling of reluctant acknowledgement came from the

young Dragon and the young woman pressed her lips together.

"Something wrong?" Jade asked.

"She's not fond of enclosed spaces."

Jade frowned as they passed one black maw in the side of the craggy hills, and then another. "This one coming up," he said, "right after the stream. It's more open than any of the others."

After much mental and emotional encouragement from Amberle, the Fledgling dipped down a bit and slowed as she sank gracefully into the cave that was low-ceilinged but wide. It was spacious enough to turn around, which she promptly did - feeling immensely better facing the exit. She pushed her legs out from her body and landed, settling gently on the earthen floor.

Amberle looked around and was strongly reminded of the cavernous hangar underneath the Last Castle of Charity de Rossi. Except here it was darker, the only light coming from the entrance to the cave, and even that was shaded by the forest of trees. And the walls were not smooth here, but carved with deep grooves as if from a millennia of water. Some of the larger grooves were wider, and blacker than night. She suspected they might be passageways that led deeper into the hills, or to other caves.

"I think this might have been a volcanic range at some point, long ago," she pondered in a hushed tone as her eyes sought out the details of the cave.

"And now they are mountains."

Amberle's lips quirked up again. "If you say so." She leaned back and regarded the elf with a smile. "Ready?"

Jade took a deep breath, the light of excitement dancing in his eyes. "We're in *your* time now?" he asked. "This is the future?"

Amberle couldn't help but laugh. "It's the future for *you*. For me, it's just now."

Now Jade laughed. "This is so crazy! But yes, I'm ready."

Together they stood and headed aft where Verdana was already creating an opening and sending down a slim flight of stairs. The pair descended and the first thing that hit Amberle was the smell.

She stepped away from the silver steps that were already withdrawing into the side of the Fledgling, trying to slow her racing heart.

The air was warm, and humid, and had a strong *earthy* smell. The smell of heavy vegetation and wet stone. It brought back the memory of the forest she had entered with Keaton, Cooper, and Tyler. The trees had been dense and dripping with vines. The forest, which had been more of a jungle, came back to her with a sharp pang. The jungle, its smell, and the temple from which they had only narrowly escaped.

The young woman could feel Verdana, feel her heartbeat quickening as well.

It's okay, she sent. *Just bad memories. For us both.*

Jade, however, seemed completely at ease. His face was lit with an enormous grin as he motioned to the young woman with dark skin and hazel eyes of green and brown. "Come on!" he urged, excited, as he led the way out of the cave. Amberle followed right on his heels.

We'll be back soon she sent, trying to assure the nervous Fledgling.

Verdana sank down a little more, settling onto her feet, and Amberle wondered if she was trying to reassure the Fledgling or herself. Her skin tingled all over, especially at the back of her neck.

From what? Trepidation? Premonition? Déjà vu? The breeze?

She didn't know.

Amberle cast her eyes about the darkness once more and,

with the sound of water dripping down the walls and rushing in a stream outside, she followed Jade out and into the light.

A river of sky ran above her head, letting sunlight stream in from between the canopy of the woods and the shade of the miniature mountain range. Jade was staring up at the trees as if he might burst with the thrill of it all. He was smiling and beckoning to her and the feeling of déjà vu intensified as she was suddenly reminded of Keaton's boyish innocence.

"What are you so excited about?" she asked, keeping her voice low but finding that his delight was infectious. She could feel a smile breaking across her own face.

"It *is* the future!" the young elf exclaimed. "Look!" he said, pointing up into the tree that towered above their heads. "Ilin broke that branch when he tried to swing down from this tree. It was just last month, for me anyway, but look at it!"

Amberle followed the direction of his finger and saw that there really was a broken branch in the tree, but it was nowhere near fresh - not from a month ago or even a year. Or a decade.

The limb hung at an unnatural angle. The rest of the mostly severed branch was dead and damp and covered with moss. The crook, where it had broken, was filled with the remnants of bird nests that had been built and rebuilt for a hundred years.

"It *is* overgrown," Amberle observed.

"And look how high it is!" Jade exclaimed with a grin that split his face in two. "If Ilin had jumped from that high he would have broken more than just the branch!"

Amberle nodded, understanding that he was gauging how much the tree had grown since the last time he had seen it. Still, she was uneasy, and eager to be done with what she was thinking of as a side-mission.

"Which way to your village?" she asked.

Jade seemed to come back to where and what they were after, sobering him immediately. "This way," he instructed with a jerk of his chin as he started off in the same direction.

Amberle followed silently. Her nervousness fell away as she followed. This was not the thick jungle or the emaciated woods of the zombie-ridden moon she had left so recently. These woods were full of deer and birds and furry creatures that leapt among the upper branches of the trees. Ones that she would not have to eat for dinner.

She hoped.

Smiling, she trailed the elf as he walked comfortably between the trees. He was obviously familiar with the forest.

Though his step seemed carefree, Amberle noticed that he didn't make a sound. She watched his face and saw his eyes move fractionally but constantly.

He would make a good hunter, she thought. It brought memories of Keaton and his brothers and she wondered what they might be up to. She hoped that their rodent-eating days were done as well.

After they had gone for what she guessed was a half mile, Jade slowed and motioned for her to stop. She peered around curiously but saw nothing but more woodland. Then, very distantly, she could make out the sounds of voices as they carried on the air as it moved through the trees. They faded as the breeze died.

His ears are as good as his eyes, she marveled.

Quick and silent, Jade stepped close, very close. Before she could move, his cheek was next to hers and he tipped his head so he could whisper in her ear. Amberle froze, but did not pull away.

"Stay here," he whispered, his breath soft against her ear.

"Why?" she whispered back. From the corner of her eye she could see Jade's lips press together and she could not tell if it was to restrain frustration or mirth.

"Because you're so loud!" he breathed, yet even his breath

was full of merriment, putting her at ease.

"I'm not loud!" she whispered back fiercely. Jade's tilted green eyes widened and he put a hand over his own mouth to keep from laughing. Amberle, to her own surprise, leaned even closer and put her mouth up to his pointed ear and lowered her voice as much as she could. "Take me as far as you can. I want to see."

She was so close that she could not see his face, but she could feel him nod. He backed away and held a finger to his lips. She nodded and he turned to lead her away.

Amberle followed as silently as she could but found herself unable to pay much attention to her surroundings. Her mind was fixed on how it had felt to have him so close to her, the feel of his breath against her cheek. Lost in thoughts and feelings, she stepped on a stick.

It was small, and so was the cracking sound it made, but it was enough for both of them to freeze. Jade turned and stared at her, his eyes wide again - this time with exasperation. But there was no anger in it, no blame. It was not the way Tyler would look at her with exasperation. Amberle held out her arms and ducked her head in silent apology, unable to keep a smile from her face. Jade laughed silently in return, then turned to continue making his way down what was becoming a narrow path through the trees.

Voices became discernible to Amberle's ears, then actually clear as the woods broke away to reveal a modest but comfortably sized home. The roof was covered with wood shingles and the sides were painted forest green. Their approach had led them to the edge of the forest. The trees stopped in an erratic line behind the house and they found themselves looking over a tidy vegetable garden bordered with a multitude of flowering shrubs. Father along, Amberle could see a similar home, and another just past it.

Jade looked meaningfully at Amberle. He pointed at her, then pointed at the ground.

Stay here, he was telling her.

She nodded in understanding.

He gave her a look that expressed doubt, but a smile still tugged at the corners of his lips. Then he turned and slipped away.

Again, Amberle marveled at his ability to keep utterly silent as he made his way to the corner of the house and then sidled up to a window. She let herself drift back to a few moments ago when the young elf had stood so close to her that she could feel his body, his breath.

The thought made her heartbeat quicken and her body tingle.

I must be over my cyber sickness, she pondered thoughtfully, *to be okay with him so close, even touching me.*

Experimentally, she imagined someone else doing the same. Possibly Faith's devastatingly handsome construct, leaning close to whisper in her ear. She felt her body go rigid in response.

Does that mean I'm still sick? she wondered. *And if I am, why didn't it bother me when Jade did it?*

She returned her focus to the elf who, meanwhile, had pressed himself against the side of the house. He had been looking in one of the windows, but now his face was turned to Amberle, his brown eyebrows pulled together. Amberle's attention snapped to the back door of the house, suddenly aware that the voices had gotten louder. Closer.

Quietly as she could, she took a step to the side and pressed herself against a tree, hoping she was hidden. Not a second later, the back door of the house opened. A pair of voices emerged followed by their owners, a pair of older (but far from elderly) women.

Amberle spoke no Elvish, so could not understand them, but could clearly hear that they were joking about something. They tittered laughter as they talked, moving about the garden.

Unable to help herself, the young woman moved her head incrementally to the side of the tree to catch a peek.

She saw the woman who had to be Jade's mother immediately. She could not see her eyes, but she had the same slight build, the same chocolate-colored hair. The same mirthful laugh. The other elfin woman was just as slight, but more fair. The two laughed heartily about something as they gathered vegetables from the garden.

Amberle's eyes went next to the house and for a moment could not find Jade. He had slipped around the corner and melted into the shadows. She spotted him when she saw his eyes, staring at her, more serious than she had ever seen them. She ducked back behind the tree and waited.

After another minute, the voices faded back into the house. Amberle was about to risk a glance around the tree when Jade was suddenly beside her. He held a finger meaningfully to his lips and she bobbed her head around as she rolled her hazel eyes to let him know she understood.

Then he grasped her hand with his own and led her away.

They went back into the woods and, after a good stealthy minute, Jade released her hand. Amberle felt the loss of his touch in more than just her hand, but she had no time to consider it. She was full of questions, one of the foremost was to inquire about what the women had been talking about, but what came out was much different – surprising her.

"Did you get what you were after?" she asked earnestly.

Jade's soft smile broadened and he nodded. "Yes. She is fine. A little melancholy, I think, but better. My aunt, too. My father's sister - that's who the other one was - is doing better as well. They're organizing a food collection, mostly of late summer roots and vegetables, for a charity food drive." He reached out to clasp her hand again and gave it a squeeze. "Thank you for doing this for me."

Amberle returned his smile, the warmth of his touch

flooding her even as a ripple of cold shimmied down her spine.

There was something wrong with that statement. Terribly wrong.

She turned her face from him, trying to keep emotion and confusion from her face as they continued their walk back to the hills.

Melancholy, he had said.

He released her hand, but not entirely. Their pinky fingers were still hooked together. Amberle could not discern if it was accidental or not. The young elf was telling her about an upcoming spring festival but she found herself at a loss trying to pay attention to what he was saying.

Part of her mind tugged at the image of his mother. She knew she needed to think about it, but what held her attention was the way his little finger was entwined with hers. She could picture their hands without looking - one light, one dark - and her pinky involuntarily tightened on his.

Melancholy.

Now, as they approached the hills, she could hear words in her head as well, but they were coming in too fast and jumbled to make any sense. It took her a few seconds to even realize where they were coming from.

They had arrived at the cavern where they had left the Fledgling and Amberle was distracted by Jade's touch and Verdana's voice, thrumming in her ears and her blood.

They entered the cave and Jade fell silent but Verdana was hammering away about others and *danger danger danger!*

Entering the cavern, their eyes had barely adjusted to the aphotic light when they saw the Fledgling, surrounded by alien bodies that were tall and bulky, smooth and crimson.

Amberle's mind had just enough time to register *Golgoths!* Before she was forcefully yanked away into darkness.

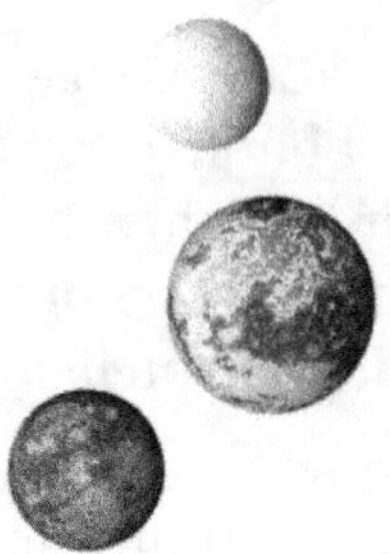

 ONE FOUR

The young woman blinked rapidly, fighting to stem the flood of panic that was trying to engulf her. Instead, she held perfectly still as she took in her surroundings.

It was dark on all sides but one, and even there it was just a sliver of muted light. The space she was in was tight, making her stand a little taller. The voice of the Fledgling was yammering away and the young woman did what she could to mentally soothe her while attempting to understand what had happened.

She had seen the Golgoths, huge and grotesque, their exoskeletons encasing them in plates of red armor. Their enormous arms cradled weapons too heavy for almost any human to carry, much less wield.

They had been standing around the Fledgling, keeping a safe distance and wary eyes on the young Dragon. Talking to each other rapidly in a language that was a strange combination of guttural and chittering sounds, they had not noticed the two that had entered the cave before disappearing into a crack in the cavern wall.

The young woman found herself looking through that crack, having been hauled inside by Jade, her eyes catching the movement of shadows as the Golgoths shifted while they chittered and chattered.

The young elf was wedged in against her.

Amberle shushed Verdana and the Fledgling quieted immediately. *Can they get in?* she sent. *Can they hurt you?*

No, they can't get in. Verdana replied, calming quickly. Amberle could feel the Fledging scanning the creatures and the weapons they held. *No, they can't hurt me. But you...* Amberle could feel the fear begin creeping back into the young Dragon, making her heartbeat speed up again.

The distress from the Fledgling seemed excessive until the young woman remembered that Verdana had already lost Jade once before, in a similar situation.

I'm okay, Amberle sent, reassuring her. *Jade is okay. Just stay calm while we figure out what to do.*

She closed her eyes, trying to ignore the feel of the elf's body against her own.

She couldn't.

Her normal reaction to the proximity of another being was to move away, and quickly. This was quite the opposite. Though he was pressed against her, she felt the urge to press back.

She could feel him and smell him and hear his breath. Yet she did not pull away in the slightest.

He was slender but muscled. She could feel it through his clothes. She apprehended he smelled like the forest where they had just been. Leaves and moss and earth and water. And skin. Warm skin.

She scrunched her eyes, closing them tighter.

"What do we do?" she whispered without moving. There was no need to move closer for him to hear her. Their bodies were so close that they were more than just pressed against each other, they were entangled. Her cheek was next to his, her lips brushing his ear.

Jade was at a loss. Moments ago he had been deeply content, knowing that his ma was doing just fine. Then, upon their arrival into the cave, he had been inundated with shock, and then filled with fury that the most dangerous and aggressive aliens in the known universe were on this moon.

His moon. *Less than a mile from his village.*

Still, he had moved instinctively, ducking out of sight and pulling Amberle with him.

The shock and anger had disappeared in the darkness.

He suddenly found he had no ability to focus on anything other than the young woman. The feel of her body, so much of it touching his own. Her hips were against his hips, her long right leg between his, so that he was straddling it. He could feel her breasts on his chest. His hands were around her waist and he forced himself to keep them relaxed rather than tightening, clutching at her.

Her lips were against his cheek, her soft breath just barely reaching his ear.

Her wild curls were tickling his neck, driving him out of his mind.

Then he found himself struggling against something else.

No no no, he prayed silently. *Not now.*

"I...I.. don't know," he stammered quietly. "Other than we need to get in the Fledgling and get the hell out of here."

"How are we supposed to get past those Golgoths?" she whispered back, opening her eyes. She tried to think, but she was as distracted as the elf. She was intensely cognizant of every part of him touching her. She fought against the compulsion to press herself harder against him. "We wouldn't stand a chance against even one of them. Is there any way to get by them unseen? Maybe a secret tunnel through the caves?"

"Not that I know of," he breathed.

His breath caressed her jaw and slipped down her neck. She could feel his heart beating against her chest and she was acutely aware of his body beneath his clothes. The swell of his slim bicep against her rib cage, the press of him at the apex of her thighs where she had become unexpectedly and terribly sensitive. She thought of what it would be like to put her lips on his neck. To see if he tasted like the forest.

She closed her eyes again and swallowed, trying to concentrate. "We need something to distract them. And we need a weapon."

She could feel Jade's smile against her cheek. "I think we already have one."

Amberle's eyes sprang open, confused for a moment, engulfed by his touch and his warmth and his smell.

Then the meaning of his words sank in and she realized they did indeed have a weapon. A very dangerous one.

She closed her eyes again.

Mentally, she opened those eyes of green and brown - and looked through the eyes of the Fledgling.

There were sixteen Golgoths, gathered into a semi-circle right in front of her nose, keeping what they judged to be a safe distance from the craft that had not moved for the hour since they had discovered it. They had closed in slowly, carefully, but the Fledgling had not so much as glimmered. They were clicking and grunting as they looked at the young Dragon.

I don't suppose you know what they are saying?

There was no answer, but Amberle clearly got the impression that Verdana had no more of a clue than she did.

Are you able to, I mean - could you...?

Her thought trailed as she found herself unable to ask Verdana if she was able to kill them. The feeling that came back was quite affirmative and without any of the young woman's indecision. Amberle watched through her eyes, reluctant to take life in such an unexpected manner.

She told herself that they were Golgoths, the worst and most dangerous enemies to the civilized galaxies. She knew they would kill her and Jade if they were discovered. Or worse, they could be captured and tortured. She knew they had to get out of there. Still, she held back.

The first Golgoth she had come face to face with had shot Cooper, without a moment's thought or hesitation. So why was she wavering?

The clacking and grunting stopped as fifteen of the aliens turned to the one with the largest weapon, the massive gun easily the size of a full-grown human. The Golgoth hefted the giant stock up to his shoulder and pointed the barrel at the Fledgling.

Kill them! Amberle sent, all uncertainty gone and replaced with a stab of fear that she might be too late.

She wasn't.

Before the Golgoth could finish taking aim and depress the trigger, all sixteen of them were engulfed in green flames.

The young woman was brought back to her own body by the feel of Jade's arms tight around her, pulling her off her feet and pivoting, driving her back. She opened her eyes to see that he had forced her farther into the crevasse and had turned them both to shield her body with his own from the heat exploding in the cave.

Amberle shut her eyes and pressed her forehead into his shoulder and waited for the heat and light to subside. The barrage lasted for another few seconds and then was gone entirely. She looked up, startled, and quickly moved her hands to search the elf's back. His clothes were hot but seemed intact.

"Are you okay?" he asked.

Amberle laughed quietly. "I think so. Are you?"

Jade voiced a nervous chuckle. "I don't know, is my hair still there?"

She reached up intending just to touch his brown locks but found her fingers sliding through them. They were very warm and very soft. "It's there." Acutely aware of their proximity once again, she let her hand drop to his shoulder, embarrassed.

"Do you think it's safe to go out?" Jade asked, not in any rush to let her go. She nodded again and he reluctantly inched back until he could turn around. "Careful," he warned over his shoulder as he peeked his head out. "The sides of the cave are hot."

Amberle could feel the heat coming off of the stone walls as she squeezed through, following the slim elf out into the cavern. The Fledgling, untouched but quite smug, was alone in the cave once more. A few flakes of drifting ashes were all that was left of the Golgoths.

"Let's get the hell out of here," she said, heading for Verdana.

"Wait!" Jade called, not moving from the spot where he had emerged from the deep crack in the cavern wall.

Amberle stopped, her eyes darting everywhere. She saw nothing. "What?"

"We need to go back to my village. We need to tell them what we found out here. There might be more."

Amberle shook her head of wild curls, knowing that there was almost certainly more Golgoths lurking about. But she had to get back to Faith. She had dallied too long wanting appease Jade and had put both their lives in danger.

"I can think of a hundred reasons why we shouldn't. Come on, let's go." She headed for the Fledgling again but Jade held his ground.

"Like what?"

The young woman turned on her heel, her hazel eyes bright and wild. The crazy spikes of adrenaline and the ensuing crashes from it were making her already short temper even shorter.

"For one," she started impatiently and then bit her tongue. *For one thing, you're dead*, was what she almost said. *And seeing you would freak everyone out.* But, even as the words turned into smoke in her mind, something else sank in.

It was the thought that had been tugging at the back of her mind as they had approached the cave.

The sight of Jade's mother, happily chatting and gathering vegetables in her garden.

Melancholy.

Not devastated.

He had just recently told her that elves never let go of their grief. And maybe a hundred years would balm the loss of her husband.

But now, in Amberle's present time, her son was dead. Only months ago.

She had not appeared to be a woman who had recently lost her only son.

Maybe she doesn't know yet, Amberle considered and then discarded the idea just as quickly. *She would have to know. Even in the sticks, there is news. And some IGC Official would certainly have contacted her personally.*

"For one what?" Jade demanded.

"For one thing," Amberle told him, patiently this time, choosing her words, "the Golgoths obviously know that no one comes here, which is why they picked this place to hide, and are still hiding – both themselves and whatever they might be doing. If they are confronted that will undoubtedly change, provoking an attack. Second, if there are more, they will be as heavily armed as the ones we found. Does anyone in your village have any kind of weaponry that could stand against them?"

"No," Jade admitted. "Nothing even close."

Amberle gave a quick nod. "That's what I figured. We need to get out of here, and alert people who can help. This is bigger than just the two of us."

Jade considered for a moment and then nodded thoughtfully. "Who are we going to tell?"

"Faith," Amberle answered without pause. "She'll know what to do. Who to call. She has the power to make a bigger difference than we can."

The normally jovial elf looked at her, his face deeply serious for once. "And you trust her?"

This time Amberle did pause. It was not something she had ever considered. "I guess so."

"You guess?"

Amberle frowned as she thought. "I do, though I can't say why. Maybe because she trusts me." Her eyes lifted to Jade's. "Most people don't."

"They don't?" he asked, surprised. "Why not?"

"Because I'm young," she speculated softly. "Because I'm good at what I do."

"What is that, exactly?"

Amberle's hands balled into fists. "Do you ever stop asking questions? We have to get out of here!"

"Right," he agreed with an apologetic smile. "Sorry. Kind of the way I'm wired."

Amberle could not help but smile back at him. He seemed to bring it out of her, somehow. She had never known anyone before to do that. Puzzled but pleased, she headed for Verdana who was already opening up and forming stairs against her side.

The young pair climbed in and retook their seats in the cockpit. The Fledgling drew in her legs and glided from the cavern without being asked. She was only too happy to leave the cave, and the moon, behind. Rising up out of the forest she banked away from the hills and the direction of Jade's village, picking up speed and altitude until she was a green glimmer in the sky.

The young elf stared out in amazement as they exchanged the atmosphere of his moon for the starscape beyond. It first came into brilliant focus before it began to blur by. "How fast is she going?" he asked.

Amberle looked through the eyes of the Fledgling and smiled. "I don't know if there is any measurement to quantify it, not in human or elfin terms anyway. But I do know that it has to do with her folding space, the way she folds time."

The silence that followed gave her a moment to reflect back on being pressed against the elf only minutes ago in the cavern. And her reaction to it. She could still feel the warmth that had spread through her body, and the places that still smoldered.

A blush crept into her dusky cheeks.

The young woman turned her face to examine the profile of the young elf - the pointed ears, the high cheekbones. The starlight seemed to infuse his green eyes, almost making them glow. The wonder in them made him seem even younger.

"You're thirty?" Amberle asked. She had gleaned almost everything about him from the Galactic Web, via Verdana. But now that she had a chance to sit back and look at him, she found it hard to believe. Though she was almost twenty, thirty seemed so old. At least to a human girl.

"Yeah," he said, his seat moving with him as he turned to face her, a smile breaking across his face. He said it with so much pride that she chuffed softly, clapping a hand to her mouth.

"And that is what?" she asked, brows raised. "Thirteen to a human?"

The smile left his face but stayed in his upturned eyes. "That's a rude supposition," he reprimanded, "Miss Nineteen-Old-And-Wise, which is not very old for a human either." Amberle laughed aloud this time as his green eyes narrowed in suspicion. "Which begs the question of why would anyone send out someone as young as you are? And how is it that you know how old I am?" he asked. "And how did you know where to find me and how..." his eyes widened before he continued, his voice suddenly lower - his tone both of discovery and accusation, "you're a trafficker."

Amberle's smile disappeared. "Now *that* is a rude supposition."

"But it's true, isn't it? You're a disseminator. An information trafficker."

"I'm an exclusive research analyst."

The young elf laughed. "You can't be serious!"

Amberle turned away, her seat turning with her as she crossed her arms over her chest and looked out into the dark of space. She jumped when she felt the elf put his hand on her knee and her face snapped towards his. She saw that his eyes, normally dancing with mischief, were solemn.

"I'm sorry," he said.

"For what?"

"I just realized what you meant, about people not trusting you. Judging you because of your age, and I just did the same. I'm sorry."

Amberle was suddenly flustered. By both his apology and the feel of his hand on her leg. He gave it a squeeze and then sat back.

"Maybe now would be a good time for you to tell me what this is all about. Can you tell me what we are going to be doing? Why you needed to come find me?"

Amberle was finding the trip back to the Last Castle much the same as the voyage to get Jade, minus the strangle ripple effect which she guessed was the result of traveling through time. They were already back to her time, something that made her worries over Jade's mother resurface. But she knew they had a few minutes. They still had a galaxy to cross.

Amberle did not feel any hesitation in trusting him. She

suddenly thought of how he had pulled her to safety in the cave, and shielded her body with his own. She felt herself warm at the memory, but this time the heat surrounded her heart.

"You said you know of GwenSeven," she ventured, affirming what he had told her earlier, and he nodded. "And you know that it is owned and run by the de Rossi sisters?" Again he nodded. Amberle gave him a nod in return and continued. "Faith de Rossi is looking for her sister, Hope, who disappeared. I need Verdana to get to her, and Verdana's only condition was for me to get you."

"Wow," he said, trying to feign disappointment but unable to with a grin splitting his boyish face. "I hope I can live up to such heroic expectations as a trophy."

Amberle gave him a ghost of a smile. "She loves you, Jade."

The elf, for the first time in his life, found himself at a loss for words. After a moment of silence, he stretched out a leg and gently kicked her foot. Her smile widened and she playfully kicked him back.

His mother had been so happy, she thought. *Was there a twinge of melancholy in her voice? Maybe. But grief? The horrible sorrow that should have been tearing her apart? Not a trace.*

"Look," she said, jerking her chin towards the windows. "We're slowing down."

"How can you tell?"

"Everything is coming back into focus."

Jade frowned at the stars and realized she was right.

Seconds later, they were bursting into the atmosphere over the Distant Shore and headed for the Last Castle of Charity de Rossi.

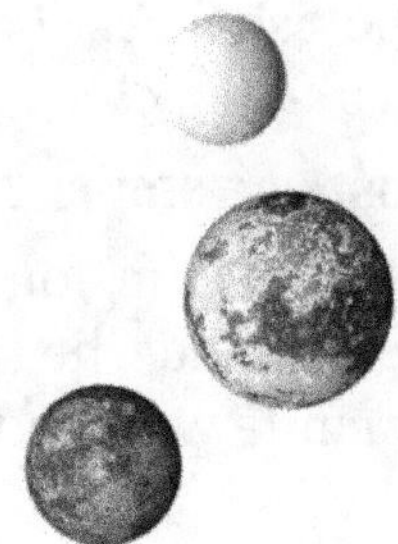

ONE FIVE

Amberle announced their arrival to de Rossi security and Verdana flew them over the watery moon of the Distant Shore. Jade stared, his green eyes wide as he caught a glimpse of the castle itself – its black towers thrust towards the sky – before they dove for the waters and the hangar hidden beneath the fortress.

The young woman's mind finally let go of thoughts of Jade for a moment as they were engulfed by darkness. The expression on her dusky face hardened as she considered the situations she had found herself in while employed by the ersatz Faith de Rossi.

Dangerous situations. Life-threatening kind of dangerous.

Verdana turned and landed.

They were being awaited by the same party that had seen Amberle off - the de Rossi sisters, the dark-haired construct, and the extraordinarily tall Engineer with the ginger-colored beard.

Most of them were even dressed the same, or very similar to, the last time she had seen them. Faith was in a suit of white with gold chains hanging from her neck and ears. The construct wore a tight-fitting shirt, pants that were slightly more loose, and military boots. The lanky Engineer was once again, or still, in pale mechanic-style coveralls. Charity was the only one markedly different, wearing a cocktail dress of silver and green that covered only her breasts, barely, and the area between her upper thigh and hips, barely.

Even the droids were there, though Amberle could not tell if they were the same ones, setting up a table with flatware and plates of food. The two adventurers disembarked the Fledgling and Amberle made the introductions. Faith greeted them with warm welcomes but the young woman cut her off, trying her best not to be rude but knowing no other way to be direct.

"I need a gun."

Faith froze, unblinking, her hands clasped tight. "Excuse me?'

"I need a gun," Amberle repeated. "I'm not backing away from this contract, but it has become more dangerous with each step I take. My life seems to be in jeopardy at every turn for this assignment, and it gets worse every time. I don't want more money, or more software - but I want a gun."

Faith began to shake her head but the dark-haired construct gave her a nod. "I'll take care of it," he assured. Faith gave him a sharp glance but said nothing.

"What happened?" Charity asked before taking a drink from a glass that was as long as her arm, filled with sparkling purple liquid.

"There are Golgoths on Erebos," Amberle told her.

"Golgoths," Faith asserted. "Like last time, on the other moon. You are sure?"

Amberle sighed through her nose and lifted her chin, realizing she did not have to turn towards Verdana or even ask. She held out an arm, palm up, and the Fledgling responded without the need for words.

In the midst of those gathered, young Dragon projected a life-size holographic image of the aliens that had gathered before her. The tall Engineer, though he was closest in height to the creatures, jumped back.

"Jesus!" he shouted, clearly shaken by the projections.

"Do they look like they could be anything else?" Amberle

queried.

"Nope," Charity acquiesced between sips from her glass, unperturbed. "Those are definitely Golgoths."

The handsome construct, who had stepped in front of Faith, fixed his dark hazel eyes on Amberle and gave her another nod.

"But that's all the way out in the Outer Banks!" Faith exclaimed. "They shouldn't be there, not in that system!" She blinked and sighed and continued. "But then again, they shouldn't be here in the Jovian system either. Especially on an IGC owned moon."

"And at the same time," Charity noted aloud. "Is that just by accident?"

"There are no accidents," Jade told her.

Charity returned his somber expression and sipped her drink.

"Please," Faith implored as she gathered her thoughts, "have something to eat while I make some calls."

She moved away quickly and Amberle glanced meaningfully at Jade as if to assure him that she had made the right decision. He looked back at her. More than just satisfied, he placed his hand over his heart as he stared into her eyes, showing he was in her debt. Amberle's dark face blushed and turned away.

Seeing the places being set for them by the droids, she jerked her chin towards them and headed away, the elf on her heels.

"Thanks," Jade said as they sat down at the small table, facing each other. "For not wasting any time on that."

"What can I say?" Amberle asked. "I'm wise beyond my years."

Jade laughed as he sat down and gave her a kick under the table. Amberle kicked him back and loaded her plate with mashed potatoes and dumped a ladle full of gravied meat over them.

Charity disappeared back into the castle while the tall Engineer slowly circled the Fledgling for a quick inspection. The handsome construct stood apart from everyone, arms crossed over his chest, keeping watch everywhere at once.

Faith returned to the hangar after only three calls, the only ones she really needed to make, and saw the young pair eating dinner. Watching them, she was filled with a feeling of compunction and dismay.

Jade was covering his mouth, which was full of food as he laughed, and delivering a kick to Amberle under the table. Amberle laughed and threw a slice of cooked squash at the elf as she playfully kicked him back.

They're children, she thought. *Practically babies.* Faith herself was over three hundred years old and, for her race, not even middle-aged.

She knew Jade was thirty years old, which was barely an adult by elfin standards. She was not sure of Amberle's exact age because there was no record of her birth that she could find, but knew it could not be more than twenty human years.

What am I doing? she asked herself, wavering for only a moment before she answered herself - and quite firmly - *I'm doing exactly what Faith de Rossi would do.*

She lifted a glass of champagne from the tray of the butler droid as it floated by and took a large and rather unladylike gulp.

Faith watched them joke and laugh as they ate - like a couple of kids on their first date. She felt another stab of guilt and quashed it immediately.

"Are you going to let them get a night's worth of sleep?" a voice asked from behind her. She did not need to turn to know to whom the voice belonged. Nonetheless, Jasyn stepped forward and into her peripheral vision and took a sip of dark liquid from a short glass he had also taken from the floating droid, his eyes also on the young pair enjoying their dinner.

"It's the least I can do," Faith answered, taking a drink from her own glass – a more ladylike sip this time. Jasyn snorted softly and she ignored him.

When dinner was done, Faith approached the table, a second glass of champagne in her hand.

"We have rooms prepared for you upstairs," she told the young pair. "You are, of course, welcome to rest for as long as you need."

"That's okay," Amberle assured her. "I'd rather stay with Verdana." She looked at Jade who agreed with a bob of his head. "And a bit of sleep will be fine. We can get underway in the morning."

Faith acquiesced with a nod. "I'll send the droids down with blankets and pillows."

The young programmer stood, smiling. "Thanks, but everything we need is already in there."

"Very well. I'll make sure breakfast is ready for you in the morning and the Fledgling is restocked."

Amberle laughed softly. "I didn't know it was stocked now. But I never had time to check. It's been a busy day."

Faith smiled. "It has," she agreed. She gave the young woman another nod and one to the elf before turning and heading for the lift that would take her back up into the castle. The black-haired construct followed her silently as Jade followed the girl towards the Fledgling.

"You can have the bed," the young woman told the elf as they boarded Verdana. She tried not to sound overly uncomfortable but her thoughts were besieged with the idea of lying close to him as they slept. "I'm fine sleeping up front."

Jade shrugged and climbed onto the raised mattress in the aft end of the Fledgling, deciding beyond a doubt that it had been the most exciting day of his life. Something inside told him that it was just the beginning. He laced his hands beneath his head and closed his eyes, trying not to think of the young woman sharing the close space with him.

Amberle sat herself in the pilot's seat and placed her hand firmly onto the armrest. Silver tendrils snaked out of arm of the chair and slipped over, under, and between the young woman's fingers, forming a mesh glove. Amberle smiled and jacked into the Galactic Web.

Sleep, Verdana urged.

I will, Amberle assured as she felt the seat beneath her recline. She thought back over the day, almost unable to believe how many things had happened. *Was I really sleeping here, in this same spot, only twenty-four hours ago?* she wondered. *Was it only just this morning that I left to find Jade?* It seemed incomprehensible that so much could happen in so short of time.

Thinking about it made her realize just how tired she was. Still, she started a search for trending holos as something else occurred to her, but she was getting sleepier by the second.

Are you doing that? she asked as her eyes drooped.

There was no answer, just a feeling of satisfaction as the young woman's eyes closed altogether.

The Fledgling Dragon reshaped the seat into a bed and wove a silver blanket over the sleeping form of the Fledgling human. Protecting her two passengers in a soft emerald glow, she rested fitfully as well.

⋈

In the morning, Amberle and Jade awoke to find a breakfast laid out on the table in the hangar. The two said little to each other but ate quickly, hurried by their excitement more than the by the press for time.

Amberle was decidedly distracted, thinking about Jade's

mother.

She's not devastated because it's not just been over a hundred years since she lost her husband, but a hundred years since her son disappeared as well.

The realization made her whole body go still and she jumped when Jade spoke to her.

"You seem nervous," he remarked, then chuckled when her body jerked at the sound of his voice. "Jumpy, even."

Amberle almost replied with a scathing remark, thinking for a moment he might be making fun of her. His voice was soft but there was a sparkle in his pale green eyes that held nothing but kindness. She gave him a lopsided smile.

"Jumpy? That's a laugh. I'm always like this," she told him, "though I'm getting better. You should have seen me a month ago."

The young programmer wasn't nervous, but her thoughts certainly had her on edge. She wiped her mouth with a napkin and rose from her seat. Jade did the same and together they made the short walk back to the Fledgling Dragon where the de Rossi sisters waited along with the dark-eyed construct. There was no sign of the lanky Engineer.

Faith stood before them in an impeccable cream-colored suit edged with gold, her hands clasped in front of her body. The skirt of her suit was short, exposing long, pale legs. She wore golden shoes with high heels, and a heavy gold chain necklace. There were hectic patches of color on her face and her eyes were red from lack of sleep.

"Bring back my sister," she commanded, "or any trace of her."

The young woman and the young elf both dipped their heads in solemn acquiescence. Charity de Rossi was possibly in the same attire as the night before but it was hard to tell as she was covered with a silver robe. One that covered very little of her. She had a drink in her jeweled hand, though it was still not even eight on the clock, and she raised it in salutation.

"Good luck finding her," she said with a smile that showcased perfect teeth behind her red lips. "And even more luck if you do."

The young adventurers gave her uneasy smiles in return.

But it was the devastatingly handsome black-haired construct that surprised Amberle the most when he approached and put his arms around her.

The young woman froze, not just from his touch - which she was learning to bear without panic yet still did not like - but from the fact that he was fastening a belt around her waist. He cinched it and pushed it down to her hips. Then he held up a gun, its wide muzzle pointed at the ground, and turned his eyes to where he held the grip. Amberle followed his gaze and saw that his thumb was on a small lever.

"This on safe," he instructed. "It's a double safety. You have to press it in before you push it down. Also, it's a photon pistol, not laser, so your aim doesn't have to be exact. Just point and shoot."

Amberle stared at him, amazed. "How did you know I can't..."

The construct shook his head quickly to silence her as he leaned close and slipped the weapon into the holster that hung from the leather strap.

"Don't trust anyone," he advised softly in her ear before he pulled away and took a step back.

Amberle's shoulders sagged. "But I was just starting to trust people!" she hissed at him with a frown.

Jasyn shrugged apologetically as he smiled at her. "Life is all about knowing who deserves that trust, and who does not."

His dark eyes gleamed while, at his side, Faith stood as still as a statue, her lips pressed together into a tight line.

"Good luck and Godspeed," Charity bade them, raising her

drink in salute once again.

Amberle and Jade glanced at each other and then boarded the Fledgling without another word until they were seated.

Verdana snaked safety webbing over both of them.

"Wow," Jade finally whispered. "That felt pretty tense. Or intense. I'm not sure."

"Both," Amberle agreed as Verdana lifted off the tarmac, tucked in her legs, and dipped out of the hidden cave and into the bright light over the crashing waters of the Distant Shore.

"Any idea what's going on with them?" Jade asked.

"With Faith and her construct?"

"That guy is a construct?"

"Yes. You couldn't tell?"

"I haven't seen very many of them. Not in real life."

Amberle snorted. "Have you seen *any*?"

"On my Podunk moon?" Jade pressed, defensive.

"Calm down. I wasn't laughing at you. That phrase, *in real life*. I thought that was funny. But to answer your question – no, I don't know what's going on with them. And I don't think I want to."

"Fair enough," the elf acquiesced with a shrug and a smile. He rubbed his hands vigorously over his thighs in anticipation. "What's the distance from Jupiter to Venus?" he asked.

With smooth and uncanny speed, the Fledgling had taken them up and out of the artificial atmosphere that surrounded Charity de Rossi's private moon. Verdana floated gracefully through the dark of space, the great gas giant of Jupiter looming at their side.

A hologram appeared above the smooth silver dash console. It showed both Jupiter and Venus, along with strings of numbers between them.

"Do you want miles, kilometers, light years, astronomical

units, or what?" Amberle asked.

Jade laughed. "I guess I was just wondering how long it would take us to get there."

Amberle smiled. "We are about to find out. Verdana?" she queried, looking at the hologram of the planet of swirling golden gas.

Without another word, the Fledgling tipped slightly - seeming to slide a bit to port - and then straightened before she shot off into the open sea of space. The distant stars around them distorted and then disappeared altogether.

Amberle lifted her hand and pointed a slim dark finger at the set of numbers that represented kilometers. The largest number, which had started at close to seven hundred million, was decreasing with blurring speed.

The girl pulled what remained of the tracking device Faith had given her from the small bag of personal items she carried. Amberle had made some adjustments, which included taking out most of the wiring and finding the program chip. She had transferred the program to a modern t-chip and retrofitted what was left into a micro acrylic. It was now much smaller, about the size and shape of a spades poker card made of black glass, but faster and more accurate.

Jade leaned across the space between their seats to take a peek and his green eyes grew wide. The green blip on the screen that indicated them, and the Fledgling, was zooming towards the slowly pulsing red light. It was the only indication of their speed which the elf now realized was even faster than he had imagined.

"Dragons are even more mind-blowing," Amberle said, seeing the look of astonishment on his face.

Though the Fledgling could not yet travel with the near instantaneous velocity of a full-grown Dragon, it did not dawdle. Still faster than any ship that could be made by man or elf, or any other known species of the universe, it traversed the

Solar System with ease.

Neither young woman or young elf spoked as they traveled within the grip of space, awed by the means with which they journeyed.

It was not as far as Amberle had traveled to find Jade, and not just because she had to cross a century to get him. It seemed to her that crossing from her own galaxy to his took much longer than going from her time to his, or back again.

So when it came to the Solar System, going to other planets – in a Dragon - was like visiting a neighbor.

Within minutes they were almost to their far-flung destination.

Jade looked up and the view outside the eyes of the Fledgling came abruptly into focus as they slowed to a near stop. Stars winked into view, crisp and bright against the black beyond. The main star of the system, the sun, glowered in the distance. But what dominated the view was now Venus herself. Not the beautiful planet named by the Earthlings as they saw her in the sky thousands of years ago.

Not at this distance.

Close-up, she looked malevolent and baleful. Cloaked in swirling, poisonous gases with a crushing gravity that lurked beneath. The atmosphere of sulfuric acid eddied and churned below them by winds whipping well over two hundred miles per hour.

Though the temperature in the Fledgling had not raised by even a single degree, Jade knew that what he was looking at was hotter than the fires of Hell.

Not a beauty but a Siren, to lure men to their deaths.

"We're supposed to go in there?" he asked.

"Yep," Amberle answered. She did not share Jade's trepidation because she could feel nothing from Verdana except for a confident pleasure in the ease of the voyage from the

Jovian System. She glanced at the tracker and then lowered it till it rested on her knee. They were definitely in the right spot, or close to it. But first, she wanted to take a look around. "Take us in," she said softly.

Jade swallowed but did not protest. He flicked his brown hair away from his face and watched as the Fledgling descended into the murky yellow atmosphere. The clouds swam past, swirling as if watching them. All around, lightning flashed.

"Did Faith say anything about the elves leaving traps, or any kind of magical protection around the planet?"

Amberle tipped her head of pinkish curls and looked him, her hazel eyes bright and curious. "No. Why?"

Jade shrugged. "They wanted to be gone. They wanted to cover their tracks and not be found. It stands to reason that they might want to protect it as well."

Amberle nodded. "We're safe in here," she assured him, throwing him a glance and noting his pale face. "Are you okay?" she asked.

"Yeah," he replied, still staring out the glass. "It just makes me nervous."

"Really?" Amberle asked, turning her eyes back to the windows and the dark gold swirls of mist outside flaring constantly with forks of lightning. "I think it's fascinating. But I don't want you to be uncomfortable. Verdana?"

The Fledgling responded before the girl could voice the command, dropping down through miles and miles of atmosphere in a few short seconds.

"Wait!" Amberle exclaimed as they broke through to see what lay below. The Fledgling paused, hovering under the bank of yellow gas.

Beneath the poisonous blanket of fumes miles deep was another world.

It looked as if it were encased in a glass bubble, but Amberle knew it was just where the atmosphere changed from noxious carbon dioxide to nitrogen rich oxygen. Under the curve of a clear blue sky was a world of ice and water and, far away, where the planet curved - land.

"Look," Amberle said. "It's spinning."

Jade nodded. "Just like the Earth does. Though, with the sun at our backs, it's going in the opposite direction." Though the world was indeed turning, its great size made the movement look slow and ponderous, yet graceful - like some great beast of the sea migrating to warmer waters.

"It looks slow," Amberle said, "but only because of its size. It's going fast enough to generate its own gravity, but likely perfectly timed to keep the days between twenty-four and twenty-six hours long. Perfect for a human, or an elf, to keep a circadian rhythm."

Jade gave her a sidelong glance, his green eyes bright as he smiled. "Are you sure you're not a construct?"

Amberle chuffed a soft laugh. "You know, you're not the first person to ask me that. And I'll ask you the same thing I asked him - how does one know if they are real or not?"

"Love," Jade answered without hesitation.

Amberle's feathery brows went up in her dark face. "So, you're saying that if a construct feels love, then they are real?"

Jade shrugged. "If love is not what sets us apart, what does?"

Amberle laughed. "I don't know. But you certainly better figure it out. You are the one who is going to be fighting them. Right, Verdana?"

Hmmm?

It was not a reply of surprise, as if the Fledgling had not been paying attention. It was a feeling of genuine puzzlement. It gave Amberle a terrible jolt, and she froze as something occurred to her - for the second time. She had the same thought last night, but she was too sleepy then to ask. It was along similar lines that had been bothering her about Jade's mother.

You don't talk to Jade like you talk to me, do you?

Why would I?

The young woman looked at the young elf but he, of course, had missed the exchange.

"Look," he said, pointing at the globe as it rolled slowly beneath them.

As they watched, the small bit of land they had first spied slipped away over the curved horizon.

"Take us down, V," she whispered.

The Fledgling dove gently, slicing through the invisible barrier without causing so much as a wrinkle. The young elf and young woman stared at the upcoming planet, this one breathtaking in its beauty, as they dipped down through the clean, clear air towards a world of white.

Verdana took them down and down and down, waiting for the girl to let her know when to stop. When Amberle did not offer up what she desired, the Fledgling probed her feelings and leveled off at thirty thousand feet above the surface.

For a long time there was nothing but glaciers, great mountains of white and blue, still and frozen - too cold for even the hardiest of trees. As they flew on, they could see slopes of snow abraded by seracs reaching skyward and cut with crevasses so deep they appeared bottomless.

After twenty minutes of flying over the frozen continent, Amberle and Jade finally got a peek of brown, and then green, on the horizon. Long before they reached the obviously warmer land, they crossed mountains that began to show some rock, along with scrub trees that had been brutalized but somehow survived the cold.

They crossed a river that was wide and wild, icebergs colliding and grinding together as they were tossed by the furious current. Peering out the left eye of the Fledgling, they watched as a great chunk of ice calved away from the glacier. With a colossal splash it hit the river, forming a tidal-sized wave and sent another huge berg slowly bobbing across the tributary.

"The world is warming," Amberle murmured.

"Mmhmm," Jade agreed. "Though it's protected by that atmospheric field, what light and warmth do get in from the refocused sunlight is producing a greenhouse effect."

They came to a ridge of snow-choked mountains that stretched across the horizon. The peaks were so high that Verdana had to gain altitude to clear the summits.

Amberle gave Jade a sidelong glance from the corner of her eye and the elf shook his head, his lips pressed into a line.

"Don't say it," he cautioned, but she could hear the light-spirited tone under his warning. "I can see how big these mountains are. The ones on my moon are still mountains, they're just smaller."

Amberle kept her eyes front and her own lips pressed together to restrain her smile. Jade gave her a gentle kick in the foot and she used the toe of her boot to give him one in return.

At long last, the snowy mountains dropped away and gave way to fields and forests and more mountains to their right. Though life was obviously more abundant and thriving, they saw no signs of people.

Jade was about to ask sarcastically if she was planning on doing an aerial search of the entire planet, which could take forever - even in a Fledgling - when Amberle seemed to remember the small pane of glass she had lowered to her knee.

She lifted the transmitter and eyed the red blip. It had gotten much brighter after they had entered the atmosphere. They were closer, very close by the look of it, but her thoughts mirrored Jade's - it would take forever just flying and looking.

Amberle debated whether she should ask Verdana for a keypad or just speak the coordinates aloud. On impulse, she simply placed the dark rectangle on the smooth silver skin of the dash. It dropped forcefully at the last second, sucked down as if it were magnetic. She thought silver tendrils might slip out to wrap the device, or that it might be swallowed whole by the console, but it just sat there - securely fastened.

The young woman could feel an expectant anticipation coming from the young Dragon and knew she was awaiting her command.

Amberle looked at the blip. "Take us there, V."

Though the two inside could feel no discernable movement, the world outside disappeared in a blur. It reappeared a second later, bursting out over what looked like Hell.

# ONE SIX

The young elf and the young woman had come upon the sunrise as it slid over a range of mountains, pouring the gentle light of dawn over a broad meadow that had become a killing field. Blood soaked bare earth and trampled grass. Bodies lay everywhere - broken, unmoving and stiff, rooted in their death throes - eyes staring and mouths open in screams that had been forever silenced.

Strung out on the fringes and at the rear of the battlefield were so many bodies that the corpses lay in heaps. Carrion birds circled and swept down to alight on faces, pecking at eyes and lips.

In the midst of the fray, blood still sprayed and men screamed their last.

Amberle's body jerked back at the horror of it all, then it was all gone in a blur. She craned her neck, her forehead pressed against the glass, trying to look behind.

"Back," she commanded. "Take us back around."

The Fledgling banked, circling around for another fly over the battle that had come to a sudden stop. She slowed considerably, letting her passengers take it all in.

The young pair gaped at the sight, mouths hanging open.

Jade could see elves and humans, crouching and staring at what had burst into the air above them. Fighting the small band of survivors were the most hideous beasts Jade had ever seen outside of a holo movie, though most had turned tail and were now running pell-mell in all directions.

They were of epic proportions to the young elf, being over twice as tall as he was. Indeed, most of the creatures were over eight feet tall - with giant heads, Cyclopean jaws, and mammoth sized bodies. Massive slabs of arms and prodigious bellies sloped down to trunk-like legs that topped huge, bare, nasty feet.

They were clothed primarily in dirt and grime, though the most private of their parts were cloaked with animal skins that had been crudely fashioned into clothing that looked as mangy as the creatures wearing them.

Jade's green eyes quickly discerned what was happening.

He knew not why and did not care. It had nothing to do with race. All he knew was that a smaller and weaker force was being pulverized by an army of brutes.

"There!" he commanded, pointing to the line of battle where the combatants had backed away from each other as the sky was torn asunder. "Put us down right there!"

Verdana paused for half a second, unsure of who should be giving her orders, and then complied. She, too, could see they had come upon a losing battle. And it seemed for all the worlds like the wrong side was losing.

She pushed out her legs as she came to the bloodied, blackened ground and landed with a roar. She parted her jaws to drop a splash of green Dragonfire in their midst to help speed the monsters on their way.

It worked.

The brutish creatures ran screaming in all directions save for towards the line still held by the small band of humans and elves. Upon closer look, there were other races too. Jade spied a group of wild looking elves that could be nothing but Sprites. There was also a sprinkling of giant men that Jade could not place. There were others, ones who looked like humans, but Jade knew were not.

Despite the dirt and the wounds, they were too perfect to be human.

"Those are constructs, aren't they?"

Amberle's eyes flicked over a number of those still standing and nodded.

From inside the Fledgling, the elf and the young woman surveyed the bleak scene. With the foe suddenly gone, people were helping each other up, dusting each other off. No one seemed terrified of the young Dragon in their midst. A few elves were smiling up at them. Yet there were no cries of victory, no elation on the faces outside. Only exhaustion.

Jade and Amberle had both seen quite a few pictures of Hope, even a few recordings from family holos that Faith had shown them. Even filthy, she would have stood out in the crowd.

No one outside sported the wild, copper colored hair and bright green eyes of the youngest de Rossi sister.

Bloodied and bedraggled, the band of fighters coalesced into a tighter group and waited. They were armed with swords, knives, and spears. A few had bows slung over their backs.

"Well!" Jade exclaimed cheerfully. "Who goes out? You? Me? Both of us?"

Amberle opened her mouth to say they both should go when Verdana spoke inside her head.

Though the Fledgling had driven away most of the foul creatures, the air was ripe with the smell of blood. Of death. And the ones waiting outside held weapons.

Stay, she commanded. *Send the boy.*

Amberle's green and brown eyes widened slightly in surprise. *The boy? You mean Jade?*

Jade? Verdana queried and then paused as if considering, or confused. It was not for long, but long enough to make Amberle's feathery brows draw together in consternation. *Yes*, Verdana agreed. *Jade. Send Jade.*

The young woman turned her eyes to the elf, trying to mask the concern she felt.

"Why don't you go first?" she suggested. "You're dressed a lot more like them. And maybe they'll be less freaked out if we come out one at a time."

Jade's green eyes sparkled with mirth. "If seeing a Fledgling Dragon land right in front of them doesn't freak them out, I think they'll be fine. But I'll go first."

The young elf rose eagerly and headed aft, pausing before he reached the galley. "What do I...never mind!" he chirped as the side of the Fledgling seemingly melted open and a slender set of stairs formed on the outside.

Amberle watched him disappear through the newly made door and then turned back to look through the eyes of the Fledgling. She saw him approach the group and address them in his usual cheerful manner.

At first nothing happened. No one moved.

Then a woman stepped forward. She was young, though not as young as Amberle, with hair as red as blood that had bound in a single braid. She was dressed all in black and strapped with bladed weapons.

I wish I could hear what ... Amberle started thinking when, suddenly, she could.

"I am Hope's daughter," the woman said, her voice allowed in and slightly amplified by the Fledgling.

Amberle glanced down at the tracker and saw that they were right on top of the red indicator light. She gave her head a quick shake, hardly able to believe she sent Jade out by himself.

Out into a group of armed people that were obviously well trained in battle. Jade was armed with nothing but his smile and his unflagging optimism.

Without another thought and disgusted with herself, the young programmer left her own chair and headed aft. As she reached the doorway she had the sudden idea that Verdana might close it, and not let her out. She had the distinct feeling that the Fledgling was trying to protect her.

A warming pulse confirmed her thoughts, but the door remained open.

Amberle stuck her head out into the bright morning sunshine. Every face on the ground turned up to look at her, making the young woman want to yank her head back inside. Instead, she took a deep breath, forced a small smile, and turned so she go down the stairs the same way Jade had.

She reached the ground and turned to look at everyone. There were small elves and tall ones, along with humans - a few of which were the biggest and tallest ones she had ever seen. Tall as Nathan, Faith's Engineer, but broad shouldered and thick with muscle. Every warrior, from big to small, was cut and bruised and dirty. They were on the brink of collapse, even though it was early morning.

Amberle looked at the woman who had stepped forward. Her eyes looked like multi-colored jewels and even her slight movements marked her with a lethal grace. She looked older up close, but it also could have been the etchings of exhaustion and sorrow that lined her face.

An elf with ears poking out of sand-colored hair stood close on her right side. One of the extraordinarily tall humans stood behind her.

"I'm Amberle," she said, introducing herself.

"Ember L'chiross," the female warrior answered.

"Is your mother here?" Amberle asked, feeling like an idiot. It was a question someone would ask a child. But Hope had to be near, very near, for the tracker to have pinpointed the location.

Ember shook her head. "I haven't seen my mother since I was very small."

Amberle frowned in consternation for a moment and then

her face softened with understanding. "Then you must have her rings," she said, the words coming out in a quiet rush of breath..

The redheaded warrior stood perfectly still for a second, then dug the fingers of her free hand under her sword belt and retrieved a small leather pouch. She passed her sword to the elf by her side. She worked the pouch open and pulled free a rawhide lace that had been tied at the ends to make a necklace. Threaded onto it, were two rings. The bands of the rings had markings that were tribal in appearance, and each was topped with a ruby that gave off a barely perceptible glow.

"They glow brighter," Ember informed her, "if I put them on."

"Were there always just two?"

Ember nodded. "My father wore his, on this, around his neck. I took it when he died, and added mine."

Amberle sighed through her nose. "Your mother must have the third. She probably divided them up so she could find you again."

The woman in black swallowed. "Is she dead?"

"I don't know," Amberle replied softly. "I was hoping you could tell me." She watched as the sharp-eyed fighter weighed her words and then returned the rings to their pouch and the pouch to her belt. "But," she continued, "your family has been looking for you. For a long time. They would like you to return home. And find your mother as well."

The elf returned the sword to the warrior. She switched it to her left hand and used her right one to grasp his. A glimmer of a smile surfaced on his face, though Jade noted the stiffness of his body and could see the clench of his jaw. A tall, red-bearded human with icy blue eyes took a step closer to the black-clad fighter and laid a hand on her shoulder. Jade could see her throat bob as worked to swallow.

"My family is here," she said, her voice firm. "This is my

home."

Now, Jade saw the smile reach the eyes of the elf that grasped the warrior's hand. His chest swelled and that smile seemed to run through his whole body. The man standing behind her made no effort to contain his grin as he gave her shoulder a squeeze.

Amberle, however, deflated like a balloon. Hope was not here. Her daughter did not want to return. Faith was going to be less than pleased.

She was getting a really strange feeling about Verdana. She was grappling with her own feelings about Jade.

Th young programmer felt a powerful urge to get back into the Fledgling and jack in. Disappear into the Web, even if it was only for a few hours.

Responsibility is a heavy burden she remembered. But what could she do? Take charge? Force Hope's daughter to come back with them?

It was certainly an option - the small crowd was armed, but with swords. Amberle had a photon pistol, and a *Fledgling* for the love of Pete.

The eyes of the bloodied warrior glimmered and her lips thinned in a smile, as if reading her thoughts, and Amberle knew that even with technology and firepower on her side - she was no match for the woman in front of her.

Ember's eyes, green and brown like Amberle's but also flecked with gold, flicked up to the Fledgling.

"My father spoke to me of Dragons when I was young, but I thought they were just children's stories. I had no idea they were real, or that you could actually ride inside one." Her eyes went back to Amberle. "Maybe someday I will, but not today."

A tall elf with white hair cleared his throat, drawing everyone's attention. "And as you have now ascertained," he announced, "we have kept our existence here hidden for a century. We wish to keep it that way."

Jade gave the older elf a disarming smile. "Your secret is safe with us," he assured him.

Amberle was still at a loss for words, for action.

Ember let go of the elf's hand she was holding and stepped away from the giant man behind her so that she stood alone before Amberle, her face somber. "You really did save us today," she said. "All of us. It is something I will never forget." She held out a hand that was still sticky with drying blood but Amberle did not hesitate to grasp it with her own. The warrior's expression was lifted by a smirking smile. "And just because I'm in no position to leave now, does not mean I won't be looking for that adventure later." She let go of the young woman's hand and stepped back, giving her a wink. "And now, you know where to find me."

Amberle returned the smile as best she could and looked to Jade who was grinning from one pointed ear to the other. His eyes glanced at her hand then back to her face. Amberle looked down to see an emerald glow swirl around her arm and then disappear, along with any trace of blood.

"Magic and miracles," Ember murmured in wonder.

"Thank you again," said the tall elf by her side, speaking for the first time.

"I wish there was something else we could do," Jade offered.

"There is," advised the giant of a man with icy blue eyes that loomed behind the black-clad warrior. "On your way out, make sure those bastards aren't coming back," he said, jerking his chin in the direction the brutish creatures had run.

"Will do," Jade agreed, still grinning. "Amberle?" he asked, raising an arched brow at her. The young programmer blew out a great breath through puffed cheeks.

"Yeah," she said. "Yeah. We can do that." She looked back at the battle-grimed woman in front of her.

"Until next time," Ember told her.

"Until next time," Amberle echoed.

More elves were starting to drift out of the forest along with woodland sounds that were returning now that the battle was done. Somewhere close, a nightingale sang.

The young woman and the young elf returned to the Fledgling and boarded her, Verdana pulling in her legs and heading in the direction held in Amberle's mind. The young woman looked out as they left and saw that the survivors were clasping hands, patting backs. Some embraced one another. Turning her eyes back front she watched in silence as the land broke into a series of cliffs and then dropped away to fields below. Amberle gasped at the sight.

It might have once been a meadow, but now was a field of carnage. Bodies were everywhere in various stages of bloat and decay. Vultures and other scavengers feasted on the remains. Amberle felt her stomach lurch even as an anger gnawed at her heart.

So much senseless killing, she thought.

"There," Jade said, pointing towards the western end of the fields. The giant creatures that had been decimating the band of humans and elves had ceased their hasty retreat and were now starting to gather in small groups. "I think they are trying to decide their next move."

"Then let's decide for them," Amberle said. "Verdana?"

The Fledgling banked and headed west.

"Let them have it," Jade commanded.

Amberle, at the edge of her senses, could feel Verdana hesitate. Waiting. Waiting for *her* command. "Do it."

The words had no sooner left her mouth than the jaws of the Fledgling dropped open, just as one of the brutes pointed, yelling a warning as he turned and tried to flee. It was too late. For all of them.

Verdana swooped down, unleashing green Dragonfire

on those that had managed to coalesce into groups. They were immediately engulfed in the flames and turned into roasting meat. A few actually exploded with the heat. The few survivors scattered, once more running for their lives, and this time they did not stop.

"Should we go after them?" Jade asked.

Amberle shook her head, curls bouncing. "I think they got the message, those that are left."

"You're right," he agreed, watching the remnants of the nasty band flee, some of them singed and smoking. "Besides," the elf added, "we don't want to start a forest fire. We have enough to worry about as it is." He turned to look at Amberle, the chair turning with him. "Like, what are we going to tell Faith?"

"I think we have one more thing to worry about," Amberle said, keeping her eyes fixed on his. Jade hoisted a brow over one those green eyes and waited.

Should we leave Jade here on this planet? she asked Verdana. *Maybe leave him to these creatures?*

She had no such intention, she only wanted to gauge the Fledgling's reaction.

The indifference was not complete, but it was close.

The elf? she asked. She gave Amberle the mental equivalent of a shoulder shrug. *What do you want to do?*

The young woman sighed. "Verdana is forgetting you," she told him.

She did not say that the use of the present tense was merely to soften the blow. She was quite sure that Verdana had already forgotten him completely. Not who he was, but who he had been to her.

Amberle could see the shoulders of the elf fold in, as if he had the wind kicked out of him. Then the right side of Jade's lips pinched together. "Balls and shit."

ONE SEVEN

Returned once again to the vacuum of space, Amberle sat facing forward, her hand encased in the silver mesh glove Verdana had woven for her out of the armrest. Her green and brown eyes flicked over the images and words that floated above the smooth silver skin of the front dash console.

Verdana had taken them up and out of the atmosphere of Venus and they now cruised away at a speed that, though it was considerable, did not blur out the stars. Earth was a distant marble of blue. Jade watched it grow, staring out into the darkness, his arms crossed over his chest.

The images above the dash faded and the silver tendrils around Amberle's hand melted back into the armrest as she turned to face him.

"It's called a temporal paradox," she told him.

"I know," he replied, his tone flat and his usual good cheer gone. "I mean, I didn't know what it was called, but it makes sense if you stop to think about it. We changed the past. If I left my time before I could go on to become the Jordan of the Green Fledgling, I never become the Jordan of the Green Fledgling. I'm nobody."

"You're not nobody," Amberle corrected.

"I am in this world - in this time. And if I really am supposed to be someone who impacts others, who impacts history, my absence will cause an uncountable number of paradoxes - one after the other!"

Amberle regarded him solemnly for a moment. He was

right. It was what Jasyn had warned them about. What the ripple effect changing the past might cause. What dug at her the most, however, was the thought of Jade's mother.

Melancholy.

Doing charity work because it was all that she had. That and the hope that her son was out there somewhere, alive.

Amberle lifted her chin, her pinkish coils of hair falling away from her face. "What do you want to do?" she asked softly.

"Seriously?" he asked, his arched brows raised high over his tilted green eyes. "I want you to take me back!"

The young woman leaned back in her chair and sighed. "That will cause a paradox of our own. If I take you back, and restore the past, then Verdana will want nothing more than to get you back."

"And you are afraid of losing control of her? Of losing your job?"

"That's a little harsh," Amberle said, scowling at him. "And no."

"Then take me back!" Jade demanded. "We didn't find Hope. You know where her daughter is, and that she doesn't want to leave!"

"Why are you so eager to get back?" Amberle asked, cocking her head.

"Because I feel that the longer I stay, the more things are going to get out of whack. I can't spend the rest of my life in limbo - a nobody, doing nothing. I need to get back. I need to find my purpose for living, and fulfill it!"

Amberle bit her bottom lip, holding back a remark that would have been more than a little harsh, something about going to his death if he returned to his time. "Then who will be the Jordan of the Green Fledgling now?" she asked instead. "Verdana shouldn't be alone. She's more vulnerable than one might think. She needs someone."

Jade's hard expression finally softened. "I think that's you," he said quietly. His green eyes looked into hers and saw what she could not see.

The young woman laughed softly. "I can't be a Jordan," she chuffed. "Jordans are trained fighters, and the most experienced pilots in the universe."

"I think all you really need," Jade countered, "is to be chosen by a Fledgling. Everything else, you can learn."

"She didn't choose me, she found me."

Jade smiled. "Kind of the same," he told her. And, when she frowned at him, "There are no accidents," he added.

That had Amberle stumped. And dazed. And intrigued.

A Jordan.

Jordan of the Green Fledgling.

Something that she never would have imagined, even in her wildest dreams.

She would never have need of software, of hardware, of implants. No outdated systems. A single hand against the Fledgling would have her jacked into the Web anytime she wanted. All of the information in the civilized galaxies, literally at her fingertips.

It was tantalizing beyond belief.

And frightening.

She had been jacked into the Web for so long when she was working on the Elba moon that it had made her sick. But perhaps Verdana could keep her safe from that.

"But what about Faith?" she argued. "What about Hope? What about the IGC and the war?"

Jade laughed and spread his hands. "That's for you to figure out. You need to live your life, in your time, and I need to live mine."

Faith would be angry, Amberle was sure of that, but she was going to be angry anyway. But what of Verdana? The young woman had a feeling the young Dragon was not going to take it well. Not at all. But maybe there was a way she could talk her into it, get her ready for it.

Amberle looked at the elf and weighed his words. She had never before thought about things like destiny and fate. Jade really believed he had a purpose. What kind of person would she be if she denied him that? And how many more paradoxes would begin to ripple if he was not returned to his time?

Besides any of it, she liked him. She trusted him. She could not make him a prisoner.

"Okay," she agreed. "I'll do it."

A grin had barely surfaced on the young elf's face when a shriek ripped through the Fledgling that they both heard. But it was Amberle who understood her words.

Jade! the Fledgling cried out. *No!*

"What's happening?" he asked, his green eyes darting around in fear as the living ship shook and shuddered. "Are we hit?" The words sounded so stupid once they left his mouth but he could not think of anything that would cause such distress to the ship.

"She knows," Amberle said, her face tight in a grimace of sympathy. "She knows you now. She remembers you."

"Just like that," Jade whispered, incredulous.

"Just like that," Amberle echoed. Another tremor shook them as another scream came from Verdana.

The elf clapped his hands over his ears. The young woman tried to send feelings of understanding and consolation to the young Dragon who was now reliving the loss of her Jordan.

The elf looked at her, ducking his head under the onslaught. "This is what you were mainly concerned about," Jade asked, "wasn't it?"

Amberle nodded and scrunched her own eyes closed as the living ship around them screamed and juddered in agony.

Shhh, shh, the young woman sent, trying to console the young Dragon. *It will be okay. Everything will be okay.*

"But to be honest," she said as the screaming faded, "I was surprised at how fast it happened. I thought it wouldn't happen until we actually took you back. I thought I would have more time to figure it out. Maybe get her used to the idea."

Jade shrugged and took his hands off his ears as the Fledgling's screams turned into sorrowful weeping, his young face full of empathy. "That's how it works."

It's okay. Everything will be alright, Amberle promised.

"How what works?" she asked aloud, her brows drawn together over her green and brown eyes.

"Reality."

Her eyebrows shot up. "What the hell are you talking about?"

Jade smiled. "You usually know so much, sometimes I forget how young you are."

"Stick it up your ass, Jade."

Jade laughed. "You spend so much time, what do you call it - jacked in? - that you have an incredible base of knowledge. But no real life lessons."

"In elf-years, you're really not that much older."

The vessel shook with its silent keening and Amberle sent out waves of comfort as best she could.

"I know more than *you* do," Jade assured her.

"The hell you do," Amberle scoffed with a lopsided smile. "You have no idea how much..."

"How much do you know that didn't come from the Web?"

Amberle blinked owlishly, her smile gone. Her mind was suddenly as blank as a slate.

Jade nodded. "That's what I thought. You might know everything that is going on, and every that has happened in the past. But you have no life lessons."

They began to pass Earth, breathtaking in its beauty. The pair stared, mesmerized.

Its moon a perfect - if cratered – globe, hung in the distance.

The Fledgling convulsed in a series of quiet sobs. Amberle opened her mouth to argue and then closed it. She reached out a hand and laid it comfortingly over the skin of the dash console.

"Sshhh," she whispered. "It's okay."

They could see Mars ahead in the distance, a red eye in a sea of darkness, as the shudders of the living ship subsided into occasional shivers.

Dragon sniffles, Amberle thought with affection. The mournful tremors continued for another minute before she heard the Fledgling inside her head.

You'll stay? Verdana asked, hesitant.

Of course, Amberle answered. *If you want me to.*

The Fledgling's only answer was a feeling of relief and gratitude so overwhelming that it brought tears to the young woman's eyes.

Was Jade right? she asked, tentative. *Do you want me to be your Jordan?* The reluctance that came from the Fledgling was unmistakable. *I mean,* Amberle sent right away, *I understand if you don't. I haven't been trained in any way.*

No, no, Verdana sent back. *It's not that. It's...* she halted, trying to find the human words. Then she paused again, afraid to say them. *I...need a boy. I wanted Jade...*

The words were as puzzling as they were shy, which made them more puzzling. A feeling of discomfort, of *embarrassment* came from the young female Dragon, but she said no more.

Amberle frowned until the understanding dawned inside

her and her eyes became as round as saucers in her dusky face.

You mean...? Amberle stammered mentally. *You need...?*

She felt the skin of her cheeks and neck warm and knew that, through her, the Fledgling was blushing.

Not now, Verdana replied. The young Dragon knew it was too soon, that it was not even possible until the future. Far in the future. The images and feelings passed to the young woman. *But someday. It was why I chose him.*

There was feeling of love and loss and, yes - of destiny - so strong that Amberle became aware that her body was thrumming like a tuning fork. Her skin tingled, so much so in her fingers and her lips that they trembled.

I don't even know how it happens, Verdana told her.

Well, I know how it happens for humans - and elves.

It's not the same for us. It has something to do with the Captain's body.

The Captain? But Jade's not...

I know. It is supposed to be later, much later, for the both us.

That's why you wanted his body.

Yes.

Do you know what to do with it?

No.

The last was delivered with another flood of embarrassment and something close to despair.

The young woman's eyes shifted so she could see the elf in her peripheral vision. She could see his profile - slim face, strong jaw, dark hair hanging over his jade-green eyes. She swallowed and shifted her gaze back to look through Verdana's eyes. They were passing Mars and its lumpy moons.

Maybe...maybe I can think of something.

But what she was thinking of was being pressed close against Jade in the cave. The way her body had responded.

The way her body was responding now just thinking about it. About him.

She glanced at the elf, suddenly self-conscious, and saw that he was staring at her.

"Are you okay?"

Amberle frowned immediately. "Of course I'm okay. Why wouldn't I be?"

"You look more than nervous, maybe a little scared. I've never seen you look that way before."

Amberle didn't know whether to snap at him or laugh off such a suggestion, but the look was likely still on her face. She gave him a lopsided smile.

"I'm just trying to calm Verdana down."

Jade nodded. "I figured you were communicating with her. Seems like whatever you said, it worked."

"It did," she said, letting out a shaky breath.

Amberle planted her elbow on the arm of her seat and dropped her forehead into her hand and massaged her temples. It felt like instead of solving problems one by one, she was gathering them like flowers.

"You look tired," Jade commiserated.

"I am."

"Do you want to rest? Lay down in the back...?"

The elf could see the young woman go perfectly still, so still that it looked as if she had even stopped breathing. Then, slowly, Amberle's face came up and her eyes met his.

"Yes," she said. "I do want to rest. In fact, I think I need a good night's rest." She swallowed against the dryness in her throat, almost afraid to press on but the elf gave her a nod of understanding. "Since I'm doing this for you, taking you back, I mean - would you do something for me?"

"Of course," Jade agreed. "Anything. What do you need?"

Amberle tried to keep her eyes from widening and her face from blushing as she considered her need. Verdana's need. "I could use a night of sleep, but not in here. One real night of sleep, in a real bed. Before I have to go back and face Faith."

Jade nodded emphatically. "I know just the place! It's a bit out of the way, but it shouldn't matter much, considering our transportation."

Amberle drew in a deep breath and let it out between pursed lips. "So," she pressed, "back to your time?"

"Back to my time," he agreed with a grin. "About halfway between my village and the university."

Amberle could not help but return his grin. His enthusiasm was infectious. "All right. V? Do you need.." *coordinates* was what she was going to ask but apparently the Fledgling found them unnecessary.

The young Dragon banked and began to fold space and time, taking the young pair of adventurers across the galaxies. They stared out the windows as everything blurred. Amberle swallowed again and tried not to think about where they were headed. She had never been a person to fill silence with idle chatter, but she had to take her mind off what was ahead.

"Well, oh great and wise one," she chided, "why don't you enlighten me with a magnificent life lesson?"

"What do you know about reality?" he asked with a smirk.

Amberle smirked right back at him. "I know I don't like living in it."

Jade laughed. "Exactly. But you should. Life is the best."

Amberle made a face and shook her head in disagreement. "Life is scary."

"Thrilling," Jade corrected.

"It's hard."

"Challenging."

"Sad."

"Emotional."

Amberle exhaled in a huge, exaggerated sigh and let her head roll all the way back on her shoulders. "You're impossible!"

"I'm visionary."

"Ugh!"

Jade laughed and nudged her foot with his boot. "Back to reality."

"Ugh!" Amberle repeated with a laugh and gently kicked his boot.

"What do you like so much about being jacked into the Web?"

Amberle's hazel eyes lost focus and her expression became dreamy. "Oh," she sighed, "everything."

"But if you could narrow it down to one thing, what would it be?" the elf asked. He expected her to shrug, unable to answer, but she surprised him.

"That's the thing," she said, her eyes finding his. "There is no one thing. It's endless possibilities."

Jade straightened in his seat. "But that's exactly what reality is!" he told her. "Everything - life, consciousness, the future - is all just a vast expanse of endless possibility. Except, instead of using your finger to click something on a compute, all you have to use is your mind."

"That's all it takes to change reality? A thought?"

"Not just a thought. Intent. Choice. They are what shape reality. They change everything, every moment. They can turn on the head of a pin. You, and all beings in the universe, are where you are right now as a result of all the choices you've made."

Amberle did not have to think about it long to know he was right.

I am here, right now, because of the choices I have made.

Every decision has led me here, to this moment.

Even now, as she pondered over what he had told her, she could feel Verdana passing from her own galaxy and into Jade's. Taken there by choice. Guided by her intent.

Her decisions.

Responsibility is a heavy burden.

The young programmer finally grasped that the heavy burden meant you were making decisions not just for yourself, but for someone else. Possibly more than one.

It was simple. And frightening.

"But sometimes I can get cornered," she argued, "get trapped, by the choices others have made."

Jade shrugged. "You still have a choice on how to deal with it."

"The Web is safer," Amberle said, her voice barely above a whisper.

"I'm not saying reality isn't without risk, but the reward outweighs it. By a lot. Life is feeling, touching, enjoying. It's living!" He smiled at her dubious expression. "What would you rather do, watch someone on the GW eating a bowl of ice cream, or eat a bowl of ice cream yourself?"

Amberle's face split in a grin. "Eat it myself." She kicked his boot. "As I'm sure you know." She glanced over her shoulder, towards the galley, and her smile widened. "Speaking of which..."

She rose up from her seat, meaning to help herself to a serving of her favorite frozen dessert, sure that Faith had stocked the refrigerated larder - when the Fledgling braked, and banked sharply.

Outside, they were plunging into the atmosphere over Jade's moon and heading west. Inside, Amberle was thrown off balance, stumbled, and found herself in Jade's lap. His arms went around her protectively and, once again, they found themselves face to face, bodies, close.

Amberle felt her hand clutched tight around his arm and heard the echo of her earlier thought: *I am here, right now, because of the choices I have made. Every decision has led me here, to this moment.*

Then there was the sensation of being pushed through something like a wall of water, that strange feeling as they rippled through time.

ONE 8

"Looks like we're here," Amberle said.

Jade pulled his eyes away from her face to look through the eyes of the Fledgling. They were dropping down through a thin layer of clouds and leveling out to cruise high over acres of lakes.

"Not quite," he said. "I think we are too far north. I don't know the coordinates for Mary's Meadow, but..."

Once again, it appeared Verdana did not require coordinates. She dove and the vessel yawed again, hard to starboard. Jade's arms instinctively tightened around Amberle to keep her from tumbling off his lap. She drew in a quick breath but, once they had leveled out again, she gave him a sheepish smile and carefully extracted herself from his protective embrace.

"I guess the ice cream will have to wait," she said, retaking her seat next to him. "Which is too bad. I'm getting hungry."

"Me too," Jade agreed, regarding her thoughtfully for a moment before refocusing his attention on the world outside. "Which should not be surprising. We haven't eaten since breakfast. I don't know how much time has passed, but the sun is going down here. I'll make us dinner when we get to the house."

"House?" Amberle asked with a sidelong glance at him and a smile. "Make dinner? You're going to cook for me?"

"Yep."

The Fledgling dipped lower and slowed even more as they

sailed through a valley between low, rolling hills. The meadows below them had once been green but, at this time of the year, were as gold as the hills. From one end of the basin to the other was a patchwork of shorn Timothy fields.

"There," Jade said, pointing as they neared the end of the shallow vale.

Amberle leaned forward in her seat as they decelerated. The Fledgling flew lower and she saw that they were nearing a large farmhouse flanked by a huge barn on one side and an enormous fenced-in yard on the other. It appeared to be deserted but she was not taking chances.

Any signs of life? she asked Verdana. The reply was immediate.

None.

"The barn?" she asked Jade.

"The barn."

By the time they reached the farmhouse the Fledgling was gliding leisurely and silently over the raked earth before the farmhouse. She slowed to a stop and hovered before she stretched out her legs and landed lightly, sending up puffs of dust.

Jade was up and out of his seat with his usual grin, stopping first at the galley to retrieve a few boxes from the refrigeration system. He handed one to Amberle and she saw that it was a pint of ice cream. The corners of her lips turned up as she followed him to the exit that Verdana had made for them, then out and down the silver stairs that stretched out from her body.

The sun was setting on the far end of the vale, filling the air with golden light and shadows of lavender and rose.

"What is this place?" Amberle asked as she followed the elf across the yard.

"Remember the woman you saw with my mother, when we went to my village?"

"Yes."

"She's my aunt. This is her place."

"How did you know there wouldn't be anyone here?"

Jade grinned at her from over his shoulder as he ascended the steps to the covered porch that wrapped the entire house. "Because we locked it up two weeks ago."

"We?"

"I come help her and my cousins every year when they harvest the hay and stay to help until it's baled and carted off."

They reached the door and Jade knelt down, overturned an old pot, and retrieved a key made of brass.

"Clever," Amberle remarked sarcastically as he straightened and used the key to open the door.

"Don't start," he told her, returning her smirk as he held the door open for her. "This place is so deserted in the off season that I don't know why my aunt even bothers to lock it."

Amberle smiled at him then turned to look, curious, inside the house as he flicked on the lights.

To her eyes, it was enormous.

She had been raised in a high-rise podment where everything had been compact, if not downright tiny. Her home had barely enough of a kitchen for two people to be in it at one time. There was room for her in the common room with her parents to watch the holo-v, if they squished. There was a single washroom and the bedrooms were merely pockets for humans.

Here, the kitchen was spacious, and then some. It had cabinets with long countertops. There was a cooktop *and* an oven. Not a micro-warmer but *an oven*. The refrigerator was as big as two men. There were shelves and cupboards. There was a dining area with a long table and benches for seats. The other side of the house had couches and low tables, along with a hallway that she supposed led to the bedrooms and bathroom.

She turned to Jade and the elf, seeing her wide eyes and raised brows, mistook her expression.

"Yeah, we have electricity," he told he told her as he headed for the kitchen with a look of exasperation on his young face. "You don't have to look so surprised. There's running water, too, if you can believe it."

Amberle laughed and followed him. "It's not that," she said, handing him her ice cream. "I know it's not some Podunk moon."

Jade gave her a dubious look as he took the ice cream and put it in the freezer unit.

"I'm serious," she assured him. "I just can't believe how big this place is."

"Now I *know* you're making fun of me," he chided, kicking her boot.

"I'm not, I swear!"

Though his expression was still suspicious, Jade opened the door of the oven and put in the two foil boxes he had brought from the Fledgling. He straightened and turned the appliance on, adjusted the temperature and glanced at his watch.

"The podment I grew up in," Amberle explained, "was hardly bigger than just these two rooms."

"Really?"

"Really. It was definitely smaller than your house in the village. This place is huge by comparison. What is it? Why is it so big? And why isn't there anyone here?"

Jade, his cheery demeanor restored, opened a cupboard and started pulling out dry foodstuffs.

"I told you. It belongs to my aunt. We help her harvest hay in the late summer." He took out bowls and cups and spoons from a different cupboard before glancing at Amberle to see an expression so blank that it made him laugh. "Hay grows in the valley meadows in the spring," he told her. "At the end of summer, we cut it down. We spend about a week drying it and then another week tying it into really big bundles, called bales."

"Hay?"

Jade pressed his lips together to suppress the chuckles bubbling up inside. She really did know so much that when she came up clueless on something it tickled him. "Hay," he repeated. "It's a type of grass."

"And you cut it down and save it?" she asked, suspicious that he might be pulling her leg, especially because it was plain he was trying not to laugh.

"Yes. People feed it to their horses and cows. Especially in the winter."

Amberle lifted her chin. "Why don't the horses and cows just eat it from the ground, where it grows?"

Jade had to bite his lip, which drew another scowl from Amberle, but he kept the chuckle down. "It doesn't grow in the winter, because it gets so cold. Sometimes there's even snow."

That last seemed to resonate with her and the young woman's face softened. "Ohhh," she breathed. Her eyes focused on the elf and she jerked her chin towards the items he had gathered. "What are you doing?"

"I am going to make biscuits. And you are going to help me."

"I am?"

Jade nodded and motioned for her to join him on the kitchen side of the counter. He pulled open a drawer to retrieve a utensil and handed it to Amberle. He began measuring and dumping ingredients into a large bowl. The young woman held the item he had given her up in front of her face, feathery eyebrows raised high over her green and brown eyes as she examined it.

She had never seen anything like it in her life. The closest thing it resembled was a pair of brass knuckles she had once seen in a pawn shop while searching for used lithium chips. It had the same kind of handle, but where the knuckles were supposed to be, was a metal grate.

"What the hell am I supposed to do with this?"

Jade grinned as he added a spoon of salt into the bowl. "Use it to mix everything together." He began dropping white, greasy-looking cubes into the powdered ingredients and motioned for her to get going.

Amberle began mashing the ingredients together, wondering why he didn't use a mixer, or just a spoon. "What is that stuff?" she asked instead.

"Shortening," Jade answered, drawing water from the sink. "And this should be milk, but water will have to do. At least it's cold."

"Shortening?"

"Yeah, it's like fat, but from plants."

"That's ridiculous."

Jade laughed, adding the water to her efforts and pulling out a wooden board and a rolling pin. Amberle kept mashing and mixing with the tool and, to her amazement, dough began to form. Jade smiled at her look of wonderment and, when he decided it was the right consistency, he put flour on the board and showed her how to knead and roll out the dough.

By the time the biscuits were cut and laid out on a metal sheet, Amberle's dark skin was powdery white up to her elbows. She washed it off in the sink while Jade put the pan in the oven. He straightened and turned to see her drying her hands on a dish towel.

Smiling, he leaned forward and wiped off a streak of flour from her face and held her cheek cupped in his palm for a second. One second became two, then he stiffened and abruptly dropped his hand away as he realized he had been about to kiss her.

Impulsively, not seriously, but still...

"What do you want to do with Verdana?" he asked quickly.

"I know for sure the valley is safe, and I'm pretty sure no one is going to just happen along, but I can open up the barn if you feel better putting her in there."

Amberle was silent for a moment. She could feel the shift in energy, the spike and sizzle of intensity as it occurred over a few brief seconds and it confused her, but his question sank in. She sent the thought out to the Fledgling and received only uncertainty in response. A slow smile spread across Amberle's face.

"Let's open up the barn. If she wants to go in, it's her choice."

Jade returned her smile and headed for the door. Amberle followed him out and down the porch stairs.

The shadows were deepening into twilight, yet the air was full of warm buoyancy.

The barn door was massive and made of painted wood planks, but it was on wheels set into a track and together they rolled it open.

A wave of air blew across their faces, hot and smelling of hay and making them feel young and childish. Making them laugh all the same.

"Go ahead and see what she wants to do," Jade said, "I don't want the biscuits to burn." He winked at her then hurried back to the house.

Amberle stayed long enough to lay a hand on Verdana and speak with her for a few moments. Thoughts of choice and intention passed between the young woman and the young Dragon. They were deep thoughts, new to both of them, but reassuring to them both.

Amberle returned to the farmhouse to find Jade putting food on the counter. He handed her a round ceramic platter and together they mounded their plates with what he had brought from Verdana's galley and heated in the oven - chicken and potatoes – along with the biscuits they had made together.

They sat themselves at one end of the long table and dug in.

"These are really good," she told him. "The biscuits, I mean."

Jade nodded, smiling. "They would be even better if we had some fresh butter." He looked up as something occurred to him and he snapped his fingers. "Wait!" The young elf jumped from his seat and went to one of the many kitchen cupboards and brought back a small glass jar. "Preserves!"

Amberle's dark, slim fingered hand came up to cover her mouth as she laughed. "Preserved what?"

Jade held up the jar and examined its interior. "Peaches, I think." He twisted the top and it gave a small pop as it opened. "Here!" He took Amberle's biscuit from her and used his own knife to scoop up a generous amount of golden jam and cover it. Carefully, he gave it back and watched as she took a bite. His smile widened as her face lit up.

"Oh my God!" she cried around the food in her mouth. "That is amazing!"

Jade laughed. "There's more to this life than just ice cream," he told her. Amberle laughed.

"Until now, I might not have believed you!"

Jade helped himself to the preserves and they ate in silence for a while, drinking cold water from glass jars.

The young woman watched the elf and felt something twist inside her, making her feel weak. She rested her biscuit on her plate and took a deep breath.

"Are you afraid of dying?" she asked.

Jade looked at her as if she had asked if he was a Golgoth.

"No," he blurted, almost laughing in surprise. "Why would I?" Amberle shrugged and Jade regarded her with his arched brows raised high over his green eyes. "Are you?" he asked.

That had Amberle surprised. "No, I guess not. But I've never really thought about it before."

"Young people never do," he said, giving her boot a playful

kick, which she promptly returned.

"Just because *I* probably won't live to be over..."

"AHHH!" Jade shouted, covering his pointed ears with his hands. "Don't tell me!" He scowled fiercely at her and then, as he slowly lowered his hands, a mischievous grin spread across his face. "Over one hundred?" he asked. Amberle pressed her lips together to keep from smiling or saying anything but the young elf could read it in her eyes. Jade nodded in satisfaction. "Over one hundred," he assured himself before raising his brows at her again. "Over two hundred?" he ventured.

Amberle laughed and kicked his boot. "You said you didn't want to know!"

"That's a yes!" he exclaimed, laughing. "But I won't ask anymore." Jade tipped his head back and sighed as he regarded the ceiling. "I couldn't ask for anymore."

"But it doesn't bother you? Knowing that it is coming?"

Jade shook his head and again looked at her like she was crazy. "Life is an adventure, death is another – just one that we don't know about. But life is for living. Whether you live to two hundred or twenty, it's what you do with the years you have that counts. You need to live every second and love every breath of it, no matter the situation."

Amberle leaned forward. "And what is living?" she prodded, feeling she was on to something. Something essential.

Jade blinked and shook his head as if overwhelmed with so many answers to her question. "It's riding in a Fledgling," he told her, "but it's also baking biscuits, and the taste of jam. It's jumping out of tree into a mulch pile, even though you might break your leg, or worse." He closed his almond-shaped eyes and Amberle felt her breath hitch in her chest. "It's the sound of children and the crackle of fire. It's the feel of wind and the smell of grass and the vastness of the stars." He opened his eyes and looked at her. "It's filling yourself with love and gratitude for every moment you have - risking everything and expecting nothing."

Amberle felt the hitch in her chest move to her throat and she swallowed it down. She breathed deep, thinking it might have been the biggest breath she had taken in all her life. It took a few more seconds before she could rally a smile and the words to go with it.

"I hope it's also doing the dishes, because - as big and fancy as this kitchen is - I don't see a dish cleaning machine in there."

Jade laughed and kicked her boot. She kicked him back and finished her biscuit. And helped with the dishes.

After the dishes were done and the kitchen cleaned, Jade showed Amberle to the room in the house reserved for guests.

"There are a few rooms for the adults," he said as he lead her down the hallway.

"And at thirty, you're not an adult yet?" Amberle teased.

Jade rolled his eyes as he opened a door and tuned on the light. "There's a bunk room, where I sleep with my cousins, and we are *all* adults now. But we still like being together like we did when we were kids."

"Mmhmm," Amberle remarked with sarcasm as she looked around the room. It had a double size bed with an iron bed frame that had been painted white and a mattress covered with a patchwork quilt. There was a small wooden dresser, two well-worn rugs, and a doorway that led to a washroom.

"Well," he told her "oh-so-old-and-wise one, enjoy your good night of sleep."

He gave her a smile and had already turned to leave when he felt Amberle's hand grasping his wrist. Surprised, the elf turned back to be downright astonished as he felt her step close and slip an arm around his waist before she pressed her lips against his own.

Her kiss was tentative at first, but then built slowly as it became more intense, forceful and passionate. Jade felt his body respond in kind, pressing close against hers. Still, he broke the kiss and blinked at her.

"What are you doing?" he asked softly, not letting her go.

"Living," she said, as she reached behind him, and cut off the light.

ॐ

Later, their bodies naked and entwined on the bed, Amberle rested her face on Jade's chest and listened to the beat of his heart. It was strong.

"I *have* had adventures, you know," she told him.

Jade pressed his smile into her wild hair. "Really? Do tell."

"I was stranded on a moon and chased by zombies. I made friends and ran through a labyrinth in a temple and got away from an entire company of Golgoths."

Jade's smile widened. "That story sounds made up."

Amberle yawned. "All stories are."

Jade chuckled softly and kissed her forehead. After a few moments of quiet, his lips like feathers against her dark skin, he asked, "any life lessons?"

Amberle moved her face slightly against his chest in a nod. "Responsibility is a heavy burden. But it's worth it."

Jade smiled into her pink coils of hair. "I can't argue with that."

ॐ

When Amberle opened her eyes again there was bright sunlight streaming through the curtained windows. Her hand slipped between the sheets but there was no one else there. She sat up, gathering the quilt around her as she looked around. There were splashing sounds coming from the washroom.

She held the blanket against her neck, intensely aware of the feel of her naked body – her skin against the linen sheets – of her awkward angles and strange new curves.

Before she stood, her hand gently sought out her abdomen and rested there.

Don't be ridiculous, she thought, *I'm human and he is an elf. The odds are greater than a million to one.*

Her hand spread out over her flat belly.

Still, those odds are there. Possibility is there.

Her eyes went to the door of the washroom as she heard the sound of water shut off. She left the bed and dressed. She was lacing up her boots when Jade came out, freshly scrubbed and wearing only his pants.

"You're up early," she remarked, unable to restrain a smile as she looked over the plated muscle on his narrow chest, his strong arms.

"I'm not going to lie," he said. "I'm eager to see the look on my friends' faces. I'm eager to start college and learn new things." He dropped down next to her on the bed and laughed. "I'm eager to go out and live every second of my life." He gave her a nudge and the mischievous look she now knew was entirely his own. "Unless you want to spend a few more seconds here," he suggested, glancing meaningfully at the bed.

Amberle laughed. "If all you have is a few seconds, I think I'll pass."

"I could manage a few minutes."

Amberle kicked his bare foot. "Get dressed. You don't want to be late for your grand entrance."

Jade put his hand behind her head and pulled it to his own and kissed her.

Twenty minutes later, the house was locked and they were in Verdana, streaming towards the university. Classes were not scheduled to start until the next day, but the campus was full of students that were suddenly craning their necks to see the Fledgling Dragon streaking across the sky.

"Don't think I'm dropping you off in a crowd of people," Amberle warned with a smile as she looked out and past an oncoming forest.

"Don't worry, I'll hoof it."

"*What?*"

Jade laughed. "I'll walk."

Amberle shook her head in amusement. "There's a narrow vale coming up which should be perfect. V?"

The Fledgling obliged, banking and gliding in before landing carefully between the wooded area and the rising hills.

Amberle smiled at the elf as she stood. "Come on, I'll walk you out," she said, motioning with her chin to the door already opening for them.

They went down the set of steps that had formed against the side of the Fledgling and stood in the grass, facing each other.

"I hope my mates brought my stuff," Jade muttered and then sighed heavily, but happily. "If not, I'll figure something out."

Amberle was acutely aware of the feel of the breeze ruffling the curls of her hair, the sound of birds, the smell of the grass - and the elf in front of her.

"What are you going to do?" he asked her, his green eyes unnaturally serious.

"I'm going to live. But not jacked into the Web. Well," she corrected with sheepish grin, "not all the time. I think it is time for me to stop watching life and the lives of others, and start living my own."

Jade reached out and cupped her cheek in his slender hand.

"You do that. *Jordan.*"

Amberle laughed. "I still don't know how that's going to work. I don't know the first thing about being a Jordan."

"Are there Jordans in your time?"

Amberle nodded.

"Find them. Learn from them."

Amberle nodded again. She had the feeling that Faith would help her do that. "And you?" she asked.

Jade laughed. "I have to take the long road, I guess. Starting with changing my major area of study on my first day, to flight!"

Amberle's smile was bittersweet. "Thank you, Jade. For everything."

He pulled her close and kissed her. When their lips parted, he still held her close, pressing his forehead against hers. "Live it to the fullest, every second of it. Take everything you can from this world, and all others. And give back twice as much. In that way, you'll live forever. We both will."

Still holding him tight, their hips pressed against each other, Amberle closed her eyes and nodded. "I will." She kissed him again and let him go.

He moved away slowly, and then turned and began his short trek towards his future. Amberle resisted the urge to press her hand against her abdomen. She was glad she did, because he looked back and flashed her his most mischievous of grins before he disappeared from her sight into the sun-dappled woods.

Amberle closed her eyes and let herself feel the air around her, taking in the smells and the sounds before climbing back into Verdana. Both the stairs and the door disappeared into the Fledgling as she eased herself into the pilot's seat.

"Well," she said aloud, "I know the chances are more than a million to one, but...in case this is that one...well, I'm less ready than you are."

The young woman was not sure how to express herself to the young Dragon but her feelings were clear, as was her condition. Despite the odds, deep inside, she knew for certain.

Verdana did as well. The Fledgling was literally glowing with joy.

"Go ahead," the young woman told her. She took a deep breath and nodded in reassurance.

Amberle felt a stab of pain, a cramp in her lower belly, and then it was gone. A green glow surrounded her abdomen and then coalesced into a small, emerald-colored ball. In its center was a spot, a pinprick of light so tiny that she could barely see it.

"Holy shit," Amberle whispered. "You're going to take care of that, right? Until you're ready for it, or I am, or we are?"

There was a warm feeling of acknowledgement from the Fledgling as the green swirl of light with its glowing spark disappeared into the smooth silver skin of the console dash.

Amberle smiled, feeling like she never had before.

She drew in a great breath of air, held it for a moment, and let it all out in a rush. Her body trembled with excitement and anticipation. Unseen tendrils from the Fledgling caressed her temples, gently moving the faded pink coils of her hair, silently probing for what she wanted - encouraging her to ask anything.

"Let's go find Faith," she suggested. Experimentally, she reached out her hands and a small wheel pushed itself out of the dash. "But, maybe first, I should learn to fly."

As she took hold of the wheel, however, she found that she already knew.

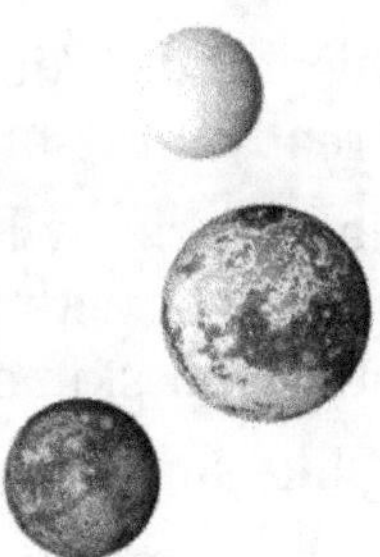

AUTHOR'S NOTE

I can hardly believe I started this story ten years ago. I guess the question at the end of this tale is - where does the time go?

My avid followers know that I wrote the first half of this book for my daughter when she was a sophomore in high school. Subjugated to the living room couch after a surgery that put metal plates and screws into her ankle.

Though I stay true to the copyright page statement (..this book is a work of fiction. Names, places, characters and incidents are products of the author's imagination or are used fictitiously...) as much as any writer can and should, the story was about my daughter so it was impossible for me not to include a number of her traits and quirks.

Looking back at the time, while I wrote the second half of the book, I recalled those habits and peculiarities and realized they were not exclusive to her (though many were and still are) but simply encompassed who she was as a teenager.

I did not set out to write a "coming of age" story but, as with most of my writing, I try to let the story evolve on its own and not jack it up too much. A coming of age is what I got. Doing so, it is impossible not to recall my own teenage years. Ick.

All of us go through it (the changes, the awkwardness) to varying degrees, but what amazes me is the range of emotions and how raw and incredibly strong they are. Insecure and afraid to the point of suicide one day and the next nearly bursting with a feeling of immortality.

This strange psychosis between childhood and adulthood fills us with both exhilaration and terror. Romantic and sexual feeling feelings are exploding during a time when we can hardly recognize the face and the body in the mirror. And what we see there, we rarely like. The idea of responsibility we squint at like a tidal wave on the horizon.

And the worst – we feel like we are going through it alone.

What you need to know, no matter what age you are now, you are not alone.

And, wherever you are, don't give up. You need to see what happens next. Not just in my story, but your own.

Nonetheless, back to my story – only because I refuse to leave you on such a heavy note. I am actually looking forward to getting back to the other brave Jordans, the beautiful Chimera, and the other happenings in the InterGalactic parade.

I know a lot of what is about to happen, but not everything. I am being honest when I tell you I like to let the story evolve on its own. It's more fun that way.

And, honestly, I've found Faith. I'm still looking for Hope.

Where do you find Hope?

Where do any of us?

Maybe in the realization that we are not alone.

# AUTHOR'S NOTE #2

A REMINDER THAT LIFE (REALITY) IS HOW YOU SEE IT.

The young Dragon banked and began to fold space and time, taking the young pair of adventurers across the galaxies. They stared out the windows as everything blurred. Amberle swallowed again and tried not to think about where they were headed. She had never been a person to fill silence with idle chatter, but she had to take her mind off what was ahead.

"Well, oh great and wise one," she chided, "why don't you enlighten me with a magnificent life lesson?"

"What do you know about reality?" he asked with a smirk.

Amberle smirked right back at him. "I know I don't like living in it."

Jade laughed. "Exactly. But you should. Life is the best."

Amberle made a face and shook her head in disagreement. "Life is scary."

"Thrilling," Jade corrected.

"It's hard."

"Challenging."

"Sad."

"Emotional."

Amberle exhaled in a huge, exaggerated sigh and let her head roll all the way back on her shoulders. "You're impossible!"

"I'm visionary."

"Ugh."

Just remember, life is an infinity of possibilities.